D1343917

9037724310

Trap Door

Dreda Say Mitchell

Print ISBN 978-1-913419-25-7

Praise for Dreda Say Mitchell

'Yet death is never a wholly welcome guest.'
Faust, Johann Wolfgang Von Goethe

Prologue

How do you clear up after you've murdered someone?

That's what ran through the killer's mind as he turned his head away from the body. He trembled with shock, fear and an acidic horror about what had happened.

Thirty minutes had come and gone since he'd passed through the curtain of fire that divides those who have taken a life from those who have not. He'd already learned in that brief time that it didn't matter whether the death was accidental, what your original intent was, or how sorry you were afterwards. It didn't matter how many times you thought things through again and again, desperately wishing and pleading with yourself, 'If only, if only…'

It was too late for soul-searching regret. There was no way back through the curtain.

The body was slumped in the driver's seat of a German model 29 Nash saloon. One of a number of classic cars that sit side by side in this purpose-built garage complex. Ex-wives and girlfriends claimed the victim cared more about his shiny boys' toys than he did about people. He'd certainly spared no expense housing them.

The gears in the killer's mind turned, finally piecing together how to answer his horrific question. How ironic that it was the victim's obsessions that led the killer to the point of understanding how to cover up this unspeakable act.

The victim had installed sealed tanks of specially formulated fuel to pump into his much-loved vehicles. And that meant when the place was set on fire, at some stage it was going to erupt like a volcano and destroy everything in its path. But how would you know when that moment would come? That you'd left enough time to run and run from the scene without the fire catching you too?

The killer turned back to the car. Peered inside. The dead man looked serene and unmarked as if he was having a quiet nap. At rest, his head tilted to one side. The fatal wound to his temple oozed something nasty through the congealed blood. If the blow had been anywhere else on his body this man would still be alive, probably raging and lashing out. But the temple is the thinnest and most vulnerable part of the skull. A thumping blow is all it takes to crack it.

The killer splashed petrol over the body until the clothes were soaked through. Did the same to the interior and bodywork of the car. Lashings more poured over the floor and on the fixtures and fittings in the building. Petrol everywhere, the place stank to high heaven. He doused one of the many 'no smoking' signs in the greasy liquid from his jerry can. Of course smoking was strictly forbidden in this building, so how to account for the inferno that was to come? He put down his can and ran back to the house.

There was so much to remember, so much to easily forget.

In a bureau in the office he found what he was looking for, a box of Havana cigars. Took one out. Put the flame of the lighter to it but it didn't catch because of his fumbling fingers. He tried again. And again. He shook so badly he was seconds away from falling apart. Finally, finally the tip of the cigar sizzled as it glowed orange-red-hot. He placed the cigar to his lips and inhaled. A hacking spluttering cough erupted from his chest. But then your life is never the same after you've smashed someone's skull in.

The killer choked his way down the cigar until it was half its length. Outside, he chucked the Havana not too far from one of the garage's opened windows. The investigators would find it. The killer already had an explanation for that. The dead man was smoking a cigar in the garage and threw it out of the window. What an idiot. Case closed.

Or perhaps the case wouldn't be closed. Maybe he should have placed a tissue around the end of the cigar before he put his mouth over it? He'd seen the TV docs and the grisly true crime shows where forensic science seems to have X-ray eyes.

There was so much to remember, so much to easily forget.

Standing by the door, he found a classic car exhibition brochure and rolled it up. Dipped it in petrol. Took the lighter out of his pocket. Glanced around the building for one final check, set the brochure on fire and then threw it onto the fuel-soaked floor. The flames skipped and danced towards the saloon like a child running on a beach. The car was soon consumed in fire, the dead man's face blistering and creasing in the flames. It was time to go before the whole place went up.

He ran out of the door, across the grounds, greedily gulping in the fresh country air, running through what he was going to say to the police.

'When I smelt smoke I rushed around to the front of the house and saw the garage in flames. I tried to get in and rescue him but the heat was so intense I was driven back. That's how I got the cuts and bruises on my face. I told him a thousand times not to smoke in there but he wouldn't listen, he just wouldn't listen.'

He stopped abruptly. Frantically patted his pockets. Where was his lighter? Behind him, the garage windows were already in motion with leaping orange and yellow flames. In his head, he heard the police saying, 'Our team recovered the charred remains of a brass lighter from the scene. We've established that it had your name engraved on it, along with the words 'Las Vegas'. We understand you were holidaying there last year. Have you any idea how that item came to be in the garage?'

He ran back. Pulled open the door and was thrown onto his back by the rush of heat and fuel-scented flames. But he struggled to his feet, pulled his jacket over his head and plunged into the inferno and headed towards where he'd started the fire. It didn't take him long to find the lighter. The sweat soaking through his shirt exposed a brass lump in its top pocket. He hadn't dropped it at all. It was there all along.

He never heard the explosion. He only saw blue, white, a flash of lightning tear across the garage from one side to another. He somersaulted through the air like a leaf twisting in the wind, crashed hard into a burning wall before sliding down onto the floor below. Molten drops of fuel rained down upon him, burning holes in his clothes and flesh. But he felt no pain, only numbing disbelief as his body began to smoke and smoulder. He was inches from the door that the blast had slammed shut, and was able to lift his arm and rest his hand on the door handle. But there was no life left in his fingers to pull it open and crawl out. His arm slowly slid and dropped away.

In a moment of searing clarity as death closed in on him, there was an unearthly relief at what was happening. This was the right turn of events. Because he knew in the long run, he'd never be able to cope with life on this side of the curtain between those who've killed someone and those who have not.

And in death there's nothing to remember and nothing to forget.

One

I'll do anything. ANYTHING. I'm facing the abyss and don't have a choice. That's why I sit with crippling desperation in this trendy coffee bar, an island of stillness among the rushing parade of Londoners blurring in and around me. Waiting for a stranger who has the power to yank my life back to safe ground or shove me deeper into the hell my life has become.

'Rachel?'

The hesitant-yet-commanding voice catches me unaware, even though I'm expecting him. I'm up and out of the chair with such force the top layer of my latte splashes across the table. Idiot! Idiot! Idiot! What a way to start a job interview.

My hand scrambles towards the solitary napkin, but he gets there first, mopping up with a rhythmic flicked efficiency of his wrist that has the table back to right in no time at all. I feel such a first-grade fool the honourable thing to do would be to hit the exit and keep walking. But someone in my situation doesn't have space for chivalrous ideals like honour. Ideals are out, facts are in. And the fact is I need this job. Badly.

'I'm so sorry.' The required apology sounds high, too breathless. What happened to the laboured confidence I practiced, this way and that, in front of the mirror in my room for a full hour this morning? Gone the same way as the coffee; soaked up into oblivion.

'No, it's me who should be apologising,' he says with an easy smile, 'for asking you to conduct an interview in a café. I didn't want you seeing my office with the plumber around fixing the leak. The last thing I want is for you to think you're joining a company that's disorganised.'

Michael Barrington stretches out his hand, which I quickly take, praying he doesn't feel the sticky sweat on my palm. He's the CEO of a boutique-style management consulting company. A Steve Jobs wannabe in his black polo neck and black pants, hair flicked and buffed back to perfection, a face groomed and moisturised to within an inch of its life. I suspect he's closer to thirty-five than my twenty-eight. He doesn't look it.

But it doesn't matter what he does or doesn't look like. Priority number one is snagging the job he's interviewing me for. I have to get it. If I don't I'm facing catastrophe with a capital C. My life is a house of cards teetering on the edge of tumbling down. *Please help me*, I silently plead with this oh-so-perfect man who holds my salvation in his hands.

When the pleasantries are out of the way, my nerves twist into a medieval torture device when he pulls out and studies my CV or resumé or whatever the business buzzword for it is these days. Is he impressed or not? I can't tell because he shifts the gears of his expression into neutral. The truth is, my work history has been nipped and tucked with fibs and exaggerations. We all do it. Pretend the time we helped Mum organise the garden shed was our first attempt at a start-up. Here's another truth – I'm not really qualified to be a management consultant. Correction: ~~really~~. I'm not qualified to be a management consultant. That's not me being modest like many women are prone to do. Hand on heart, I've never done the job or even one similar. I've made my work history very long, hoping he'll become bored before he figures out my employment record is a roll call of bartending, delivering pizzas and the annoying robotic 'I want to talk to you about your accident' intrusive voice from a call centre.

Michael doesn't look up from his reading as he asks, 'Tell me, Rachel, how's Jed?'

I'm caught off guard. It shows. It's the last thing I expect Michael to say. Shouldn't he be hitting me with a firing squad of questions?

'*Why do you want this job?*'

'*What experience do you have?*'

'*What do you know about this company?*'

Then again, it was Jed who lined me up for this job in the first place. Of all the friends I'd begged for help in finding me proper employment with proper money, Jed was definitely on my 'won't come through' list. When Michael Barrington rang me out of the blue and said Jed had spoken to him, at first I thought it was a sick prank. Then Michael invited me for a coffee and chat and here we are.

I paste on a smile. Hope it doesn't make me the spitting image of a creepy clown. Gut breath. Exhale. 'Jed's good. Such a great guy. Salt of the earth.'

Michael carries on reading. 'Is he still playing in that indie band?'

'I've heard his band is pretty good.' My voice is shaky, losing the perilous thread of confidence I'm clinging on to for dear life.

Michael's bark of sudden laughter startles me. Pushes me back in my seat. The couple at the next table look over as if laughter is some type of miracle drug they wouldn't mind an injection of. 'You're joking. They're amateur hour on speed. Saw them in some fleapit and they sounded like an abattoir on a busy day. They had some dopey girl with blue streaks in her hair on the bass. She couldn't play a note, even though Jed put coloured tabs on it to show her where her fingers should go.'

I join in with the laughter, my staccato ha-ha-haing sounding rehearsed. Obviously I don't let on that I was the dopey girl with the blue clip-ins, standing in for Jed's regular bassist who'd come down with food poisoning.

The blue's long gone. I'm wearing one of two smart suits I own. My weight loss means it swallows me, leaving me the picture of a sad girl playing dress-up. The cuffs of my blouse are tucked up inside so Michael can't see they're as frayed as I feel.

Michael sighs, folds the pages of my CV in half and keeps folding and folding until it's the size of a postcard. He drops it in his open rucksack. My hopeful heart plummets too.

His magnetic eyes make contact with mine. 'I don't think we need to let that farrago detain us any longer.'

It's over. I'm finished. Wish I could cry. My last hope... and I blew it. My life's over. Over.

Michael looks baffled. 'Where are you going?'

I'm standing, unsteady. Convinced I'm going to tip over. I knew this was a forlorn hope but it was hope, and when you're in a situation like mine, hope is all you've got.

Michael gestures with his finger for me to retake my seat. But I've had enough of this. Want out. I'm sick to death of it all. If I still had my car, which I sold a few months back, I'd do everyone a kindness and crash it into a brick wall at illegal miles an hour.

But he repeats his gesture and I slump back into the chair.

Michael settles back. 'Rachel, it's time for some home truths.'

Truths? If he knew the kind of truth I exist in I suspect he'd tell me to exit through the window.

'I'm not very impressed by qualifications and experience,' he continues, tone measured and even. 'They can all be invented anyway. I've hired superbly qualified guys who couldn't tie their shoelaces. On the other hand, I've had work experience kids who got into the consulting groove in the first couple of days. You just can't tell, can you?'

His fingers lock together as he leans forward, his eyes meeting mine. 'Are you reliable and loyal? Because that's what matters. I do a lot of confidential and sensitive work for my clients. I can't afford to employ disloyal and unreliable people. Can't risk employing anyone who will let the firm down.'

'I'm loyal. Reliable,' I state with quick-fire assurance. And I am. But I'm not telling the whole truth. There was that summer... *Don't go there.* I eject out of the damning past.

Michael's got a twinkle that softens his intent stare. 'And let's face it, you can overdo the honesty is the only policy mantra. I'm running a business here, not the Sally Army. Sometimes you have to cut a few corners if you want to get on – you get me?' There's a smile playing on his lips that bring out deep dimples in his cheeks.

I reach for the lukewarm coffee and gulp it down, soaking through the dryness in my throat.

Michael studies me for a few seconds. 'Jed was right to tell me about you. I like you, Rachel. I've got a good feeling about you and I trust my good feelings. Here's what I'm going to do. I'm going to start you off on a one-month contract. Come to the office tomorrow morning and if you pick up the basics over the next four weeks, we can have another chat about giving you something longer term. If not, you'll still have made a few thousand pounds out of it, plus a grand bonus on top. Would that work for you?'

I'm stunned. Can't answer. Thousands? Bonus? Michael's a money tree with multi-coloured leaves – brown tenners, purple twenties and red fifties blowing in the breeze from his branches. Hell yeah, that works for me. Is this where I make a spectacle of myself by twerking with delight round the tables because I can't believe it? But there's a niggling warning at the back of my mind – if it's too good to be true...

So, I sombrely say, 'But my career history doesn't exactly fit with the job that's on offer.' I swallow heavily despite the constriction in my throat. 'I don't want to let you down.'

A steady stare is what I get in return that increases my tension. Makes me want to grab back my honest words, press rewind and start all over again.

'That's where we disagree,' he finally tells me. 'You've worked in call centres, which means you know how to talk to clients on the phone. Not only that, but you will have learned the art of persuasion. And if working in a bar isn't a highly pressurised situation, I don't know what is.' His stare deepens. 'That's the type of skills I need in my organisation. If you're up for the challenge, I've got the job.'

A warm heady feeling of appreciation spreads through me. I feel giddy with it. Rachel Jordan, who set out to conquer the world at eighteen but instead ended up piled on the scrap heap of other nothings, has finally been given another chance. This job will not only get me out of my tricky reality but also give me an opportunity to redeem myself. Two birds one stone.

I tell him, 'I'd like to join your company.'

Michael nods with satisfied understanding as he pulls out a stapled set of papers from his bag and hands them to me. 'It's a short-term contract with the standard T&Cs. Take it away and read it first. I wouldn't want you to think you're signing your life away.'

Signing my life away? If only he knew he was giving it back to me.

He gets to his feet, signalling the interview is at an end. 'I'll see you tomorrow morning then, bright and early, hopefully with a signed contract.' He slings the strap of his rucksack over one shoulder and turns. Then hesitates. Oh heck, maybe I should've offered to buy him a coffee. I get ready to apologise – yet again – but the face he shares with me when he swivels back makes me stop. There's a carved intensity to his handsome features that tells me what he's about to say is important to him.

'We're like a family at my firm.'

That's it. Nothing else. Then he's gone, leaving me clutching the paper lifeline to solve all my worries. Slowly, and with a peace I haven't known in ages, I smile.

I got the job. Nothing can go wrong now.

Two

A s soon as I'm inside my room, the window silently calls to me as it always does. I begin the ritual. Stride over to the window. Look out at the overgrown back garden. Tilt my chin down to get a better view of what's directly below. A bashed-about concrete patio that's been broken and shattered by weeds and lack of affection. It's about a thirty-foot drop. Death would probably be the result if I fell. A motionless twisted tangle of limbs leaking blood. I turn away, ritual over.

After leaving the interview, I came straight back here, a house I share with six others, mind buzzing with yee-haw delight at hitting employment bullseye. But when I'd closed the front door, the shabby unloved hallway instantly snatched my cheeriness away. I hate this house. Dislike most of the people living here. The woman in the communal kitchen who had sensed my entrance, her head twitching my way like a vulture scenting prey. She'd caught my eye, her mouth crimped with sourness. The hostility vibrating off her was the smell that reached my nose, not the aroma of the tangy food she was cooking. Nothing new there; most of the others living here don't give a toss about me. *Yeah, well, I don't wanna be in this fleapit either, lady,* I was tempted to yell. Or play a game of 'bring it on' and stare her down. But I didn't. The gut-wrenching truth is I've got nowhere else to go.

So, I sucked up her disdain and headed for the staircase, my grip tightening on the rickety and wobbly bannister. Sooner or later, some unfortunate fee-paying soul will go hell for leather over the top, breaking their neck. It's that kind of house. Who the landlord is no-one knows, so the tenants have the letting agency on speed dial for an arm-long list of repairs that rarely get done. The renters making their own makeshift arrangements. Like the radiator, pockmarked with rust, I passed on the first floor landing that slants drunkenly despite the block of wood jammed under it. Or the quiet deadly patches of rotten timber my feet took care to avoid on the floor above that leads to my room.

My room. Controlling my shallow breathing, I study the room that has become my home. It's not too big, not too small either. Enough space for me and my material world. A narrow bed pushed up against a blank white wall in one corner and my clothes and other necessities in a good-sized rucksack that sits on a carpet that was once cream but is now a shade dimmed by the excesses of life.

It was Jed who stepped in when I was thrown out of my last place. A friend had let me sofa-surf at hers for a few weeks. When the weeks turned into a couple of months, her patience wore thin and eventually her temper told me I had to go. Another friendship bites the dust. Jed saved the day and fixed it for me to temporarily lay my hat here where he's lodging too. Once again, I'm on the treadmill of a few weeks that have spun into a number of months.

The worst of it is I could solve all my problems with a single phone call. Make all of this disappear. But that's a phone call I can't ever make. My mobile must sense I've just walked over its grave because it rings. It's Dad. My heart rises and sinks in one fluid motion.

'Hi, Dad!'

'Hello, love.' I hear and feel the broad smile I know graces his face even though I can't see him. 'How's my little princess? And why doesn't Her Royal Highness Rachel call her poor old lonely da anymore?'

I take a deep breath. 'I know, I know, I'm a terrible daughter but I've got so much going on at the mo, I don't get a second to myself.'

As always, he understands, never gives me a hard time. 'You don't have to apologise to me. You don't have to tell me about making sacrifices to get on a rung on the ladder of success.' I flinch slightly at the old regret he can't disguise. No way in hell do I hold it against him the number of times he was away during my childhood as he worked like a man possessed to create the best life for me and Mum.

He continues, 'But if you could find a five-minute slot in your busy schedule to check in with your old man occasionally, you know how much it would mean to me.'

I feel terrible because I do know how much it means. Dad hasn't only gifted me everything a daughter could wish for, above all, he's loved and cherished me. I wander over to the framed holiday photo that takes pride of place on my mantelpiece. Me and him. He's grinning despite the Spanish sun in his eyes, his arm draped over my shoulder like he never wants to let me go. My expression is more grimace than grin; that's a teenager for you. No photos of Mum. It's still too painful even after all these years.

I turn away and say, 'I've really been meaning to call but I've just changed jobs and joined a management consultancy, so it's busy, busy, busy my end.'

'Fantastic! Good business to be in.' He covers up his disapproval of management consultants. In his book, you don't consult in business you roll your sleeves up and crack on with it. 'Which firm is it? I'll probably know them.'

'Not likely, they aren't in the construction sector.' To my intense relief there's a strong three-beat tap on my door. Jed; the others keep well clear of me. 'Got to run, Dad, there's someone at the door—'

'A new boyfriend?' he teases.

The infectious joy from the outcome of the interview seeps through me again. 'Not enough minutes in the day for one of them too. Call you later. Love you!'

'Love you more!'

I hate faking a busy and successful life on the phone with the one person who loves me unconditionally. I'm such a fraud. Maybe I won't have to be for much longer with the new job.

When Jed comes in, I sense something's wrong. His locks of unruly hair and big broken nose are what grab you about him first of all. He's not exactly made of puppy dogs' tails, but he bounds about like a huge shaggy dog, eyes mischievously shining at the wonder of the world around him. And I adore him. A heart of gold never came more solid than his. Usually he's grinning like an idiot born under a full moon. Not today. The seesaw action of his lips rubbing together, combined with sombre eyes levelled over my head, speak volumes about how uncomfortable he is.

As he moves towards me, I see the disaster that's about to happen. I open my mouth in warning... Too late. He kicks over the bucket of cold water I keep by my bed.

Oh hell! The water meanders aimlessly across the dirty carpet, leaving a sodden trail in its wake. Jed looks stupefied as he stares at the overturned bucket, window wiper eyes jerking up at me and then back at the bucket.

I'm in there quickly with an explanation. 'I know that looks odd but I've been watering my plants.'

The dried withered cactus on the mantelpiece, the solitary plant in the room, tells another story. Jed nods as if he understands perfectly and picks up the bucket, placing it upright by the wall.

I'm on my feet heading for the door. 'Just let me clean up the mess—'

'Don't bother with that, sweetheart, it will dry up soon enough.' He clears the back of his throat, a jittery noise that fills my stomach with dread. 'I need to have a quick word.'

I perch on the camel stool, a solid memory of a better time, a better life on holiday in Cairo, while he sits on the edge of the bed. Jed is one of these animated talkers, all waving hands and arms, but now his hands are paralysed together, listless, almost dead.

'So, how's tricks, babe?'

I've been his babe since we were in school together. Despite going our separate ways after senior school, there's always been a tight bond between us. He's what most ladies call a stunner, but there's never been any lovey-dovey heartache between us. Okay, there was that time he threw himself on my lips after assembly when we were ten, receiving an outraged sucker punch to the belly for his romantic troubles. We're Rachel and Jed. Mates who look out for each other.

I'm about to answer when I remember. 'I got the job with your friend Michael. I can't thank you enough for putting in a good word for me. First pay cheque I'm taking me and you out to celebrate.' Fun lights up my voice and features.

Jed's not listening. Instead he's still staring at the bucket, frowning with extreme concentration as if he expects it to start talking. Share with him why I really have a bucket of cold water every night in my room.

He brushes off my words about Michael Barrington with an offhand, 'That's great, that's great... Listen, Rachel... the thing is this.' His big eyes flick up, hook up with mine and speedily skid away again. 'There's no rush obviously but I was just wondering, you know, if you've got any plans to move on from here at some stage? It's, you know...' His voice trails off. He finally makes his gaze stick to mine. 'I did say you'd only be able to have this room for a month. It's been two. So...' His tight shrug says the rest.

My heart's racing to the rhythm of the treadmill I find myself back on. I won't prolong Jed's agony by making him give me chapter and verse about how the other renters put the screws on him to kick me out. *Weird*, one called me. *Oddball*, another.

'Don't sweat it.' I hate that he feels bad. 'You did me a good turn when others wouldn't. Now I'm earning again I'll be able to sort something else out. Give me a week or so and I'll be out of your hair.'

Jed's face transforms into a glitter ball of brightness switching on. 'You sure? There's no rush, obviously, in your own time.'

Relieved that his work is done, he gets up. Squelches over the wet carpet. But as he gets to the door, he turns. That frown of concentration's back. 'Can I ask you a question?'

I playfully scoff, 'As if you've ever needed my permission to ask anything, Jed Harris.' My attempt at lightening the mood doesn't work.

'Your...' Jed hesitates, fingertip unconsciously running down the crooked slide of his nose, 'dad's loaded. Why don't you give him a bell and ask him to bail you out? I'm sure he would slip you some cash if you asked.'

I'm defensive as cold breaks over my skin. 'He's not that wealthy.'

Jed shakes his head. 'He's a millionaire, Rachel.'

When I don't answer, Jed sighs and shrugs, looks at the bucket one last time, before closing the door behind him.

Shortly after, I hear someone talking to Jed on the landing outside. It's the vulture from the kitchen. Bitch! Perhaps she's been waiting for him. Her voice is deliberately loud so that I'm witness to every nasty word.

'Have you told that nutjob she's got to move out yet?'

Three

The building has me thinking maybe I got the wrong address. It's not what I expect. A rapidly cooling breeze frosts over the back of my neck as I stare up at the place where I'll be working. It started life as a tenement, I'm guessing, part of a set of buildings all lined on the street like a Victorian family. The others have been given a twenty-first century makeover bringing out their rosy-cheeked bricks.

My new place of work is different. Its façade is blackened with age, tarnished and dark as if it hasn't been washed in a hundred years. Brooding and looming, the bad tooth in the mouth of the street. It casts me in its shadow, leaving me feeling overwhelmed. As if I need to be more skittish than I already am on my first day in my new job.

This part of London is on the border of where the East End meets the financial City. Twenty years ago it would have been run down, desolate, a byword for poverty and desperation, now it's a marker of innovative businesses and start-ups, all the rage bars and clubs and eateries where avocado on toast is a delicacy. Still, I can't forget that it was once Jack The Ripper's favoured hunting ground.

I shake off the murderous past as I move towards the huge arched wooden doors and press the entrance bell.

It buzzes. 'It's Rachel. Rachel Jordan.' I see no evidence of the lens of a security camera but I get the impression someone's watching me.

'Rachel. Yes.' The voice is sparky, female, slightly breathless. 'Be right down.'

I like the sound of her. Super friendly. It relaxes the highly-strung muscles in my tummy. The back of my neck warms up. As I wait, my side-eye catches sight of something. Positioned on the wall near a window on the left-hand side of the door, it captures my curiosity with a strength that compels me to walk over. A plaque. Not round-shaped like the honoured blue ones that pop up on London's buildings but square. Made of brass, if I'm not mistaken, but has been painted over in a fading coat of white. The writing is barely visible. I lift up to read:

In Memoriam
In the basement of this building on 29th April 1908
22 garment workers lost their lives due to fire
Requiescat In Pace
London County Council 1958

A shudder worms its way through me. What an awful story. This area of London was once teeming with sweatshops, horribly crowded places where poor people toiled for their daily bread in dreadful conditions.

'Miss Jordan?'

The call of my name snaps me back to the present. A woman stares at me from the doorway. Good grief, the last thing I want is for her to think I'm already slacking on the job. I step to it and shake her hand with solid commitment I hope doesn't hurt.

'I'm Joan Connor. Most people here call me Joanie. I'm Mr Barrington's PA.'

Joanie's a young person's name, like the freckled Rock 'n' Roll Cunningham daughter in *Happy Days*. This Joanie's middle-aged. Petite, carrying a plumpness around her hips that suggest she's comfortable in her age. Despite the lines criss-crossing her face, there's a smooth curve to her skin. Her skirt suit is bang-on formal, but her black flats with the bows on the front remind me of slippers. Professional cosy. Is that even a style?

We enter a reception area that's an eye-grabber with its bright walls and wooden floor and does dizzy stuff to all my senses. The staircase continues the hardwood theme, along with a sparkling chrome bannister rail. Clean and ordered is the impression that stays with me.

As she leads me up, Joanie starts talking. 'Mr Barrington is ever so pleased to have you on board.' Her head twists sideways to look at me, her eyes lively. 'I really hope you're going to love it here.'

'I'm sure that I will.' I end with a wide smile I don't quite feel. Truth is, until I get through this first day, I won't be taking anything for granted.

The older woman keeps up a chatter of bubbles and froth until we reach Michael's office. He waits behind a commanding desk in a contemporary office painted white. A carpet deep enough to lose your toes in and a ceiling you have to stretch your neck to fully appreciate. Huge wide windows frame him in a cityscape portrait of the go-getter CEO. The windows hold my attention until Michael's on his feet moving towards me. He envelops my hand into a solid warm shake.

'So pleased you decided to take up my offer.'

By way of reply, I give him the signed contract. After that Michael gives me the grand tour of the first floor. A creative estate agent would probably describe it as 'in need of renovation' or perhaps 'full of original features'. It's a strange mixture of old and new. On the one hand this building seems to have been untouched since Queen Victoria was on the throne. I half expect to see Oliver Twist emerge with a bowl asking if he can have some more. The heavy wooden doors look like panels in the wall while the panels look like doors. Whereas the staircase and its fixtures and fittings are contemporary. Fixtures and fittings; listen to me sounding as if I'm said estate agent on a mission to sell the place. Not far from Michael's office is a door that leads, I suspect, to a staircase to an upper floor. A twisted purple cord ropes it off with a 'private' sign hanging from it.

'Let me show you to your office,' Michael announces, diverting my attention back to him.

I'm so shocked I stupidly sputter, 'I've got... my own office?'

I've never had one of those before. Usually it's all open-planned with the cover story of 'so we can network more easily' instead of the truth: 'We don't want to spend any more than we need to on the workers.'

The broad smile he displays brings out his dimples as he leads me to my own private space.

I'm quietly delighted. The room is on the other side of Joanie's office. It's small, bog standard really, with bare white walls and bare wooden floors, a chair, desk and computer.

Michael surveys the functional space. 'You might want to think about putting up a calendar or something. You know, personalise it a bit.'

But I don't hear him. The windows are calling to me.

My ritual begins. I drift over. The view is out over a back street, scruffier and less trendy than the one at the front. The drop is a single floor onto a pavement below. Too far to jump? I try to open the wrought iron window but it's painted over. Stuck.

'Have you got the key for the window?' Seeing the baffled expression on Michael's face, I realise I've been too abrupt. I should've weaved it more naturally into the conversation.

It's Joanie, peeping in the doorway, who comes to my rescue with a jaunty, 'I'm exactly the same. Problems with the old internal thermometer.'

I haven't got a clue what she's going on about.

Her tone lowers meaningfully. 'This menopause – menohell more like – is driving me up one tree and down another. One minute I'm as cold as Santa's grotto, the next I'm boiling like a fish sunbathing in the sun. I'll go and get you that key.'

'You'll have to forgive Joanie, her mouth sometimes runs away with her,' my new boss tells me when she's gone.

'She's lovely...' I'm talking but my mind's on that window.

Michael gives me one of those one hundred watt smiles again that he seems to be more than happy to keep dishing out. 'Welcome on board, Rachel. It's great to have you as a member of the family.'

I can't believe how I've landed on my feet getting this job. How did I get so lucky?

Four

'Bumped In The Night! London's Top 10 Most Haunted Houses For You!!!'
#No. 8
'A Stray Dog Tried To Save Them! But Too Late! Too Late!'

That's what stares back at me from my computer screen inside my office. A website I hope is going to provide me with more details about the sweatshop fire here over a century ago. The memorial plaque outside has been gnawing away at me. Demanding I dig up the full story of what happened here. So, I'm taking a breather from summarising the restructuring report Michael has got me doing for a client.

Being a management consultant is surprisingly easy. I had an image of hard-sell phone calls, an in tray of mounting paperwork that had to be rubber stamped by the end of the day. Definitely not taking my sweet time rejigging a report. Is this really what Michael's willing to pay me a mouth-watering salary, plus bonus, for? Hey, who am I to question good fortune come a-calling?

I turn my attention back to the eighth most haunted building in London. Surprisingly this website is the only online information I can find about the fire. I suppose the death of poor folk fades from society's memory. The website is full of the usual gruesome tales of beheaded monarchs and grey ladies walking through walls. But at number eight on the list is an account of the fire in this building in 1908 and its aftermath. I read:

Locked into a sweatshop in a dungeon below an East End tenement block, earning a pittance a day for sewing clothes, some urchin girls rescued a stray mongrel dog from starvation on the streets! Unknown to the landlord, they kept him in the basement where they worked and hid him among the benches and sewing machines. Though hungry themselves, they kept their dog alive by feeding him scraps – so he became known as Scrap the dog! Scrap repaid the girls' kindness by performing tricks and barking a warning whenever the foreman came to check up on them.

Next to the text is an ink drawing of thin girls slaving away at their benches. There's another drawing of the owner of the sweatshop but it doesn't look like a very faithful one to me. It's a caricature of a classic Victorian villain with top hat, bulging belly, monocle and spats. The only thing this Lord Jasper Coldheart-type isn't doing is twirling his moustache.

Scrap barked a warning! One cold and stormy night in 1908, the girls noticed that Scrap was running around the basement, barking and frantically tugging at their dresses. What could this mean? Did his sixth sense mean that danger lurked below? But the girls knew if they left their benches their pay would be docked and their families would starve! Blind as to what was to happen, they worked on!!

The author certainly loves his exclamation marks.

Consumed in a fiery inferno!

Smoke was smelt! The basement was on fire! The girls were trapped! Scrap's frantic warnings had come to pass! As the lights went out and they were plunged into darkness, the girls screamed and howled for help!

Scrap to the rescue!

As they ran in circles and panicked, only Scrap kept his head! Barking at his girls to follow, he led them to hidden passageways in the building in an effort to get them out! But in vain! The passageways were blocked and the doors locked by the landlord. As the flames drew closer, their faces wreathed in choking smoke, prayers for divine intervention were feverishly howled by the doomed girls. The heroic dog that had led the way, keened in helpless anguish. All twenty-two perished. Only Scrap managed to escape!

It seems a bit mean to wonder how, if all these urchins died in the fire, the author of this website knows what happened in 1908. Perhaps Scrap told him.

For years after the fire, Scrap sat outside the tenement, keening and howling for his lost friends. Residents and neighbours claim that on stormy nights, he can still be heard keeping a lonely vigil in the darkness while echoes of the girls' sewing machines, feverish prayers and cries still carry within the building itself.

Of course, there's also a moral to this story.

And the landlord? Years later, in 1940, he was living in his luxurious mansion in Kensington when the German air force dropped an incendiary bomb on his house and he too was consumed by flames! No trace of his body was ever found! Justice at last for Scrap and his sweatshop girls!

It all sounds a bit like playing to the audience to me, especially considering the website's frequent irritating reminders for visitors to 'Like this page'. Still, it leaves me unsettled with a chill skating along my arms and spine. The window calls to me. I'm out of my chair and looking through it seconds later. Checking the drop to the ground beneath as usual. There would've been no windows for the sweatshop girls to escape from in the basement.

Suddenly my office is airless, suffocating, so I leave and head out to the kitchen, opposite Joanie's office. She senses my presence. Lifts her head and smiles encouragingly over her reading glasses. I smile back and step into the room that would go down a treat on a TV cookery show. Cosy and compact, every item in its place, immaculately turned out. The shiny red of the kettle, fridge and microwave match. Shelves containing see-through airtight jars of all kinds of health conscious goodies –

nuts, seeds, dried berries, brekkie cereals including organic oats. Different types of tea, free trade brands of coffee. I feel like a kid in a sweetie shop. I know, a big-time cliché, but this room leaves me in a state of a wide-eyed giddy pleasure. Maybe I can have breakfast here in the morning if I get in early enough. No more roughing it on the hunt for a crust back at the shared house. More importantly, I'll be saving myself a wagonload of money.

The mugs hanging off red hooks gleam with the sheen of the brand new. I select a bright lemon-coloured one. Pop on the kettle, stick in a teabag. Milk's always last of course. Plenty will disagree with me, but that's how you make a decent cuppa. Anyone who says different should stick to coffee. I swing open the fridge. The cool air melts over my skin as I pull an opened carton of semi-skimmed milk from the door. It's back in its chilled home once I've poured.

I lean against the counter, near the microwave, cup warming my palms, and inhale the rising steam. Pure bliss. Take a mouthful.

A terrible shudder of disgust ripples through me. My tummy spasms as I desperately try to close my throat. Tart. Nasty. Horrendous. A mixed taste of revulsion invading my mouth. My cheeks balloon as I gag. Eyes widen. Heart zooms into overdrive. Heavy air whooshes through my nostrils like a bucking wild horse.

I'm gonna be sick. Gonna be sick. Gonna...

The cup slips from my hand, crashing to the floor. I just make it to the sink in time before I'm throwing up. Can't stop. Heat and chills pull the temperature of my body in different directions, intensifying my stunned state.

Nothing left to give, I dry heave, my tummy painfully cramping. Blindly, I turn on the tap and stick my open mouth under the running water. Spit. More water. Spit. Continue until the taste is only a remembered smell in my nose, my breathing back to my own.

Shocked, I raise my head, water dripping off my chin, my hands clutching on to the twin sides of the freezing sink. What the hell was that? The boiling water? Tea? It comes to me what the suspect must be. Still shaking, I open the fridge and pull out the milk. Sniff. Recoil in disgust. Sour, but not spoiled enough to leave yucky lumps in my drink.

'Goodness me, Rachel, what the hell's happened here?'

A horrified Joanie is in the doorway, her anxious eyes shooting between me and the beautiful shattered cup.

'It's all my fault,' Joanie chokes for the umpteenth time, close to tears as we sit facing my new boss in his office. 'I should've checked the sell-by date, I must've forgotten to ask Keats to buy me a new carton on the way in.'

Keats? Who's that? I don't ask; this is certainly not the time for me to be lobbing out questions. I feel like an absolute damp dimwit. What a fuss. And over what? Soured milk. All I had to do was spit it out, wash my mouth, leave Joanie a note on her desk and return to work. Simple. But what do I do? Perform a scene that belongs in a third-rate daytime soap. And on my first day on the new job no less.

I can't let Michael think he's taken under his wing an attention seeker. 'No problem, Joanie. It was just one of those things.'

Her face is tense and drawn. 'I only went downstairs to collect the post or I would've heard you in the kitchen.'

'Stop worrying about it.' Michael's tone is gentle, rounded with an edge of insistence. 'As Rachel says, it's just one of those things. Would you do me a favour, Joanie – tidy up the kitchen.'

After she's gone, I try to recover the situation. 'I didn't mean to kick up a commotion—'

He cuts over me. 'Don't sweat it. These things happen—'

'Not on your first day in a new job.'

He leans back, a tiny smile licking at his lips. 'You've got nothing on me. I pranged the boss's Ferrari once on my first day in my first job.'

'You didn't.'

'For the next three months I lived on lentil soup and bread so I had enough cash to pay him back to fix it.'

We chuckle together. Any other boss would be railing at me for being a proper nuisance, not Michael. He has a way about him that puts me at ease. I'm going to enjoy working here.

Suddenly his face changes as something over my head grabs his attention. I turn to find his PA standing awkwardly just beyond the door. In her hand is the carton of milk. Something passes between them, a sixth sense people who have worked together for a long time develop.

Not taking his eyes off the other woman, he says, 'Excuse me,' and leaves me alone.

Something's wrong, I know it is. I hear their voices. Rapid, whispered, his deep, hers high. Can't catch what they're saying. I want to get up to find out, but it's as if I've been stitched into the fabric of the seat, trapped, no way to break free and move. Then I catch a word coming from Michael.

'*Rachel.*'

Why's he mentioning my name? The chair tightens. Squeezes. My ears prick up, but all I hear is the rustling of their voices mingling together.

'*Rachel.*'

It's Joanie's voice this time. What's going on? My heart's thumping against my chest, sweat breaking above my top lip.

Words continue running. Running. Then:

'*Rachel.*'

Like a song going up and down, my name's the only lyric that reaches my ears.

Rachel. Rachel. Rachel.

I'm a screaming mess by the time Michael comes back. He's not on his own. The carton of milk is in his hand.

'Michael, what's wrong?' bursts from me. I watch the milk he holds every step of the way as he retakes the chair behind his desk. He places it on the table. Doesn't let go.

His lips spread into a smile that doesn't change his watchful stare. 'Nothing. Go back to work and I'll touch base with you just before five.'

I'm about to get up. *Go on run, Rachel, like you did that summer,* the other me taunts inside. No, I won't do it. I look at my new boss. 'I wasn't eavesdropping, but I couldn't help hearing you and Joanie saying my name. Have I done something wrong?'

His smile stretches to his eyes as his palms tighten on the carton of milk. 'There's nothing to worry about. We'll touch base later on.'

I don't have a choice. The chair releases me and I leave.

I hover inside the door of my new office, listening. I hear him. Michael's firm footsteps in the corridor. I don't know for sure but I think he's gone into the kitchen. The slam of the fridge confirms my suspicions.

I give it half an hour before I cautiously head back to the kitchen. Thankfully Joanie's door is shut. With steps quick and sure, I open the fridge. The milk's back in its place. I take it out. Sniff. I reel back in shock. No sour smell. I pick off a cup from a hook. Pour. Hesitate with the cup's rim hovering on the outskirts of my mouth. Close my eyes and drink. Swallow. The flavour is rich, wholesome unspoilt milk.

I'm mortified. No wonder he and Joanie were talking about me. Sending me back to work with no fuss was Michael's way of trying to help me save face. Good grief, I hope they don't think I am what Jed's housemate called me – a nutjob.

For the rest of the day the memory of the taste of sour milk sits with the power of a deadly infection on my tongue.

Five

After work I arrive at the place that should be my real home. My house. It leaves me feeling so ashamed. My greatest gift, yet my biggest mistake. So lovely on the outside, so rotten within. It feels like a zillion years ago when I was twenty-three, deciding with youthful exuberance that it was time to stake out my own place in the world. Dad wasn't happy, I suppose not wanting his only child to flutter away from the family nest, especially with Mum gone for the last five years.

Not only did he cave, he'd also agreed to join me on my property hunt. We'd argued good heartedly, back and forth, me wanting a flat, his professional knowhow firmly in the court of a house near a tube station. In the end it was Dad who'd sorted it all out when he'd told me that a friend of his was downgrading his property portfolio, which included a small house.

As soon as I'd seen it I knew it was *The One*. Nothing grand, a two-up two-down perfect for a couple starting out. Dad – wonderful Dad – had so generously put down the deposit and the cash for the first year's mortgage. It should've been so easy after that. God, how had it all gone so hideously wrong?

I open the door and refuse to look down at the mini-mountain of letters I step over. Then stand so still in the hallway, arms criss-crossed tightly over my middle. It should be inviting, warm, but it isn't. Cold is ingrained so deeply into the fabric of the walls, floor, the ceiling, that it leaves an icy skin over my already goose-pimpled flesh. The electricity, gas and water were cut off months ago. A frightening urge to bolt out of the front door suddenly overwhelms me. *That's your MO, isn't it?* My inner voice snipes. *Always running. And running. Letting people down. Your dad down.*

I shake off the sensation of escape and move towards the lounge. Hover on the threshold. Hell, this is so hard. So crippling hard. The acid flavour of bile laces the back of my throat. It remains lodged there as I force myself to confront the physical devastation that was once my favourite room.

Radiator ripped from the wall. Ornate ceiling border hacked off. Some floorboards forced up and out. Light fixture gone. Furniture gone. TV system gone. Every room in the house the same – gutted of what a young woman of twenty-three had found so very special. Even the taps in the kitchen and bathroom and pipes in the walls are gone. Gone. Gone. Gone.

Defeated, I slump down to the naked floor. Pull my knees to my chest, arms wrap around my legs as if to protect me from further damage. I look at the place where the cast iron fireplace had lived. Now a misshapen, grotesque, gaping hole, the wall's screaming protest that its life companion has been forcefully taken away. I feel like screaming too. Banging my head against a wall that also offers support. How could I have been so stupid?

Then again, debt makes people do the dumbest things. If only I hadn't followed the dazzling seductive neon-lit 'Easy Way Out' sign. Rent out my house to a couple of mates to pull in money to dig my way out of my financial hole while I sofa-surfed about town. Easy. What could go wrong? My so-called friends deciding to use my house as their own moneymaking scheme, that's what. If I hadn't turned up here unexpectedly one Thursday night I'd have never discovered they were sub-renting it out for triple the amount they were giving me.

That Thursday, the door – my bloody door – had been opened by a guy who should've been sporting a T-shirt with the slogan 'Thug Number 1' in huge print across it. The hard faces that had hovered in the background behind him had looked like they'd written the rulebook on how to throw a punch. That had been one scary, scary night. Jed had rounded up a few bouncers from the club he gigged at and got rid of the lot of them. But not before they took every last thing of value from my home and trashed the place.

I did move back in, but one after another the utilities had been disconnected. I tried, I really did, to bed down on the floor of my one-time dream house that had turned into a freezing shell of concrete. Most mornings I'd wake, teeth chattering, no water to wash in, no fuel to cook. For two weeks I kept going, refused to give up. Until the day I awoke with a hacking cough and a chest so heavy with cold I knew it was time to quit. I'd grabbed the few belongings I had, fled, and thrown myself on the mercy of Annabelle, a friend from the bar scene, and then Jed.

I know, I know, I hear Jed's question — what about going to my dad? He'd have given me the money to reconnect myself to life, paid the mortgage arrears, put me straight. But Dad's a smart man: if I tell him about this, somehow he'd dig deep and make me confess the rest. The past. Plus, I don't want Dad losing his cool. Not a pretty sight.

I can't do that. Just like I still can't stay here. I've only come to get one thing. I ease up my aching body, go back into the hallway and stare down at the pile of post. I don't want to do this but what alternative do I have. I open my bag and pull out the bulging thing that's always with me. The self-inflicted sore that pusses with more poison every time I come here.

Minutes later, I leave, the thing I carry with me bulging bigger with more venom than ever before.

Before the whisper of courage deserts me completely, I pull it out. My poisonous unwanted bulging friend. The cheap carrier bag that stays with me twenty-four-seven. Tip it upside down. The contents scatter onto the table.

There. Done. Now the real trouble hits the fan.

I meet the unwavering stare of my newly assigned debt counsellor. It's my first appointment with her. Polly doesn't so much as blink; I suppose she's seen it all before.

'It certainly looks like we've got our work cut out,' Polly remarks in a very matter-of-fact attitude.

Our attention is hooked on to the mountain of letters I've unleashed. My dirty laundry laid bare on her pristine desk. Red letters, warning letters, threatening letters detailing exactly what I owe to whom and how much. I'm #Broke #InDebt #Can'tAffordToHaveSex.

My debt counsellor is one of these happy souls and plump like a Christmas pud that can't wait to be lit up. I suppose that comes with the training, full-on upbeatness so that clients don't feel even more crap about their financial shit show.

I'm grateful she doesn't request chapter and verse on how I ended up in this desperate situation. How does anyone end up in debt? To give myself credit – correction: ~~credit~~ – definitely the wrong choice of word – I wasn't one of those big spenders, splashing out on the high life. I'd merely been trying to keep my head above water when I couldn't find a job. Pay the bills, put bread on the table, cash for everyday travel. You end up borrowing from Peter to pay Paul and Paul and Paul… I shake my head as I drop on the seat opposite Polly. What a catastrophic, awful mess.

Polly stands up and I change my first impression of her. She's like the head of a troupe of Girl Guides ready for action. I like that. I need someone who's going to help put me straight.

'Right,' she announces, leaning over the table. 'The first thing we need to do is organise these letters into some type of order.'

A half-hour later there are three piles: final warnings concerning maxed-out credit cards, mortgage arrears, and one that sits on its own.

Polly resumes her seat. Her chin tips down. 'I can call your credit card providers and keep at bay potential court action, but your mortgage company won't be so easy. We need to show good faith, so you'll have to start paying the money back almost immediately. The last thing you want is to find yourself homeless.'

My house. Debt. The Big Bad Wolf threatening to huff and puff my house down. How could I have jeopardised the house Dad helped me buy out of the goodness of his heart?

Polly continues, 'It will be easier for me to contact the relevant organisations if I can keep all your correspondence.' I nod. She can keep the evil plastic bag. The sooner it's gone from my life the better. 'Rachel, you've come this far, so I'm not going to patronise you and say this will be easy. But, heads together, we will get this sorted out.' Her chair creaks as she arches her back ever so slightly. 'What about family? Can they support you?'

My throat muscles constrict, my troubled stare flickering momentarily away from this kind woman with shame. Thinking about Dad finding out about this leaves me cringing. If I tell him I'd have let him down – again.

'No. There's no-one.' That voice surely can't be mine. It belongs to someone who's been battered black and blue.

'No matter,' she musters with cheerfulness, 'we'll get this done and dusted the best we can.'

Then her fingertip slides the letter sitting in its own pile towards her. I'm riveted by the action. It's like watching the *Titanic* sailing ever closer to the iceberg. She taps it once before asking, 'Why haven't you opened this?'

I swallow. Tell the truth. 'I know it's cowardly, but I couldn't face it.' My head dips. I've spent so much of my life gazing at the ground lately I sometimes wonder if I truly know what the sky really looks like.

Seeing my dejected pose, Polly softly enquires, 'Are you feeling depressed? There are other services I can refer you to.'

Are you happy? would be the more revealing question for her to ask. What would she say if I answered that I haven't really known the melting abandon of happiness since that summer I was eighteen?

I ignore her kind enquiry and force my head up. 'Will you open the letter for me?' That's why it remains sealed; I know whatever's inside is bad.

The chopping sound of the paper, as her finger saws through the seal, leaves a tiptoe trail of chill bumps climbing my arms. I want to disappear. *Can't hide forever, Rachel,* my sensible voice informs me with the rhythm of a skipping game. Polly pulls out a single sheet of off-white paper. Silently reads.

Places it carefully on the table and smooths it out with her fingertips like it's the most delicate thing in the world. 'This is a letter to inform you that since you've had a county court judgement against you relating to the non-payment of one of your debts, you've now been placed on a register—'

'What?' I can't believe what she's telling me. 'What register? Like I'm a sex offender or something.'

Her fingers release the letter. It doesn't lose its smoothed-out shape. 'Let me explain. The register is not made public. Once your name's on it, you have a month to pay off what you owe.' She coughs delicately. 'If you don't pay, you'll be on the register for six years.'

I squeeze my eyes tight. Want to slap my hands over my ears. *See no evil, hear no evil, stuff evil in a cheap plastic carrier bag. Yeah, that's worked out a real treat for ya, Rachel.* What a complete fool I've been.

'Are you in work?'

I nod.

For the first time her tone sharpens. 'I need to be honest with you. I wouldn't be advising you properly if I didn't. If you're going to keep your home, you need money to pay off your mortgage arrears.' Her voice tightens with the power of a screw in my brain. 'If you end up on this register it could affect your future employment prospects. Employers have been known to check it. You'll have that hanging over you for six long years.'

'But I—'

Her stare is direct. I realise that Polly's not all jolly hockey sticks, but as tough as the seasoned leather of work boots. 'You're not in a position to pick and choose, which means you have to keep this job. Having a regular income is the one thing that's going to work in your favour. So, the job's got to stay.'

Polly's right. Debtors can't be choosers. My new job is a lifeline. My only one. Thank God Michael is such a generous and caring boss.

Six

I finally get what Katrina and the Waves meant by *Walking On Sunshine*. Because I feel the thrilling freedom of a bird as I stroll – swagger – up the stairs towards my office the following Monday morning. My step is jaunty, my hair allowed to go loose for once in its restrained life. And my heart… my heart's practically singing inside my chest. I'm even showcasing my other smart suit, my Stella McCartney pinstripe blazer and wide-legged pants I bought a few years back. That's how H.A.P.P.Y. I am.

If someone had told me I'd make it to my second week as a management consultant I'd have replied, straight and upfront, they were talking about some other Rachel from an alternative universe.

There have been no more sour moments after Milkgate. Things have settled down in my new job. Maybe it was because it had all got off to such a rocky start that Michael frequently popped his head into my office, asking how things were going. Really sweet of him, but if I'm truthful, he did it so much that it was wearing on my nerves. It wasn't like the tasks he gave me called for the rebirth of Einstein. Still, thanks where thanks are due, I appreciate him thinking of my welfare. And Joanie, bless her, is writing, in bold black marker, the use-by date on the cartons in the fridge.

I've felt the backhand of the gig economy so know this job is pitch-pure paradise. No managers bawling anyone out, no written warnings, looming redundancies or backstabbing petty office politics. Just me working at my computer, and occasionally surfing the net or doing some personal e-mails. If this is how the coming three weeks of my probationary period pan out, and Michael offers me a long-term contract, I've pretty much landed in a pot of jam.

I leave the stairs behind and head off towards my office. Say a cheery, 'Morning, morning,' to Joanie as I pass by. Open the door to my office. I rock slightly backwards, stunned speechless. The room's empty. No desk. No chair. No computer. Only the lived-in floor, four walls and my cherished window with the static buildings of London's skyline beyond imprinted in the background. A room wiped clean of me.

I stand in the doorway, palm rubbing with agitation over my bag. I don't understand.

I frown with a thought. Maybe Michael told me he was moving me somewhere else and I… forgot? Maybe my work's not up to scratch and he's giving me the push? No money means no cash to pay off my debts means I lose my house means I end up on that blasted register of financial rejects means my precious dad will find out. Butterflies beat in my belly, not the type you get when you fall in love, but the kind that visit when you're going to throw up.

Anxiety levels off the scale, I tap a single knuckle softly on Michael's door. My boss. Yes, my boss, I convince myself that's what he'll continue to be. No answer. Try again. Same thing. I have this insane urge to boot his door in.

Joanie's voice behind me saves me from the meltdown I feel coming on. 'Mr Barrington hasn't come in yet.' I don't face her, instead try as hard as I can to get the shallow air pumping out of me under control. 'Is there something wrong?'

Finally I turn. She's as mumsie as ever in a pretty floral print dress whose summery feel-good vibe is at odds with the dipped scowl depressing her forehead.

'All the furniture in my office has gone.' It comes out a breathless string of words stuck together.

She steps closer, her eyes widening with dumbfounded surprise. 'What do you mean, it's all gone?'

I decide there's no point us having this two-way chat, best to show her the conjuring trick that's been performed in my office instead. Joanie makes no comment as her gaze jerks around. Then her shoulders shift as if to fit the shape of her dress more snugly like a pair of shoulder pads. I've seen her do this before, a personal tick I suppose she's developed when trying to be ultra professional. 'Although Mr Barrington never told me about this, there must be a reason.'

'What reason?' I snap. *Calm down, Rachel. Use your lungs the way you're meant to.* I do exactly that and don't speak until calmness is back balancing my breath. 'What I mean is surely he would have told me something on Friday.'

Michael's PA brightens. 'Don't worry about it. I'll give Mr Barrington a ring. He's probably out getting you some new furniture; he likes his staff to be comfy. Why don't you wait in his office, Rach. I'll sort this out.'

My back teeth grind. I wish she wouldn't call me that. *Rach.* It's not that I don't like it, but it belongs on the lips of another person. Another time. Another summer.

Zooming back to now, I move towards Michael's office, the rhythm of my feet changing to a drag. Reach out and clasp the Victorian door handle, but don't turn it. It doesn't feel right stepping into his office while he's not there. It's his space, his private domain. It's like I'm poking around in his mind without him knowing I'm there. But still, I can't lurk out here like a naughty kid outside the headmaster's office.

As soon as I enter, the glass wall of windows calls to me. The unnatural magnetic pull draws me into the inevitable journey across the room. I gaze down the dizzying drop. Twenty-five, thirty feet? No coming back from a fall like that.

'What are you doing snooping around the boss's office?' Oh hell, it's Michael. My heart kicks up as I quickly swing round. Heart slows down when I see the cheeky grin that lifts his whole face. 'You're not trying to hack into my bank account, are you? Don't bother – all my cash is in the Cayman Islands.'

He laughs. I try to join in the fun but can't. I move to the employee side of his desk as he takes off his jacket and neatly drapes it on the back of his chair. He doesn't sit though, instead settles into an even stance by the side of his desk. Why this makes my nerves itch under my skin I don't know.

'There seems to be a problem in my office,' I tell him.

Correction: ~~seems~~. There *is* a problem, no seeming about it. We English do love our polite verbal tiptoeing dance of skirting the issue.

He looks genuinely baffled. 'Problem? I don't like the sound of that.'

Without warning, he marches out and I follow him into my office. Ourselves stare back at us, faint phantoms reflected in the window. Michael rubs the inside of his thumb against his temple, mouth skewed to one side as his gaze makes the rounds. Then he looks at me with such force I back up slightly.

'It's all coming back to me now. Please accept my apologies. I had the boys clear out this office.'

What boys? There's only the three of us in this building.

He walks and talks back to his office, me trying to keep up with his lengthy stride. 'I should have mentioned this to you on Friday. I'm reassigning you to a bold new project where you'll be summarising reports. You'll be joining a new team headed up by my top guy.'

My brain buzzes, trying to keep up with the new information he chucks my way. What top guy? What team? Before I can quiz him, he's back as lord of the manor behind his desk picking up his phone.

'Keats? Can you come to my office please? I want to introduce you to someone.'

Are there other people in this building? Have they been here all the time? I know the answer to both questions and an uneasy crawling, itching sensation travels up and down my spine.

Michael leans forward when he ends the call, his gaze trapping mine. 'The thing you have to remember with Keats is that Keats is a little eccentric and can take a bit of getting used to. A software whizz and they're not nine-to-five people, are they? Cost me big bucks to poach Keats from one of my rivals. But these software guys are all artists and you have to cut artists a bit of slack. So just humour Keats, okay?'

Eccentric? I don't like the sound of that. I've got enough strangeness already in my life. It seems like an age before I sense a presence in the doorway. I do a double take and almost recoil at the man standing there.

I lose the will to use my tongue. Keep gaping. Downright rude, I know, but I can't help it. He's about my height, I suspect in his twenties too, wearing military fatigues and heavy boots. It's not the type of dress code I'd assume would be permissible in a company like this, but that's not what's bothering me. It's his face. Over his head lies a low-hanging hoodie that obscures the top half of his face. Below that a pair of oversized sunglasses conceal his eyes and a good portion of his cheeks. Beneath that... I'm still trying to process what I'm seeing here. I think it's a bandana. Midnight black. It covers the whole of his mouth and the bottom of his nose. In a nutshell, except for a partial slice of the bridge of his strong nose, this man is faceless.

How the guy's maintaining that even soft in-out push and pull of air lifting his chest behind that piece of cloth I'll never know. He looks like a throwback to a Western outlaw including the six-shooter style mobile phone on one hip and small water bottle on the other. He's either about to set out on a terrorist mission or rob a stagecoach.

I'm stupefied and horrified all at once. Is this a joke? Am I the butt of some sort of peculiar practical-joke-cum-workplace initiation rite?

Obviously not because the boss introduces us. 'Keats, this is Rachel – Rachel, Keats.'

My hand shoots out awkwardly as I mumble, 'Pleased to meet you.'

He ignores my stretched hand, in fact puts his behind his back. Mortified, I let mine drop limply to my side. Holy hell, what have I let myself in for here? Then a relieving thought occurs to me. Maybe he suffers from one of those immune system attack diseases where the only way to avoid an excess of germs is to protect his mouth and eyes and limit what he touches. Or he's disfigured. Or protection against London's pollution. Whatever's going on here leaves me off balance. Off kilter.

'Keats, take Rachel to the systems room and settle her into her workstation and computer. And keep an eye on her.' A twinkle lights up his eyes. 'I don't want her hacking into the Pentagon like you do…'

Yeah, hahaha. Not amused. But I slap on my best employee grin.

Keats turns and begins to leave the office, gesturing with his hand that I'm to follow. Michael mouths at me, 'Eccentric… but… brilliant.'

Only when we go down the stairs does something uneasy occur to me. 'Is this systems room on the ground level then?'

I get no answer. We continue walking. I can't help but look back at my surroundings as we go. Yes, it's a dead ringer for the set of a Victorian costume drama or Fagin's lair but it's bright and light. Has windows. We cross the foyer until Keats stops near the back to the side. I look around dumbfounded. Don't understand why we've stopped because I can't see any evidence of a door or another office. Then he hunches down. Reaches out towards a round wooden handle in the floor. My stomach flip-flops, the air in my chest speeds up. He pulls, releasing a trap door flush with the wooden floor.

You've got to be kidding me! I figure out now where we're heading. Down to the place where twenty-two poor souls perished in a fire over a hundred years ago. Where a heroic dog tried to raise the alarm.

The basement.

Seven

Down and under.
Down and under.

That's where this masked man is taking me.

Anxiety hits. Panic grips. I can't do it. Can't. I have a fear of being trapped underground. Going down and under. No windows.

My jittery gaze skates over my shoulder to the building's entrance that seems to be beckoning me urgently. Whispering, warning me to run, run away. I know it's not real, a figment of the familiar paranoia and disorientation that's hijacked my mind and body.

But you need this job, Rachel. It's a necessity, not an option.

What do I do? Go down and under? Bolt away? I make myself look at Keats's back, who's unaware of all the dramarama behind him. Make sure he doesn't see what I do next. I tap the pad of a finger just above my right eye. Yeah, I know, looks crazy but it isn't. I'm stimulating a pressure point that helps to calm me. Because you see, I need to be calm. I'm going down. And under.

Keats heads into a yellowy gloom, down a long narrow staircase, hemmed in by twin walls of naked chipped centuries-old bricks that have a disjointed relationship to each other like overlapping mismatched discoloured teeth. I can do this. I've *got to* do this.

With a final tap and a prayer, I follow. Instinctively search out the light.

There it is. A naked muted-coloured light bulb, dusty, fixed to the wall. Focusing on the light is like focusing on air, a sensation of lean fresh oxygen coming through. My gut sucks and pushes air in a more regular motion.

I begin my descent. No polish on these stairs. Scuffed and scarred is their pattern, from the footwear of the living and those that are long dead. A tired rusty handrail to guide me, carefully I place my black flats on stairs that were created for smaller feet than mine. It's a break-my-neck steep fall if I lose my footing.

Every cell in my body rebels with each step. My stomach threatens to splash its contents over the walls. The bones in my knees tremble. The coldest sweat breaks, running into my eyes. My parched throat spasms, begging for water. It's barely twenty steps down but this journey feels like a martyrdom.

Keep going. Keep going. Keep...

Finally – praise be if I was a churchgoer – I reach the bottom. Teeny tiny balls of trapped dust drift in the air like drunken fairies. I cough lightly behind my hand. It's then I figure out we're in a corridor, a tunnel that would fit in a coal mine. *Coal mine, coal mine*, my mind hysterically grinds. *Down and under. Deep in the earth.*

The horror storms back. My senses become heightened, go into overdrive. I start smelling things that aren't really there. The foul aroma of death lunging up through the ground shackling about my ankles, twinning up my legs. The damp decay riddled in the age-old walls sticking and choking to the flesh inside my throat. Hearing things that aren't really there. Icy-cold water drip... drip... drip to the synced beat of my troubled heart. Start seeing things that aren't really there. The way ahead a wonky narrowing tube of darkness that leads nowhere. The lumps and bumps of the bricks growing, slimy tumours that threaten to engulf me on both sides.

What horrifies, claws at me, most of all are the screams. Of the twenty-two dead sweatshop workers. Terrifying. Deafening. Joining together until they're the raucous squealing noise of the wheels of a train, its death journey a head-on collusion coming straight for me.

My fingertip rushes above my eye. Tap. Tap. Tap. This isn't real. It's all in your head. My feverish gaze latches on to the weak light of yellow lamps fixed to the ceiling.

Air. Air. Air. Breathe. Breathe. Breathe.

Keats's stride is confident – he's done this walk many times before. I haven't. I continue to follow, breathe easier as I see there's a portal of escape waiting ahead – a steel door. I nearly lose my footing when I barrel into a large object. Instinctively, my palm touches the wall for support and I wish it hadn't; the overpowering wet chill from the bricks worms into my body. I snatch my hand away and gaze at what I've hit. A series of barrels stacked against the wall. Barrelled into barrels. Yeah, that would be a lol moment if I weren't so freaked out.

Keats stands by the steel door waiting for me. He gestures to me to follow. With his features hidden, framed in the half-light of the doorway, he's the double of a demon. I look backwards, towards the heavy shadow that marks the way to the staircase, my means of escape. Then I remember there are demons waiting for me in the outside world as well. My body stops protesting, heavy and inert as I follow Keats into the basement.

The basement is a cavernous space. Correction: ~~cavernous~~. Mustn't refer to spaces that are dark, enclosed. Underground. It's rectangular and large and probably goes beyond the footprint of the building and out under the street. The walls are whitewashed with bare bricks poking through in places. I think I can see scorch marks from that murderous blaze all those years ago. But of course I can't, my overdramatised mind working overtime again. The lighting is a blend of blue neon lights on the ceiling, flickering screens and red pinpoints shivering away on servers and routers. In other places its shade is outright gloom. The ceiling is pure Chicken Lickin' sky falling, so low that it's almost as if I can stretch on tiptoes and touch. Or near enough to crush me. Suffocating overheated stale air presses down on me too. Tap. Tap. Tap. Against the pressure point in the crease of my arm this time that I hold behind me so Keats can't see.

There's other tapping in here, the sound of fingers against keyboards. There are rows of desks arranged like a classroom where my darting gaze estimates sit about a dozen guys. Some are dressed in suits and ties while others wear clothes that are so untidy even calling it casual is being generous. No-one looks up or acknowledges my presence, like I'm a ghost passing through. Suddenly it hits – they're all men. Not a solitary woman among them, which means I'll be the only one of the opposite sex working here. Unease slithers menacingly through my bloodstream.

Keats introduces me to no-one.

A man with no face, workers who ignore me, a room that is intimately acquainted with death, what a contrast to my earlier carefree mood. So much for walking on sunshine.

Keats leads me to a desk in the middle of the back row where he switches on a computer. As it comes to life, he gestures for me to sit. He sits at the desk next door, which I'm assuming is his own workspace. His head goes down, the edge of the bandana over his lower face flapping once. Am I really sitting next to a man with his face almost concealed? Surreal.

He types on his keyboard. A high-pitched whooping sound draws my attention to my own screen. There's a dialogue box with a message.

Keats: *Mr Barrington would like you to finish a report in a folder on your desktop called 'Project' by the end of the day. Any problems please send me a message in this box.*

I scowl over at Keats, not that he's looking my way. Why isn't he just telling me like other human beings do via the mode of moving their tongue and lips? That's when I figure it out. Keats hasn't uttered a word to me yet. Not a 'good morning', a 'how do you do?', a basic 'hello'. No face. No talking. What the bloody hell is this?

Then I feel guilty. Perhaps I'm being unfair, even cruel. Maybe his illness prevents him from speaking. Or he's on the spectrum. A genius tekkie but socially very awkward? Still, it leaves me feeling like whatever control I've clawed back is once again slipping through my fingers. I write back.

Me: *Thank you. Will do.*

I consider popping on a smiley emoji, one of those with a full mouth of teeth that looks as if it's just dropped some acid, but think better of it. He doesn't respond. Cracks on with work. So do I. That's when I notice the continuous low humming noise coming from the walls. My palms go clammy as I type. As I sense the walls breathing around me, pumping blood from a stone heart I can't see.

Eight

I'm riding a horse through the surf on a deserted beach. Sand glittering a rich golden colour. The sun warming my bare arms as I hold the reins. A shy breeze cooling my face, the tangy salt it carries perfume in my nose. The sea is the bluest blue I've ever seen, its waves rippling in beautiful silence towards the horizon. I've got nowhere to go and nothing to do; the strong and wise animal I'm riding does all the work. He doesn't need leading or steering, he knows where he's going and I don't need to know. Rest back, relax and...

'Rach.' Philip's voice intrudes from that long-ago summer.

My eyes punch open with a vengeance. I'm almost choking at the unexpected intrusion of his voice as I try to cope with working in the bowels of the building. Never has Philip ever been part of the images I magic up during my mindfulness visualisations that I've learned from the Net. Maybe it's this new job reminding me of that other job all those years ago.

I've been in the basement for just over two hours, and for the last ten minutes my head's been a dome of throbbing pain. It's bowed, my hands shielding my eyes like a blinkered horse on a racetrack. Occasionally, I hear my heartbeat rattling like the beginnings of a chesty cold. Feel my calf muscles bulge and bunch. Now there's a sickness inside. Inhale deeply. Another. I squeeze my eyes and it subsides for a while.

I steal a furtive glance at the masked man next to me.

Despite the fact that I'm obviously in distress and Michael instructing him to look after me, Keats takes not a blind bit of notice as he hacks away on his keyboard. I bloody well know he can hear my small gasps of air. What does he think I'm doing, having a one-on-one orgasm? The guy's deliberately tuning me out, I know he is. I'm already regretting making excuses for him upstairs. He wouldn't know basic human empathy if it tried to tongue him through that stupid bandana. Maybe he doesn't like women.

I turn to him and ask in a brusque demanding tone, 'Where's the ladies?'

He doesn't answer my look with one of his own or answer but types on his keyboard. A message whoops into the message box on my screen.

Keats: *The what?*

Instead of using the option to digitally reply, I quietly snap, 'The ladies. You know, where women go to the loo as opposed to the gents where blokes go to have a wiz.'

I know, vulgar, but this creep's testing all my fraying resolve.

Keats: *Oh that. We haven't got one.*

I turn again to him. 'Is this how you're planning to communicate with me? By message box even though you're sat right by my side?'

Keats: *Yep.*

I hiss, 'You're an idiot.' Getting angry with Keats is making me feel better.

Keats: *You can use the gents. It's at the back there.*

My gaze finds it, a battered door at the rear with the outline of a man fixed to it, rather pointless given the male composition of the staff. I hold my nose as I approach; you can smell it's a men's bathroom from here.

When I get inside I sit on the seat and lick my emotional wounds. The lock is an old-fashioned drop latch. The cistern one of those that you only see these days as features in back gardens with plants in them. The chain looks like brass and has a porcelain knob on the end. If you took away the desks, phones and computers, this place could be a time capsule.

I try to visualise the thousands of pounds Michael has promised me at the end of the month. The debts I will be able to pay off. Going from the red into the black. I try to control my breathing as I massage my temples. None of it works. I'm trapped as securely as a caged animal. A terrified sweatshop girl.

I don't have the headspace to think things through but I already know this job is over if it means staying in this basement. Depression descends. How the hell am I going to pay off my debts now? It's highly unlikely I'll find another job that pays as well or have, for that matter, a great boss like Michael. Which leaves me where? Only one option. Making that phone call.

No, I won't do it. I can't.

The rest of the morning follows the same pattern: fifteen or so minutes writhing at my desk and when the anxiety floods inside me like foul water from a drain, heading off to the gents. Calming visualisations that don't work. Then back to my desk. Rinse and repeat.

It's nearly lunchtime and I'm on the gents part of the cycle when I hear the steel door swing open in the basement. Feel the cold breeze from the corridor sweep under the toilet door and stick against the lower half of my legs, sinking into my skin and bones.

It's Michael. 'Where's Rachel?'

When I present myself, no doubt resembling someone at the end of the ghost ride at the fair, Michael peers at my face, his dipped brows showing his worry. 'Are you all right? You look terrible.'

In fact, everyone down here looks terrible in this blue strip lighting but clearly I take the prize for most lousy-looking employee of the day.

'Not too good actually, bit under the weather.'

He nods, expression flattening and wiped blank. 'Right, well, in that case, you should probably think about going home. Do you want to go home?'

I know how damning this is going to appear, doing a sickie on my second week here, but... 'That might help.' He can't stop the spark of disapproval he snuffs out as quickly as it's come, so I add, 'I'm sure I'll be shipshape tomorrow.'

The concern for me is back on his face but I feel a barrier between us that wasn't there before. He probably thinks being sick counts as the disloyal or unreliable behaviour he warned me about at my interview. He escorts me out along the tunnel – I'm not kidding myself this is a corridor – in long strides, which I'm grateful for; I need to get out of this underfoot world like now.

I stumble up the stairs. Make it through the trap door. The squint of my eyes against the bright light of the foyer reminds me how long I'd been in that subterranean world. Hours. The light bathes me, a baptism of being reborn again. I top up my lungs with urgent gasping wheezing breaths. Michael makes no comment; probably thinks my behaviour is down to my illness.

Upstairs, in the doorway of his PA's office, he tells her, 'Rachel's unwell. She's going home.'

Joanie's immediately on her feet, her expression a picture of motherly concern. At least one person in this company doesn't view being ill as some kind of character defect. Is that being too bitchy about Michael? After all, he's got a business to run and the new girl on his management consultancy block is already playing the sick card.

'Your colour does look a tad off.' Annoyance flattens Joanie's mouth. 'I hope it's nothing any of the lads said downstairs.'

Said? I almost bark with insane laughter. They'd have to use their vocal cords, I want to fire back sarcastically. Including Michael's revered top guy Keats. That home truth is a lump I swallow back. Instead I lie. 'They've been perfect gentlemen. I'm feeling peaky is all.'

'You should go to a doctor, Rach. Don't come back until you're your wonderful self again. Isn't that right, Mr Barrington?'

Mr Barrington's lips are sealed.

Joanie accompanies me to the main door in the foyer, keeping up a brisk mummy bear comforting her cub patter that runs over my head.

Before I go, she leans in to my ear in the motion of our little secret. 'Don't worry about Michael. He's excited about the project he's got you and the others working on. It's also putting him a bit on edge.' She straightens, our just-between-you-and-me moment over. 'Maybe see you tomorrow.'

I tip out eagerly onto the street, greedily gulping lungs of oxygen. Who'd have thought London's polluted air would taste so sweet? Anything's better that the fetid air of the basement. I glance at the people I pass and wonder if any of them have ever considered what might be going on under their feet in the street? Of windowless worlds bricked up in the dark? As I stumble down the narrow street, holding my face up to the lukewarm sun, I think of Joanie's last words. One word in particular.

Tomorrow.

There's going to be no tomorrow for me here. I can't work down and under. Trapped in the windowless belly of a building that was once a burning sweatshop.

My only way out is to make the dreaded phone call. My trembling hand pulls out my phone.

Nine

I'm going to make a clean breast of it, I reaffirm yet again as the cab deposits me on the driveway of Dad's home. It's a grand eighteenth-century house where I changed from my teenage years to a young woman. Growing into my swan phase, except that's not how it quite played out.

I'm a nervous ball of energy as I push my key into the door and turn. He's going to hear the lot today because I'm tired of pretending and tired of running. He's going to help because he's a kind man and a good father who loves me. Correction: ~~father~~. Never that, always Dad. 'Father' is a stiff old-style word that implies a man who has a slight distance from his child, that's the way I see it, whereas Dad is a person who gets stuck in with oodles of unconditional love. I'm all Dad's got left since Mum died. Making me happy is his main pleasure in life.

The only thing I will *never* confess is the root cause of why I've messed up so spectacularly. He's never going to hear about that. Not from my lips.

My heart clenches at the sight of him in the large gleaming wooden-floored hallway. New lines of worry are etched near his eyes and mouth. There's a restlessness that surrounds him that suggests he's been pacing since he got my call. Frank Jordan's a big man – shoulders, hands, stature, laugh. Head, those who are jealous about his success would also say. Muscle and attitude to life honed after years of hard slog on construction sites before he established his own building empire. Still showcasing a full head of hair, vanity maintaining its original shade. But what's always fascinated me about my dad is that chipped side tooth of his. He's got enough money to turn it into something belonging to a Colgate ad, but he never has. It's as if that tooth is a symbol of the tough Yorkshire mining world he came from and he doesn't want anyone to forget.

He reaches me first, in measured strides, and hugs me like he hasn't seen me for a long time. Too many men are unwilling to demonstrate physical emotions, not my dad. He smothers me with it. 'Are you all right, pet? You look upset.' He pulls back to scan my face, not hiding the concern he's feeling.

'Not too good actually.' Hesitantly I add, 'I've left my purse at home. Do you mind paying the cabbie outside?' Beginning a visit that's all about the truth with a lie about my purse I know isn't the best way to start but I need to warm up to what I have to say.

'Of course, love,' he answers in a voice that's still threaded with his Yorkshire roots. He's a man who's proud of where he's come from, also proud of where he's got.

As he goes outside, I skim over the framed photos of him and Mum proudly mounted on the walls. Snaps that catch them in their youth at the start of their relationship. Frank and Carole.

In those early years, married life was the three of us in a semi in south London suburbia. Dad was a labourer on building sites until he decided the only way he was ever going to get the job he really wanted was to create it himself. So he set up his own construction company, working gruelling hours day and night, often coming home with tiredness threatening to pitch him forward after dropping off his crew in his van late at night. As his fortunes grew, he moved us into larger and larger homes that he often did up himself with the workers he hired.

Flashed memories flick through my remembered mind of him treading his dirty boots and overalls through the house, leaving muddy footprints behind. Mum would follow him around with a squeezy bottle and a cloth without complaint. Dad doesn't wear boots or overalls nowadays; he's a Saville Row made-to-measure gent. I'm dead proud that his catchphrase remains, 'I'm what I always was – a working man.' I study their couple pictures again. They look so happy. Especially Mum. I look like her, except her young self sparkles from the health of her skin to the shape of her pixie-like smile. Towards the end of her life, the smile had eroded away until the day it slipped away forever.

'I miss her too.'

The strained sadness of Dad's voice behind me draws a lump to my throat as I turn. He rarely speaks about Mum because I sense he thinks it will upset me. It was such a devastating time. She fell prey to an illness of the immune system that none of the many doctors she saw could cure. There I was, at the gateway of adulthood, eighteen; I wasn't ready to let go of my mum. Each day she grew fainter, thinner, fading from the picture of my life, until one day all that was left was a devastating blank page.

The year Mum passed he tried to cheer me up with a goodness that he still has no idea went completely bad. I could pretty it up with all manner of flowery adjectives but the simple fact is what happened has left me feeling like I've betrayed everything Dad has done for me. Let him down. And I've been struggling ever since.

Just as I'm struggling with what to say now as we sit facing each other at the high-legged dining table in the massive kitchen with the commanding views of the North Downs and Kent countryside in the background. In the summer it's a mash-up of green hills, sandy-coloured wheat fields, wild flowers and bees blowing around in the warm breeze. In the winter, snow lying long, fixed to the ground, reflecting the white gleam of the moon on dark evenings. Today I find it hard to find any beauty outside.

Dad cuts to the chase. He always does, priding himself on the plain speaking he learned as a child in a northern mining community where bluntness is a virtue.

'Spit it out, girl. What's the matter?'

My teeth worry my bottom lip. Rising blood flushes my face. My skittish gaze darts away, skidding with annoying panic around the room, only stopping as it settles on a small photo on the fridge. Mum pregnant with me. Her hand rests on her large bump, her teasing eyes only for the man behind the camera. What would she say about the screw-up the baby she nurtured, loved, has made of her life?

The warmth of Dad's palm over mine draws me back to him. 'Whatever's the problem we can sort it out. Together. I'm here to help. I'll always be here to help.' I look into his comforting sturdy eyes. Suddenly his expression burns fierce. I know that look; Dad's donned his battle armour. 'Is it a boyfriend? If it is, he'll be answering to me and no mistake. I'll teach him to mess my Rachel around. I'll knock some manners into him. If you're in trouble…?'

If it were only that easy. 'No, Dad, I'm not going to present you with a grandchild. I don't have man trouble—'

'Then it's got to be this new job. Are they taking advantage of you? If they are, you know what the answer to that is – work for me instead.'

Since I dropped out of uni halfway through my first year, he's run a subtle campaign of trying to coax me to work for him in readiness for the day when I inherit his construction empire. But I've run a counter-campaign with the banner 'Rachel does life the Rachel way'. Me wearing a hard hat? No, not a look I'd want to carry off. That's what I tell Dad, but my reasons are much deeper, more rotten. Once I start working for him, it won't take him long to discover that I'm as much of a wreck as the house he helped me buy. Then he might wonder why that is.

I remember the first time I decided that always telling my dad the truth wasn't such a good idea. A teacher made a joke about my appearance at school one day. A pretty harmless joke really but I was upset. Back home, after my dad persuaded me to tell him what was wrong, he promptly jumped in his Range Rover and went to the school. He threatened to do serious damage to the teacher if he ever did that to his daughter again. It was the talk of the playground for days and I was beyond embarrassed. That's when I decided that perhaps some things were better left unsaid.

And that was before everything that happened when I was eighteen, giving me even more reasons in the world to be guarded with the truth around him.

'Darling.' I hear the emotion he's trying so hard to control. And there's hurt there too. Pain.

'Dad…' I hate seeing him like this. Hate even more that I've brought it to his door. I've heard the rumours about how ruthless he can be in the business world. Formidable is what they really mean. A kid from a poor community has had to be in order to get where he is in the world. I wish they could see him now, the no-holds-barred kindness and devotion he has for me.

'Do you know the last thing your mum said to me?' He takes my hand again, his broad fingers curling into mine, bonding us together. 'Make sure our girl grows up to be like you. Independent. A fighter. The best there can be. And that's what you've done. I'm proud of you. I know things didn't work out at university, but so what? I never went to one of those snob-nob places and look at me? You've got the spirit of your mother in you.' He stabs a finger passionately into the table. 'Whatever's eating at you will never shake the belief I have in you. Your mum had in you.'

His staunch belief in me slays every last word I was determined to lay on the table between us. How can I sit here and tell him things that will demolish his unconditional conviction in me? Watch the aching disappointment in his eyes that the rest of his face tries to hide. Why isn't there a law against putting others on pedestals? We all come tumbling down in the end. A heavy depression shrouds its veil over me.

I feel the ridges and calluses in his palm as I squeeze. And go with a semi-truth. 'I wanted your advice about this character who's my supervisor at work.'

I tell him about Keats's manner of dress and remote behaviour, which Dad responds with, 'Stay out of his way as much as possible. I had this client once, him and his lady wife would dress up as Batman and Robin every Friday.'

'You're making this up.' At least I'm smiling.

'God's honest truth.' He winks at me. 'The fellow would insist I call him Bruce Wayne and they'd go around their home humming the theme song.' Dad does just that, humming the theme tune wildly, rocking his body, eyes alive with mischief ending on a resounding, 'Batman!'

I lean over, punching light-heartedly on his arm as we laugh ourselves silly. That's what my dad does for me, makes me feel great about the world again. But this time he's done something else. He's given me my mum's words to help me through.

'*Make sure our girl is a fighter. The best there is.*'

The best doesn't choose to remain on their knees when they can be standing strong on their own two feet. Sort out my financial woes, that's what I'm determined to do. I'm going back to my job. Back to the world beneath the trap door in the basement.

Ten

BBs, aka Beta Blockers, and cannabis oil are my breakfast of choice this morning. No way on this earth can I go back through the trap door, work in that dungeon-coffin-basement without their chemical assistance. I can hear the naysayers in their saintly perfect-world voices: 'I'd never go back to that job. No how, no way.' But would they really? With debt growing every day? The haunting dying words of a mother for her child to become the best she can be? Walk in my very heavy shoes first before you cast the first know-it-all stone.

Relax. I hang on to the word with the tenacity of a rosary bead as I approach the building that is my place of work. Before I press the entrance buzzer, my eye catches the plaque honouring the dead workers. Dead girls. The 22. That's what I've decided to call them. I give them a nod of respect before my finger on the buzzer lets Joanie know I'm here.

Joanie doesn't drop the lock but comes down to greet me, her features a mask of pinched concern. Inside the foyer there's a subtle twitch in her arm muscles. I hope that's not the forerunner to her hugging me to her motherly breasts, attempting to 'There, there, there,' soothe me better. I mini-step to the side so she gets the message to keep her embraces for those who request them. Don't get me wrong, open-armed physical kindness is always a beautiful blessing but I suspect this morning the only thing it will do is make me turn tail and run.

Joanie satisfies herself with a tingling single comfort-pat on my shoulder, her tongue hitting the roof of her mouth with disapproving noises. 'Rach? You shouldn't be here. You should be at home with your feet up. What are you thinking of?'

'I'm fine.'

She examines me, head-to-toe, expression grimly doubtful. 'You still look a bit off colour.'

Before I have any say in the matter, Joanie's corralled me upstairs with a steaming cuppa between my hands, doing a ten-minute chillout in her office before work really begins. We're a strange pairing, me and Joanie. Her offering me chocolate finger bikkies as she fusses and flutters recommending this herb, that potion that can kill the common cold dead, while I sit impassively with a strange strained smile. Still, anything that delays me having to face going *down and under* is welcome.

'On a tea break already, Rachel? I wish I had your job.' The sound of Michael's unexpected voice rattles my cup, splashing drops of tea over my hand. Oh heck.

Dreading coming face to face with him, I take all the time in the world turning, recalling his fleeting displeasure that I went home sick yesterday. I'm not sure what expression he's wearing. Blank-faced? Suppressed anger? I don't know this man well enough to judge.

I breathe easier when his dimples strut the catwalk of his cheeks. 'Sorry about the low sympathy quota yesterday. I had a lot on, which is why I'm off to my office now.' He turns, then shoots over his shoulder, 'Good to have you back in the family, Rachel.'

Joanie flashes a triumphant look, clapping her fingertips together in rapid glee. 'Told you he was being a tad touchy yesterday. Don't mind him. His bark is worse than his bite.'

My moment of grace is up so I stand. Smile, with heart this time. 'Thanks so much for the TLC.'

She escorts me to the door. 'Are you sure you're all right to work?'

I want to ask her a question back: will she escort me beyond the trap door? I know I'm a proper scaredy-cat, but there's a killer dread brewing within.

'Are you all right working down there in the systems room with the boys?' Joanie must sense my reluctance to go.

The systems room? A polite phrase for the basement. 'I preferred working up here with some light and space.' I can't help the internal tug that draws my gaze to her window.

'You mustn't mind the lads.' She waves my fears staunchly away. 'They're all perfectly harmless, I know they are.'

What's that supposed to mean? I don't get a chance to find out. Joanie closes her office door.

Less than a minute later I'm looking down at the trap door. This is the first time I'll be going under on my own. The spit I nervously try to swallow refuses to slither down. I notice what I didn't yesterday; the trap door has an extra-light sweep of polish, that the flooring it lies flush with has started to let go. Smooth. Entrancing. A make-believe sheen that's to lure me into a false sense of security that blinds me to all manner of horrors below.

The BBs and CBD oil have long kicked in but they can't reach that tiny screaming part of me that won't let go. It's inside my manic mind, shaking and quivering, dreaming up terror-soaked happenings I'll encounter beyond this door. Darkness. Encroaching walls. A ceiling waiting to free fall onto me. *Stop it with the silly shrieking girly drama. Right now! It's a walkway not a tunnel. The only thing moving down there will be you.*

Before I lose my nerve, I hunch down. Gather my building courage. Take the hard handle in my hand. Pull back. Stare down. Hunt the light in the naked bulb at the top to help me breathe properly again. That's it – air, air, air. I take two steps. My arm shoots up, halfway in the world below, half in the world up there. I know I have to do it. I clutch the inside handle. *Do. It.*

Pull the door shut above me.

I want to run down the stairs, but know that's an idiot idea. I'd probably go head over heels and who knows what may happen to me then. So, I remember the light above the air it brings and move steadily to the bottom.

'*Rachel. Rachel. Rachel.*' The whispered echo of Michael and Joanie saying my name as they did that first day suddenly joins my journey. It's my ears playing a nasty trick. Hearing things that aren't really there. I pick up speed, looking ahead only, willing myself to make it to the steel door.

'*Rachel. Rachel. Rachel.*'

Get out of my bloody head. Slam! I shut my ears down. Centre every part of me on the light. Air, air, air. There! Made it! You did it, girl! I touch my palm to the coolness of the steel door to verify I'm really there. I catch my breath for a few seconds. Then to the business of how I'm going to deal with my day inside the basement. One thing I have decided is to love-bomb creepy Keats with the messaging system in an effort to get some kind of conversation going so I don't feel so isolated. I also plan to do the mountaineering thing; not look up at the ceiling, down at the floor or across at the walls. Instead focus on my computer to try to forget where I am.

Nothing's changed inside the underground room with no windows. They're all in there, sitting in rows. Zombies doing exactly what they're told. Zombies? That's exactly what they're like. No surprise that not a single one looks up, or acknowledges my presence with a morning-morning, a welcome-again-to-the-club smile. I could be the phantom soul of a dead sweatshop worker.

Only Keats gives me the time of day with a glance and short nod. His choice of bandana today is green fatigue. I wonder what his eyes are like behind his shades as he takes me in.

Smiling? Rolling? Squinty eyed? Dead dull? Who was it who said, 'The eyes are the window to the soul'? Well, this man's keeping his soul under lock and key. It's what you can't see sometimes that terrorises you the most.

After a decent interval of cracking on with a report that uses stupid happy-clappy management phrases like 'blue-sky thinking' and 'out of the box', I turn my attention to my charm offensive against Keats.

Me: *Hi Keats. How's things?*

He takes his mouse, and with an elaborate swirl, clears the message and carries on working. Ah, a man who isn't into office chat. I'm not giving up. The idea of having no-one down here to talk to is crippling. I'm not looking for a friend, but that human-to-human spark every now and again would be massively appreciated.

I give it five mins then I'm pinging back up on his message box.

Me: *Do anything interesting last night? I stayed in and watched* Love Island. *Don't know why really, it gave me an inferiority complex about my body.*

A bit of humour to dent his armour. Doesn't work. Double damn.

Me: *Joanie's a real softie, isn't she? She's worried that I'm unwell. I thought she was going to make a camp bed up for me in her office and make me drink honey and lemon for the rest of the day.*

Keats sits back. What's the expression he wears under his facial mask? I suspect it's mouth-twisting annoyance. The reply I finally get proves I'm spot on.

Keats: *This is a work environment not a club for the twinset and pearls brigade. Put a cork in it and get on with your work.*

That has my mouth flapping like a fish. How rude is that. And condescending. I don't know why this guy doesn't like me. I haven't done a thing to him. Probably I was right yesterday; he doesn't like women. I side-eye him with the type of contempt I hope turns his seat into an electric chair. Okay, not really. All I want is someone else down here to be able to reach out to. But it won't be Keats.

What a nasty piece of work he is.

Eleven

It's lunchtime. And a strange thing happens. Keats stands, with the others following suit. I feel like a solitary audience watching a synchronised chorus line of male workers. I tried to talk to one of the guys earlier and he blanked me. I was midway through asking him a question about his role when he shuffled away like he was fleeing from me asking him out on a date. My teeth press into my lip as doubt and indecision play tag. Am I meant to stand too? New jobs can leave you so insecure with their unwritten rules and regs no-one takes the time to tell you about. Before I can decide on what to do, the door opens revealing a beaming Michael.

He rubs his hands together as he makes a jolly announcement. 'Who's for pizza?'

Ah! So that's why they all got up. I assume this is some kind of lunchtime office ritual, Pizza Tuesday, bonding over food and drink. What a great idea. So I stand and reach for my jacket as Michael disappears back into the corridor. But Keats puts his hand on my shoulder. I tense at his touch. I've never felt his flesh on me before. I thought it would be the sensation of forbidding cold, but beneath his imprint is a stirring warmth. How strange, I wouldn't have expected a cold creature like him to be warm-blooded. He goes over to his computer and types. I lean down to view my message box.

Keats: *Not you. Permanent staff only.*

I'm engulfed by this retched sense of isolation. It's never a great feeling being left behind. Brings back memories of Mum passing over. As they file out, leaving me alone, I try to cheer up by insisting I'm not entirely sorry that I won't be joining these zombies, or Keats in particular, for lunch. I'd love to be a fly on the pizzeria wall to see the stunned expression on the waiter's face when Keats orders his Hawaiian in his full combat desperado rig. Pineapple and ham? No, Keats will be a pepperoni and Cajun sauce guy. Hot 'n' fiery.

The steel door clangs shut. I sigh lightly and then decide I might as well go for lunch too. I push the door handle down. The door doesn't budge. I tug harder. It refuses to detach from its frame. The metal handle slips from my hands when the penny drops. I'm locked in the basement.

Alone.

All the earlier patient work I've put in to keep composed goes out of the window. Correction: ~~window~~. There's no window down here. No natural light. I fumble in my bag for my mobile and call Michael. No connection. The basement must be beyond the reach of my service provider's reception. And stupid me forgot to ask for the password for the office wifi, so I can't even send an e-mail. I turn. My edgy gaze bounces and bounces about. My chest squeezes, my eyes water as if they've been stung by a film of dust.

The walls are closing in on me, I know they are, the ceiling inching lower. The lights come alive, stabbing me with their hostile glare. I'm caught in a coffin, the bang bang of nails cementing its lid over me forever. It rushes back to me, the girls who died in this very trap room over a hundred years ago. The words on the website come back to haunt me.

As the flames drew closer, their faces wreathed in choking smoke, prayers for divine intervention were feverishly howled by the doomed girls. The heroic dog that had led the way, keened in helpless anguish. All twenty-two perished.

I panic. Thump my fist on the door and cry out. No-one comes. I flatten my back helplessly against the door, my palms spread against unresponsive cold steel. *Don't panic. Don't panic.* Didn't a character say that in the classic comedy, *Dad's Army*, as they did the opposite, panicking enough for England?

They'll be back soon, won't they? How long does a pizza take?

I hurry to the back of the basement, hoping to find a way out of this prison. The wall is shadow and whitewash over ancient wood panelling. Something catches my eye. A semi-circular wooden handle. I study the panel more closely and note the straight lines defining it. I think it's a door. I look back at the handle. Damn. It's been painted over and is stuck to the panel. Screwing up my face with determination, I dig in my nails and pull. Let out an ouch of surprised pain as I spring backwards and stumble. The handle hasn't budged an inch.

Think. Think. Think.

I rush back and rummage around in drawer after drawer until I find a metal ruler. It takes all my will and strength but I manage to jemmy the handle free. Then I tug desperately. No joy. I use the ruler to scrape away the old paint from where I think the door frame is and put my foot against the wall and pull with all my might. A thick solid oak door creaks on its hinges, gives off the groan of a dying person, opening enough for me to inch through.

I sense it's another room. Blanketed in dark, coated in a musty smell. I use my hand to feel along the wall. Touch something that's the shape of half a tennis ball jutting from the wall. A dated light switch. My fingers roam over it until I locate the on/off switch. Flick. A pasty dirty brown-yellow light throws its gloom over what appears to be an empty storeroom. The aged bulb inside is hanging by a wing and a prayer, its wiring frayed and torn. There's another door at the back. It's fastened shut with what must be decades-old rusty bolts. I won't be defeated. I bite and fight the pain that attacks my hands as I pull the bolts free. Open up.

Fresh air. Streams of natural light. I tip my head back like a convert reborn. Tilt my mouth open. Bliss. I stay like that, don't move for a while, breathing in the invigorating oxygen that I've always taken for granted. I look about me and am surprised to see I'm not fully outside. It's a kind of narrow courtyard, functional, not pretty, save for its cobbled ground. In the middle is an old-fashioned drain to catch rainwater through the large iron grill above that links the courtyard to the world outside. Two black things suddenly clatter over the grill. I jump back, grossed out it's a pair of rats swishing their tails taking a lunchtime stroll. Then it happens again and I understand – it's the shoes of pedestrians walking over.

I breathe with relief now I can holler for help at passers-by if I need to. Thank God my mobile works here because of the reception coming through the grill to outside. Now I know I can come here, it feels okay to go back inside.

I close the door to the narrow passage, fasten the bolts again but their age and rust mean they're nearly hanging off. I push the internal door to the basement back into place and try to cover where I've scraped off the whitewash.

Now I'm here on my own, naughty thoughts come to me. While the cat's away… I slip into Keats's seat and spin round. I can't resist grinning. I shake the mouse on his computer to get rid of his screen saver and look at what he's been doing all morning. He's a busy boy, no doubt about it. The guy's a whirlwind. On his recently opened files option, there's a dozen he's opened today alone. One is a policy document for a corporation that explains how to create a happy and integrated workforce. I can't hold back the nasty laugh that bursts out. Laughter dies, curiosity grows when I see a graphics file called 'P Funeral Service'. Strange thing for a management consultant to be doing. Or perhaps 'P Funeral Service' is a cover name for something else. I open it.

It is indeed the first page of an order of service programme for a funeral. The photo of the deceased, a young man, stuns me. My breathing changes, along with the beat of my heart, both high kicking to a dangerous level of acceleration. My earlier wish that Keats's chair turns into lethal electric must have come true because I swear I'm being electrocuted. You see, I knew this handsome young man in the photo. But I'm not paralysed with shock because he's dead. I knew he was dead. How can Keats be working on his funeral service programme *now*? He can't have passed away. Not recently.

Philip died that summer ten years ago.

Philip can't have died twice over.

My head, my brain, my everything is shaking in numb denial. This can't be Philip. Not my Philip. No! I've got this wrong. Being alone down here, in this stagnant vault, has mushed my mind. My head moves closer to the screen to check… I hear the zombies coming back in the corridor outside. A tribe of footsteps playing musical echoes. *Keats.*

Panic is beside me again. A fine sheen of sweat blooms below my hairline as I hurry, with shaking hands, to close the file. The footsteps beat louder. Hell, I can't get Keats's screen saver back. *Come on. Come on.* The footsteps are the intense beat of a drum as they near the reinforced door. The screen saver won't be found. Awful silence from outside. My heart lurches. I jump into my chair, head down, tapping nonsense on the keyboard as the door opens.

I run my hand over the damp sweat on my brow. Look up at Keats. Smile innocently enough, although I suspect he deliberately locked me in this room. The zombies file back on his tail. Keats takes his seat and studies his screen for a moment. He moves and clicks his mouse. He turns his head towards me slightly and pauses. What's going on behind that bandana and sunglasses of his? A patchwork of confusion? A vision of menace? Lips parted because he's going to let rip at me?

He turns slowly from me and carries on working as if nothing has happened.

I'm completely shot. The only sounds are digital hums, the walls' peculiar breathing and my own aching heartbeat.

Nothing in my life could prepare me for this moment. My eyes have just told me one thing but my searing and inerasable memory tells me something else. Philip died, was buried. Ten years ago. That's not something I'm ever going to forget. It made me the person I am, more than anything else. Now a file – a funeral programme – on Keats's computer tells me Philip's just died and is about to be laid to rest in the near future.

Both can't be true. Deep down inside my soul, someone, something is screaming at me to somehow, someway, print off a copy of the funeral programme. I can hear the screaming. But my limbs and hands are stiff, stuck still by a bitter cold as my fractured mind hurtles back into an unwilling past.

Twelve

That summer

'I've found you a summer job, Rachel. I know you don't need the money but you know how I feel about teenagers learning to stand on their own two feet. When I was your age I was labouring on building sites from dawn to dusk. It'll give you something to do before you go to university. And anyway,' her father's voice faltered, 'it'll be better than staying in the house, moping and thinking about your mother.'

In the three months since Rachel's mother had died, her father, Frank, had never uttered the words 'mum', 'mother' or 'wife'. Rachel hadn't either. She didn't want to upset her father by reminding him about his wife's death. She knew he didn't want to remind her that her mother was dead either. They were like two conspirators covering up a crime called grief. Instead of the sound of tears in their rambling country house, there was only silence. The silence of the grave.

Rachel pasted on her best make-believe smile. 'Great.'

'I met an old friend of mine yesterday at my club,' her father informed her as they sat at their special spot at the kitchen table. 'I don't think you've met my friend, Danny. He's got a big house on an estate about five miles from here. He owns a business in my line of work too, building, construction. Anyway, I had a word with him and he thought he could find you something to do around his house, filing or collating or something. You can travel there on your bike. I said you'd go over tomorrow morning. Nine o'clock. Don't be late, start as you mean to go on.'

That was all her father said before silence descended on their home again.

There was no sign of Danny the following morning when Rachel wheeled her bike up the drive of a property that certainly put the 'country' into 'house'. She rang the doorbell and hammered on the brass knocker but no-one came. The house was silent. But in the luxuriant gardens that surrounded the property, there was a sound. Someone singing along to a guitar, accompanied by the yap-yap barking of a small dog. She left the front door and followed the music. Behind a gazebo, she found a young man who her girlfriends would call 'a looker' sitting back against the structure singing Alice Cooper's *Eighteen*. A puppy gleefully scampered around, joining in with a howling harmony.

The man looked up with a warm smile. 'Hi there. Come to burgle the place? The safe's behind a landscape painting in the master bedroom.'

Cheeky guy! Though she did like the twinkle in his eyes.

'I'm Rachel. I'm supposed to be starting work today with Danny but I don't know where he is.'

The young man nodded. 'He's probably out and about putting up overpriced jerry-built flats that don't need to wait for Jericho for the walls to come tumbling down. That's where he usually is. I'm Philip, by the way. Why don't you park your backside and join me for a ciggy while you wait for the old crook to turn up?'

'I don't smoke, it's bad for you.'

Philip was laughing at her. 'Right. I suppose that means you don't want to shoot up any of the heroin I've got in my bag?'

Rachel looked outraged. 'I'm sorry?'

'It's a joke. You know what one of them is, don't you? If you're going to be working around here, best to have a sense of humour.'

'Right.' More in embarrassment than anything, Rachel sat down next to Philip and enjoyed the puppy making a fuss of her. 'Hello, what's your name?'

Philip explained. 'He hasn't got a name yet. I found him in a river on the way to work a few weeks back; I think someone was trying to drown him.' He tapped a finger to the side of his nose. 'By the way, don't tell Danny I'm looking after our little friend here. He doesn't like dogs. He told me to get rid of him.'

At the sound of footsteps approaching, Rachel leapt to her feet and stood awkwardly to attention, Philip meanwhile lounged further back. A large thickset man with a stony face came round the corner, eyed Rachel, then Philip, then Rachel again.

He spoke to her first. 'Hello, you must be Frank's girl. Come into the house and I'll find you something to do.' He turned to Philip. 'And as for you, what do you think you're doing?'

The cheeky young man shrugged. 'I'm on a tea break. I'm entitled, it's the law.'

'And what's that mutt still doing here? I thought I told you to make it disappear. I'm paying you to be a gardener and handyman – not a dog warden. Why don't you go and prune the roses or something?'

Slowly, with the insolence of youth, Philip climbed to his feet, guitar in hand. 'Yeah, I'll do that. They could do with a bit of nip and tuck. I'll see you around, Rach.'

As Danny and his new employee walked towards the front door of the house, Philip called out across the garden. 'Hey, Rach. I've got a name for the dog. I'm going to call him Ray – then you'll be Ray and Rachel – you can go on the stage together as a double act!'

For the first time since her mum died, Rachel's face lifted into a real smile.

Rachel was an only child. In the weeks that followed, Philip became the brother she'd never had. They were both eighteen. When Danny wasn't around, and sometimes when he was, her new friend seemed to be on a perpetual tea break. During those extended breaks, he taught her how to juggle apples from Danny's orchard, how to play the chords to Alice Cooper's *Eighteen* on his guitar and how to do wheelies on her bike across the gravel drive. He taught her all the names of the plants and trees and the birds that sat in them. He asked her questions that she'd never been asked before. When she said she was going to a really good university in the autumn, he looked puzzled. 'Why?'

No-one asked that question at her school or among her friends because it was the natural order of things that everyone went to university. 'To get a good job.'

He scoffed, appearing highly unconvinced. 'Right. Good plan.'

When she mentioned she'd lost her mother in the spring and the doctors couldn't explain why, he didn't react like most people. He didn't say:

'At least she's at peace now.'

'Time's a great healer.'

'At least you've still got your dad.'

Philip said nothing, just offered her his hand. When she took it, he held it softly for as long as she wanted it held. He always said and did the right thing. He always made her laugh. He always looked out for her.

Only once in those first few summer weeks did Philip turn serious. When he asked her what Danny was actually making her do, she told him she was cleaning his classic car collection in their specially built annex.

Philip's initial reaction was to sneer, 'Oh yes, his cars; they're the only things he really cares about. That and his multiple ex-wives of course.'

But when she told him, 'From tomorrow though, he's asked me to go down in his wine cellar and catalogue the vino in a notebook for him,' the muscle in Philip's cheek twitched.

'His wine cellar?'

'Yes – that's all right, isn't it?'

It was a long time before Philip answered. 'I suppose.'

'Why wouldn't it be?'

It was an even longer time before he whispered, 'No reason.'

Thirteen

'When are you packing your bags and moving out?'
Those are the fiery coals heaped on my disorientated head after I close the front door of the houseshare. It's the vulture from the kitchen. Hands on hips, standing there blocking my path like a newly constructed partition wall. She's one of those perpetually angry people. You know, lips drooling with displeasure, eyes hard that refuse to rest, a body held a hair's breath away from pouncing on some unsuspecting victim. Well, I don't need her BS. Not now. Not after seeing Philip… If it was his face that I saw. Will the shaking ever stop? The hurt go away? My hidden past leave me the damn alone? *But you know it's never gone away. It's always taunted, playing a cruel version of peek-a-boo around every corner you turn.*

The walk from work back here was a path strewn with broken-glassed turmoil. My existence spinning on a sixpence ready to capsize, upending me. I'd been frozen, transfixed in the street by a toddler crying and its mother trying to scold and tug her into a pushchair. That's what happens when I see the distress and pain of a stranger, no matter how young or old, I catch a wisp of Philip's tortured features in their face. As if he's there, amongst the suffering and heartache.

Did I see what I thought I saw in those moments at Keats's computer? Or have things reached such a pass that my imagination has replaced my reality?

'I asked you a question.' What is without doubt a reality is this woman rearing in my face. Her obnoxious tone rather than the question itself is what mercifully drags me back to the present.

'Whatever's the problem will have to wait. I'm busy.'

I try to bustle by but that bristling body of hers shuffles and shifts, won't let me pass. Who the son of a monkey does this woman think she is? My guardian demon angel? No, that's Philip. His beautiful open face swims in my mind. Then it shutters and snaps, a camera lens replacing one picture after another of him. Talking. Head tilted back, filling the world with his husky start-stop beat of laughter. Humming Alice Cooper's... No! No! No! I won't go back there.

She needs to let me pass. Can't this self-important woman see I'm on the edge? Ready to combust apart? It makes me rage, so angry, I bite back, 'Can you get out of my way.' Do I mean her or mine and Philip's past?

The only tune she's listening to is her own. 'You should've been gone a month ago. My friend's been waiting to rent the room.'

'Your mate's just going to have to wait. Now there's a rhyme you can take to your lonely bed and snuggle up to every night.'

I know, I know, I shouldn't bait her; I can't afford to be kicked out onto the street. Get her on side. Turn the heat dial down. Softly softly the mood tone. But I've had it to the gritted back teeth with her and the snide swipe of her eyes at every turn, whispering bitchy badness about me in poor Jed's ear.

Her rampant breath covers my face with the evil intent of a plastic bag. 'You think you've got him wrapped around your crooked little finger.'

'What?' Him? My snapped-together frown shows my confusion. Bloody heck, are those tears glossing her eyes?

'Jed,' she gulps, 'he deserves someone better than a user like you.'

The pattern of the air she leaves on my skin changes. Ragged with a cyclone of emotions. Ah, I get what's going on. Little Miss Vulture is jealous. No, she's no vulture, but a lovelorn lovebird who thinks I'm Jed's latest squeeze. Thinks

I'm making a play for him on her field. Utter crap. Me and Jed are buddies and that's all it will ever be. Why can't some people get it that a gal and guy can just be very good friends? Mind you, Jed's always had a large female following, including our school days too. Most want to run their fingers through his hair, detangling its unruliness, flatten the very personality out of him. Why can't most people love someone for who they really are, not what they want them to be? *Like you, Rachel? Avoiding confessing to your dad the truth about what your life's really become? About Philip?* I flinch from my own truth.

And turn the spotlight on my nemesis. 'Jed's a mate doing another mate a turn. That's all. End of story.'

She won't let it go, seething through the tiny gap I see in her cut-sized front teeth. 'I know women like you. Gobble up the goodness in a guy and then spit him out.'

I'll gobble her up in a minute if she's not careful. Oh, she wants to play get-down-and-dirty does she? Best not disappoint her. I lean in and boldly whisper, 'He's a red-hot chilli Casanova between the sheets. Morning, noon and three times a night.'

Lovebird springs forward.

'Ladies? Ladies? Is there a problem?' The interruption of Jed's anxious voice from the top of the stairs stays her attack. Just as well; at the age of seven, Dad had instructed me there were three things I needed to learn inside out – the alphabet, the times table and how to land a punch. He'd applied himself to teaching me all three.

She swings round, takes one look at her love interest's expression, probably realises he's overheard every word and bolts with mortified *Run Rabbit Run* speed into the kitchen. The air crackles out of me with a dead-on-my-feet motion as I trudge up the seesaw steps on aching and sore legs that are begging for sleep. Instead of taking Jed to my room, I draw him to a spot by the lopsided radiator on the landing. Truth is, when I shut the door of my room, I want privacy. The company of me, myself and I.

'What was all that about?' Jed's eyes are wide, his hair wilder than usual, his broken nose even more off-centre.

'You certainly know how to pick your girlfriends.'

He blusters, 'She isn't my...' He lowers to a whisper like he's scared the other tenants will hear, 'current steady.'

'You might want to think about telling her that.'

His pose abruptly changes as he shoves his hands into the front pockets of his Levi Classics and shuffles his feet. Then he captures my gaze and won't let go. 'Thing is, Rachel, Sonia,' – so that's her name – 'has got a point. I did say you could stay with the knowledge that one of the others' friends has earmarked the room to move into soon.'

This must be what people mean by the weight of the world on your shoulders. Except the sensation I experience now is a crushing pressure on the top of my head. It won't stop. Keeps pushing. Pushing. Threatening to squash me right through this scarred bare floor. Seeing the photo of Philip – or whatever that was – and having to contemplate moving out of this house is too much for me. I want to throw myself on Jed's mercy – again.

What halts me is the agonising expression Jed probably doesn't even realise he wears. Upset. Sad. Like he wants to hold me tight. I wish I could wipe it away with the words he wants to hear. But I don't have that power within me. Call me selfish, a worshipper at the altar of me-me-me, call me what the heck you like: but know this – I'm staying put until I'm forcibly shown the door.

Finally I speak. 'I'm doing my best to find alternative digs. You know I've got money coming in with this new job. Okay, it's at a place where sweatshop workers were killed in a fire—'

Jed is bug-eyed. 'What?'

'I'm happy there. It's a really great place.'

There's the nervous shuffle-shuffle-shuffle of his feet again. 'You're going to have to find another place to lay your head soon. Or go back to your house and face up to things.'

I'm already turning away as I shoot over my shoulder like a woman who hasn't got a care in the world, 'Doing my best. A girl can't do more than that.'

I'm back in my room. The door a barrier between me and a world that clearly has a beef against my very existence. I'm not alone though; Philip's there too. Side by side with me as I do my routine of casing the window. Checking the drop and the impact it will have on my body. Then it comes to me, what people call a light-bulb moment, of how I can find out if Philip died recently and not ten years ago. I pull out my phone. Hit the Internet. Type in 'Philip'. My tapping thumbs and fingers stall. Hell. I don't know what his surname is. Was. 'Philip' and 'Rachel' that's all we ever were to each other.

For the next couple of hours I try, desperately, to block out the past with the latest must-watch five-star box set streaming sensation on my handset. Doesn't work of course. So it's a pill down my throat, a squirt of thick oil under my dry tongue. The chemicals, mixed with exhaustion, start to do their work...

I wake, head heavy, dried drool caked down one side of my mouth, in a room that's long been dark, laden with a blanket of cold. I could stay here for the rest of my days, cocooned in a space of utter nothingness. No debts to pay off, no past bad deeds to account for.

No Philip.

I blink my weary eyelids open. Tap the pad of my finger above my right eye until whatever I saw in the dungeon office on Keats's computer disappears. For now. Then I go utterly still as I do most nights and listen. No noises; the others are all safely tucked up in their rooms. Judge the time to be right for my night-time ritual. Check my mobile just to be sure. Thirty minutes after the witching hour.

I leave my room, barely touching my feet to the floor, so the others won't hear me. Make my way to the bathroom. Open the door, its peeling paint shuddering as I shut it with only a click I hear. It's small, no thrills. There's a shower minus curtain or screen. It's the distastefully avocado-coloured plastic bath that holds my full attention. I pop in the plug. Turn on the tap, which lets loose a short protesting growling sound before the water gushes out. I'm hypnotised by the water. The way it dances from side to side as it streams from the tap's open mouth. The way it splutters and slaps the water already pooling below, forming tiny bubbles that burst and die quickly.

I'm not here to have a bath. When it's filled I won't get in; I never do. Just remind myself to come back to the bathroom at six before anyone else is about so I can release the water.

The unexpected ringtone of my mobile, in my back pocket, distracts me from the running water. I pull it out. The shocking brightness of the screen in the gloomy dark hurts my eyes as I check out the number. Michael. Alertness shoves the running water and everything else aside.

'Rachel. I hope I haven't disturbed your beauty sleep.' His voice is as crisply cold as the water.

I ease the door of the bathroom shut. Rush on my toes back to my room as I answer quiet and low, 'No, no, I was up anyway.'

The last thing I want is to wake any of the housemates and for them to find me lurking around the house in the dark like a spirit that has long lost the ability to rest at night. For them to realise that I fill the bath with water every night. I check the time on the phone. 00:44. How bizarre. What an odd time for him to call.

'That's good. Obviously I wouldn't have phoned unless it was urgent.' I've made it back to my room, my feet snapping past the bucket of water by the bed I sit on with unease.

His controlled tone gets swiftly down to business. 'The thing is, I asked Keats for a progress report on your work to date. He submitted it this afternoon before he left and I'm going to be frank with you, it doesn't make for very pleasant reading. To be even more frank, Keats thinks you're totally unsuited for the work. It's his opinion that you're sloppy, unprofessional, and don't seem to know the first thing about management structure and analysis, which is a bit of a problem for someone working as a management consultant.'

I picture runt Keats upstairs in Michael's office, snitching me up. Bastard. Without thinking, I retaliate. 'Yes, well, perhaps if Keats actually took the time to speak to me—'

'All you did was regurgitate my words in those reports,' is the backlash that stings me. 'I don't need a parrot on my team. I want a skilled operator who can analyse and synthesise information.'

Analyse? Synthesise? The words make my heart pound.

'Umm... Well...' I don't know what to say. How to defend myself.

He cuts me short. 'Look, Rachel, we need to sort something out here, because if we can't, then I'm afraid, and with regret, we're going to have to part company. I want you in my office first thing so we can explore our options.'

Options? The earlier sick feeling in my tummy comes back with a vengeance.

I trip over my reply, pulse going into overdrive. 'Yes, but...'

It's too late. He's gone.

I slump on my mattress. This morning I came back to this desperately needed job to stave off bankruptcy. Now I don't care about the money or bankruptcy anymore. This job is solely about getting my hands on that funeral programme, no matter what it costs. Finding out if the face on the programme really belonged to Philip is all I care about.

Adrenaline suddenly shooting through my veins like a class-A drug to a junkie, I reach for my bag. Pull out the rope

I keep with me at all times. Except during the night and the dawning of the early morning. My hand glides over it. Black, braided, above all strong and long. And knotted at intervals like fat twine jewels in a nylon necklace. I go over to the window, as I do every night. Open it. Secure one end of the rope to the radiator below and dangle the rest out of the window. I freeze. Something disturbs this other nightly ritual. A movement in the garden. A figure looking up at me from the shadows. I don't have to ask who it is. Jed's little heartbroken bird. Sonia.

She stares hot-eyed at me. Then at the rope that hangs from my window.

Fourteen

Something detaches me from sleep. What it is, I don't know. I lie in this semi-scared half-tense world, curled protectively on my side, as if expecting massive hands to shackle around my ankles before dragging me from the bed. There's a hyper alert energy about the house that leaves a strange roaring deep in my ears.

That's when I hear it. Them. Shouting downstairs. Despite seven different people with their own personalities co-existing within these walls, this has always been a relatively peaceful house, so the sound of yelling surprises me. And at this time... 01:53. The voices hike up in volume, driving me out of the bed and into my jeans jacket over my T-shirt and shorts. A big yawn accompanies me to the door. I'm exhausted, brain-weary, leg muscles aching from the never-ending marathon that has become my life. The last thing I need is domestic drama.

The landing feels inhospitable in its chilly inkiness, leaving me shivering and pulling my jacket tighter to insulate my own body's warmth. The residue of a downstairs light blurs against the staircase wall. Does it belong to someone's room or the kitchen? Even though I don't know most of the people who live here, I hope that no-one has been taken ill.

My steps quicken down the unsteady stairs, the voices getting louder. I freeze when I turn the corner at the bottom and see the backs of my housemates gathered at the entrance to the kitchen, heads slightly down looking at something on the floor as they criss-cross argue. Well, it's actually Jed involved in a right royal row with his unrequited love. I must've made a sound, I'm not sure, because they all suddenly turn my way like wind-up toys getting ready to perform a macabre collective march. Accusatory expressions maul me. Only Jed's features are set in a different way – hopeless and helpless. Whatever *this* is, it isn't good.

I stand my ground in the space I've marked as my territory by the staircase, resisting the urge to wrap a hand on the end of the bannister for the support I suspect I'm going to need.

'What's going on?' My voice is slow as if that will delay matters.

Lovebird speaks, glaring and spitting at me. 'I want you OUT. Now!'

'We've already had this conversation.' My swift comeback lacks the confidence I had earlier when us two got into a verbal ding-dong.

Wonderful Jed comes immediately to my defence but he won't touch my gaze, stirring the dread in my bones. 'Leave off, Sonia,' he snaps, reminding me she does have a name other than one that belongs to the bird kingdom. 'You're jumping to conclusions—'

She butts in, 'Are you having a laugh? Let the bitch see what she's done.'

Jed waves an irate finger at her. 'Don't you dare call my mate a name like that.'

'Mate?' Sonia lets loose with sarcastic scorn, fists balled. 'She's using you, you muppet.'

'Now you hold on—'

'Stop.'

Pauline from the attic room stops them with the commanding tone she's no doubt honed as a primary school teacher. Pretty woman, with a perfectly shaped 'fro who usually keeps herself to herself.

'I understand where you're coming from, Jed. This is your friend, but Sonia has got a point.' The others nod. Whatever this is, I'm on the losing side. 'Rachel needs to see what's happened.'

There's a Red Sea parting of the ways to allow me through. I feel no exhilarating Moses moment as I move forward with trepidation, slow step by slow step, their hot eyes watching me every inch of the way. I see it before I reach the kitchen doorway and can't help the choked gasp that disturbs the sudden stillness of the night.

It's a scene of utter destruction. There's a huge jagged hole in the ceiling where the plaster has come down, exposing the floorboards and insulating foam of the room above. Directly beneath is the debris awash with water that's turned the kitchen floor into a mini lake. Water weeps down the walls, leaving it looking like fresh dirty-white paint settling in to dry.

I open my mouth. Nothing comes out. Try again, still baffled what this has to do with me. I turn. Talk. 'I don't understand—'

Of course it's Sonia who decides she's the one to fill in the blanks. 'You left the water running in the bath tonight.'

The bath. Tap. Water. My mind skates back. Earlier. The bathroom. Triple damn. I must've got distracted by Michael's call and forgot to turn off the tap. I'm always so super careful. Make a point of giving the tap an extra secure turn that burns my fingers so that it's tight. I always leave the bathroom with the sensation of the frigid coldness of the metal of the tap imprinted on my palm. There's no such memory now.

Jed plays knight in shining armour to my dumbstruck damsel in distress. 'It could happen to any of us—'

'It happened to *her*,' Sonia fiercely cuts in.

'I mean, we've all had those moments,' Jed continues as if she hasn't spoken, each word delivered in a jerky upbeat tone, 'when we've forgotten to do something.'

'But we don't fill up the bath every night when we think the rest of our housemates have gone to bed.' It's Pauline this time, her careful reasoned teacher tone getting everyone's attention. 'That's what you do, isn't it, Rachel? I saw you do it once when I got back from a night out with my friends.'

There! Out in the cold like the water flooding the kitchen. My secret. One of my demons on the prowl in plain sight for all to see. My face is a hotbed of humiliation. Quickly, I avert my face to the side; I don't want any of them to see how this is eating me. Tearing me apart.

'Why do you do it?' It's Pauline again, soothing, like she's asking one of her kids why they smacked another child in the mouth.

'I tell you why,' Sonia storms, 'she's a bloody weirdo, that's why. She also hangs a rope from the window of her room at night.' Now they're all looking at me, except Jed who won't look at me at all, like I'm a serial killer in the making.

'She's got to go.'

Jed steps back in. 'Why? She's never late with the rent.'

Another voice this time, the man in the room next to mine whose name my tilting mind can't find. 'If we're being official about it, she doesn't have a lease with the letting agency—'

'Who we all know won't do the repair—'

'I'll pay for it—'

'What with? The pittance you earn gigging...'

On and on they go, as if I'm no longer there, a ghoul who's haunted their house for way too long. Five against darling Jed who refuses to back down. The voices of Michael and Joanie join in during Milkgate on my first day at work.

Rachel. Rachel. Rachel. The tormenting calling of my name swamps my ears again.

Voice after voice beats and bangs against the four corners of my drained mind. Relentless, painful, grinding whatever will I have left into dust until I can't find myself. The same terrible feeling I experienced when I got into debt. When Philip...

'Shut up.' They march on. Don't hear me. 'Shut. Up.'

Stunned by my screamed yell that echoes around us, I swivel back to them. 'Don't worry, I'm going. I'm truly sorry about the wreck in the kitchen.'

Jed reaches towards me. I swerve out of his reach and scramble up the stairs. I hear him and Sonia going at it.

'You're the bitch here, Sonia.'

'Screw you, Jed.'

'Think you've got that the wrong way round because I hear that's what you're gagging for me to do to you….'

I shut my door ever so quietly back in my own aching solitude. I don't need a do-gooder or mirror to tell me I'm the physical embodiment of the wreck of the century. I could lean against the wall and cry but what would be the point? Plus, there's been enough water letting for one night. I've made a decision though. I get to action, shoving my gear into my rucksack.

A gentle tap-tap sounds against the door. 'Rachel, can I come in, babe?' His jumbled breathing is audible through the door. Poor Jed. Sounds like his latest gig has bombed.

Should I or shouldn't I – let him in? He'd provide a shoulder to lean on but that won't change what we both know – my time here is up. I open the door. For the first time I see how tired my friend looks, the drawn skin that pushes the bones on his face to the foreground.

'Where you going to go?' he asks, sounding as dejected, defeated, as I feel.

I shrug. Think about popping on a fake smile to ease the tension but the very life has been sucked out of me. 'I'll find somewhere. None of this is your fault. You've been the perfect bestie a person could ever want.'

My arms hug him tight. His hard breath stains the side of my neck as he hesitantly asks, 'So what's with filling the bath? The bucket of water by the bed?'

I haul back from him as if his skin is the hottest thing on this earth. We stare at each other, friend to friend. Eventually I pivot away and move across to the window. Tease my rope with two fingers as my gaze is captured by the dark new day outside.

I tell him what I've never confessed to anyone else. 'I have a fear of fire. I know it's crazy but wherever I live I have to be ready in case a fire breaks out. So I have to have a bucket of water next to me when I sleep and the bath filled up so I can refill my bucket if I need to.'

My words run on with the speed of a river flowing. 'I have a fear of enclosed underground spaces.' My fingers twist painfully into the rope. 'I always need to know where the window is as a means of escape so that's why I hang the rope.'

I say no more. I wait, chest and throat so tight, pulse racing like mad as I wait for him to tell me I'm nuts. That it's all in my imagination. Or ask what happened to make me harbour these compulsions and fears.

But all he says is, 'One of my exes had a fear of big toes. Insisted when we were in the sack I keep my socks on.'

I look over at him, eyes squinting. 'You're making that up.'

Jed puts his hands in the air. 'As God is my witness. She saw my hairy big toes one day and raced from the room and threw up.' There's a twinkle in his eyes so I can't be sure if he's telling the truth or spinning a yarn. I suspect the latter: Jed's way of trying to put me back together. I'm grateful he doesn't dig deeper, wanting to know what turned me into such a mess. Just as well: I'd never have told him.

'The others said you don't have to go tonight,' Jed informs me. Not Sonia though, I bet. Probably waiting downstairs with a pitchfork to see me on my way. His voice lightens. 'We'll sort this all out tomorrow. Sleep tight.'

After he's gone, his footsteps padding away into the waking morning, I sit on the bed until I sense the shifting of the energy of the house back to its usual vibe, the others all retreated to their rooms. For the last time, in this room, I do my daily ritual of going to the window. Open up. Haul the rope back and place it in my bag. There will be no tomorrow for me and Jed. Not in this house anyway.

I use my toes to go downstairs. Open and close the front door. Walk away, bag on my back, empty bucket in my hand and I'm soon swallowed by the city's anonymous nocturnal shade. And walk, and walk. Where I'm going I don't know. I've run out of places to hide.

Fifteen

I hesitate before pressing the security system to get into the building the next morning. The plaque on the wall doesn't look like a memorial today but a faded tombstone of a mass grave. I nod respectfully at The 22 and then avert my gaze as quickly as possible. The lock on the door pops and I go inside.

Leaden feet take me up the stairs. I notice their polish isn't so bright today, the chrome bannister not as dazzling. But who am I to talk? After a rough night in my new temporary home, I know what I must look like. Shattered. Sore-eyed. Tousled. Clothes that need reacquainting with an iron. Hardly the picture of someone Michael would want to keep on in his company. I wouldn't be surprised if he gives me my marching orders.

I pray he doesn't. I have to find out if that was Philip's face on Keats's computer. That's what matters now. I'm prepared to grovel, eat dirt or dance in all my birthday-suit glory for the zombies on Pizza Tuesday if that's what it takes.

The boss waits for me at his usual spot at his desk. The saliva dries inside my mouth, my tongue a beached whale that can't move. The expression he sends my way is bored, blank. Immediately, the tiny atom of security I feel withers within. I grab a huge pull of air through my nose to settle my nerves.

With a flick of his wrist, Michael waves me to sit. When I'm in the chair, he begins. 'Let's make this short and sweet. What are we going to do about this situation? Because things aren't quite working out the way I thought they would.' His fingers steeple, adding to his air of deep contemplation. 'We need to think of some solutions here. You and me together.'

Two of my fingers tap-tap-tap against the hard bone of my knee below the desk in the desperate hope there are pressure points there to calm me down. I clear my throat. Sure, I'm burnt out, frazzled, but I'm not buckling. I'm my dad's daughter all the way. Whatever life has thrown at me, I've never buckled. I might have nearly crumpled the other day when I went to see Dad, but I didn't. Just as I can't afford to now.

I find my voice, which is steady. Strong. 'Obviously I'm disappointed that you're disappointed.' Dad taught me that phrase years ago. 'Everyone's Happy' is what he calls it. The other party thinks you've apologised, when you haven't really and you haven't admitted to doing anything, so saving face.

The heat of blood beneath my skin floods my face when I see the arched expression Michael throws at me. Ah! I think he knows all about the tricks of 'Happy' phrases.

He leans back in his seat as if I'm a sculpture in a gallery he's trying to get a new perspective on. 'Now, I like that. Business talk. Smart. That's one of the reasons I took you on because I thought you were smart—'

I jump in when I know I should really let his words run their course. 'But I was upfront at the interview that I'd never been a management consultant. You assured me that the skills from my previous employment would be useful to you.'

'So, where are they?' A muscle in his cheek furiously beats. 'It's not my job to bring you up to speed. I don't have to tell Keats, Joan or the others how to do their jobs, and I shouldn't have to tell you.'

He contorts his lips like a spot ready to rupture. 'Let's look at the facts here. You go sick when you're hardly through the front door. The reports you write wouldn't be worthy of an intern. Keats says that your work is slow, simplistic, and the end product only fit for the bin.'

My fingers stop tapping as they curl into a fist with deadly intent. Keats might be Mister No Speakee but he's been loud and clear enough to do a thorough number on me. If he were here right now, I'd do him some very, very serious damage.

I go on the defensive. 'Maybe I was hoping that Keats would support me in a more productive way.' I raise my hands above desk level and deliberately wring them. Turn my voice into poor helpless girly-me tone. I know, not exactly twenty-first century womanhood but I'm using every weapon in my arsenal. 'It hasn't been the easiest thing being supervised by someone who doesn't talk to me.' I add a pitying shake for good measure. 'He's so busy. Doesn't have time for me. Just the other day—'

'I get the picture.' Michael's pensive, the outside of his thumb circles his temple. 'So, what are you planning to do about it?' There's a resigned softness to his voice.

And that's what makes me realise what Michael is. A shapeshifter. I can't be sure which Michael I'll end up encountering. Caring, sharing Michael of the dimples fame with Sister Sledge's *We Are Family* as his ringtone. Or broody moody Michael who thinks smiling is a sign of a terminal disease.

So I tread carefully, talk slowly, discarding the defenceless female act. 'I accept there's obvious room for improvement with my performance. There'll be no more sickness. I'm trying my best to develop a teamwork ethic with my co-workers. This is not a situation I want an employer to find himself in where my work is concerned.'

Michael mulls this over. Then he sighs deeply and pushes some papers across the desk. 'You need to look at these online courses and videos. They should help you get a handle on what we do here. Obviously, you'll be watching these in your own time and you'll be expected to do it in the systems room after work has finished. You need to pull your socks up, Rachel. Is that understood?'

In my own time? In the systems room? 'Are you suggesting that I work late in the...?' I can't hold back the catch that yanks the words to the back of my mouth. I cough. Try again. 'In the basement on my own?' *In the late evening. Not a soul in sight. No window. With only the humming walls and the desolate blue lights for company.* Good grief, I can't do that. *Not even for Philip?* I slam my nightmarish reservations to the darkest corner of my mind.

Michael's on his feet, so I stand unsteadily too. He checks his watch as if he's on the clock, which I suppose he is. 'I usually work late too, so I'll be here when you're skilling yourself up on the courses I've selected. I know this is short notice so I want you to start at the beginning of next week.'

I hope he doesn't hear my punched air of relief.

I leave. Allow myself a tiny smile. I haven't been sent packing. I psych myself up with the confidence I need to get another day over in the basement. To figure out how I'm going to get access to Keats's computer.

I shut Michael's door, the handle hot in my hand for a mini-second before I let go. I'm stopped by the sight of Joanie lurking in the doorway of her office. Correction: ~~lurking~~. That word's unfair to her because her features are painted with grave concern and consternation as she worries her bottom lip, fingers stapled tight to the edge of the door. She doesn't speak but pulls the door back, inviting me in. She leans past me, quietly setting the door shut. Of course, initially I only have eyes for her solitary window.

Her urgent rapid-fire voice pulls me back to her. 'I'd have to have no ears not to have heard Michael's raised voice.'

The last thing I need is for the boss to think I'm bitching behind his back, creating another opportunity for him to possibly show me the door. Though I do tell her, 'It was nothing. Really. We're on the same page now.'

Joanie considers me for a second or two, blinking heavily as she gathers the right words to say next. Satisfied she has them, she nods more to herself than me. 'Park yourself in a chair while I get us some tea. And choccie fingers.'

She doesn't give me a chance to refuse.

Joanie's back less than five later, steam wafting like charmed snakes from the cups she carefully places on her desk. Tea and sympathy: the classic English solution to solving your problems. If it were that easy, the National Health Service would have stockpiles of the stuff.

'Stress,' Joanie says with conviction. 'That's what Michael's under, poor man. He negotiated hard and long to get this new project you're all working on downstairs.'

To tell her or not to tell her? Do I really want the slings and arrows of my problems littering her personal space? Besides, other than offering me obliging sounds of sympathy and a well-meaning reassuring pat on the knee, she doesn't have the power to change what's going on in the down-under world buried two flights beneath our feet. Still... suddenly there's an urgency compelling me to offload on her. Maybe it's because she's the only other woman working here. I don't really know.

'Keats has been trashing me to Michael. Telling him my work isn't up to scratch.'

'The masked bandit of Barrington Corporation,' Joanie scoffs with drawn-out disdain followed up with a twist of her compressed mouth and shake of her head. 'I thought it was a stick-up the first time I clapped eyes on him.' Her arms shoot in the air, a Mary Pickford silent-screen expression of mock-horror distorting her face. 'Don't shoot me, mister. I'll hand over my handbag and jewellery.'

My belly rocks with a laugh. What a lovely surprise; the last thing I expected after the draining tension with Michael was a chuckle or two. I really do appreciate her trying to scrub away some of my strain, replacing it with a good old-fashioned giggle.

'You don't like him?' I state the obvious.

Joanie arches a single brow, which says it all. She gives me the verbal version anyway. 'Come on, Rach, this isn't *The Phantom of the Opera* part bloody two now, is it? The guy gives me the creepy jeepies. I know you young people are into this fashion, that fashion,' she leans dramatically forward, 'though I can't see that clothing he's rigged out in gracing New York fashion week.' With a knowing look, she shifts back. 'Call me old-fashioned but I like to see the faces of the people I'm working with. The only reason he's here is because Michael says that he's the real deal. And that's what Michael's interested in, dealmakers.'

I draw the tea to my lips, pondering what she tells me. If I'm honest I suppose that Michael had been upfront about his number one priority being to grow his business, join the guys and gals in the big league. Nevertheless, I still don't understand why Keats just didn't have a quiet word in my ear instead of blabbing badness to the boss. Exercise the right to use his mouth. *He doesn't speak,* my inner self pointedly reminds me. *He's an automated message through your computer.*

Joan says with a satisfied gleam, 'If that's all that's troubling you, I wouldn't worry about…' She must see a big giveaway written on my face that screams I've got more troubles at my door. 'What else is going on down there?'

My lips rub together, sealing the words I'm desperate to share with someone else. To tell her about Philip. What I think I saw. *Come on, Rachel, is this woman really going to understand that someone has recently died who you think — know? — died ten years ago?* Inner me is right. Joanie would think I've gone crackers. Plus, there may be nothing to know if I've got the wrong end of the stick about whose face I saw.

So, I drain the last of the tea and get to my feet. 'Thanks, Joanie. Taking some time out for a cuppa and chat has really put me back to rights.'

With a heartfelt smile, I turn, but her voice stops me. I look back and notice that she hasn't touched her drink, a cold muddy skin slick on the top.

'If you ever have any problems, you come to me. Right?'

I nod. Close the door. Philip's face visits me for the first time today, leaving me trembling on my journey down the stairs. His face is strained. Anxious. Not his usual flip a finger to the conventions of the world self. A secretive drop of CBD oil helps banish him, for now, from my anguished mind.

Sixteen

I hear Keats's fingertips on his keyboard. Acutely feel his presence next to me. I want it to be me sitting in his chair. Rifling through his files until I find the funeral programme. I could simply ask, I suppose. Humbly doff my cap to him and fling myself on his better nature. But he doesn't have a better nature. *He tried to get you fired by bad mouthing you to Michael.* The gormless little twit.

Perhaps he resents me getting a job here in the first place and gatecrashing his boy-only buddy club. Gets some kind of sexual kick out of frightening women by locking them in basements. I've noticed how he runs the show down here. He gets a constant stream of messages from the zombies, which he replies to immediately, unlike his responses to me.

Occasionally, a zombie will cross the floor and whisper something in his ear and get a nod or shake of the head in reply. Or he scribbles something on a notepad and hands it over. There's no doubt that Michael must be right about Keats being brilliant, it's difficult to see any other reason why he's allowed to rule the roost down here. I don't know about eccentric though. I prefer the word evil.

The only way I'm going to get at his computer is when he's not there. I was annoyed with Michael earlier but now could kiss him on his forehead; he's given me the space to do it, going through his online courses late in the basement. Starting next Monday. Alone.

My cheer drops away when I catch the screen of the zombie in front of me, slightly to the left. My neck stretches as I peer harder. Is he playing a computer game, like the zombie sitting next to him? Although I can't understand why either of them would be doing that since Keats seems to be so red-hot on preserving a hardworking environment. My mouth twists; probably he only applies that standard to me.

What the hell? My gaze zeros closer to the zombie's computer screen. I see more clearly what he's watching. My heart thunders in shock. This is no computer game. A battered and bruised woman is sitting on a stool in a darkened room filled with shadows, tears tracking miserably down her cheeks. She looks scared witless.

There are two other people cloaked in anonymity because their backs are to the camera. The sound's turned off, but that pitiful shape of her mouth tells me she's pleading. Begging. The figures cloaked in the dark inch closer and closer, almost circling her in a menacing dance. Her mouth opens wide in a silent scream. Without warning, a hand flashes out, lashing the woman across the cheek, sending her flying onto the barren floor. I feel the power of the slap tear through me. The screams exploding from her lips booming horribly in my ear.

WTF is going on in this place? This underground world that no-one else knows is here? Right, that's it. I'm furiously messaging Keats to stop this outrage. Now.

Me: *Have you seen what this guy in front is doing?*

He clears the message and ignores me. Can you believe this guy? I refuse to go away.

Me: *HAVE YOU SEEN WHAT THIS GUY IN FRONT IS WATCHING????????*

I don't give Keats a chance to delete me this time. I lean over and tap his message box with insistent fingers. He grunts lightly behind that ridiculous bandana, which I swear to God I'm in the mood to rip clean off his face. His stone-flat black shades give me the eye, then jump to check out the zombie's computer screen.

Seconds later he's typing away so I hurry back to my screen, impatiently waiting.

Keats: *He's watching a video. So what?*

I'm on the point of slapping someone silly myself.

Me: *You think that's acceptable behaviour in the workplace, do you? Some creep watching a video of a woman being beaten black and blue?*

Keats: *Dunno. Isn't in my job description.*

Me: *You're supposed to be in charge down here, aren't you?*

Keats: *Not correct. I'm only meant to boss you.*

That makes me mad. So mad. Leaves me feeling the sensation of a slave collar biting into my neck.

Me: *What are you going to do about it?*

Keats suddenly flicks his head to the side, staring me down. I don't have to see it to know it's hard, pissed, drilling with utter displeasure. I stare him down too. Two can play the bring-it-on game. He turns away in a swift single motion. His fingers flash at his keyboard.

Keats: *Nothing. Now leave me alone.*

The rustle of whispers in front of me draws my attention. The zombie watching the video talks below his breath to the other zombie who was playing computer games. They both turn to the offending video. Watch with rapt stillness as the woman is kicked and punched on the floor by her assailants.

The zombie sharing this disgusting scene must sense my distressed eyes on them because he side turns and notices me watching. With a gesture of his thumb, he warns the other guy that I can see them and their viewing habits. He in turn moves his chair so I can no longer see his screen.

The images of the woman on the floor, attacked, battered, bruise, crying out for her life, claw into my headspace, painting a permanent grotesque picture that won't let go.

Attacked, battered, bruised.

Attacked, battered, bruised.

Trapped. Trapped. Trapped.

I feel the sick rising. I have to get out of here. Now.

I don't remember how I make it to the door; it's the goosebump coolness of the tunnel outside that brings awareness streaming back like a slap of water to the face. I run with trepidation until I reach the stairs. I've never been so glad to see that trap door. My fist bangs it open. I nearly tip backwards in my dash to scramble out. The emotions bloating inside bend me double, palms flat on my thighs, the sound of what only a wounded animal would make rasping past my lips.

I'm done. Defeated. Can't do this anymore. Even for Philip... For Philip... A thrum of solid heat beside me comes out of nowhere. Still panting, I lift up my head and look. It's Philip. Standing right there. Smiling. I know this is manufactured by my brain cells, that he's not really there. He's as dead as he was... ten years ago? Four weeks ago? I don't know. I do know I can't live without knowing. Have got to capture the truth.

And that's what makes me straighten. Vow not to let those abusive bastards beneath my feet get into my head.

'*If you ever have any problems you come to me.*' That's what Joanie had promised earlier. With backbone straightening determination, I march towards her office.

The story's barely there in Joanie's office before she startles me by erupting out of her chair and heading towards the door, accompanied by a hot rage that clenches her hands by her side.

Somehow – I don't know how I manage it – I'm at the door before her, barring her exit. 'Please don't make things worse for me.'

'Worse?' Joanie's a growling tigress, me back in my guise as her defenceless cub. She slaps her balled fists onto her hips. 'What they're doing is wrong. I'll give them a tongue lashing they won't forget and drag them by their ears to Michael's office.'

Joanie knows I won't allow that to happen so she retreats with tight fury and heavily retakes her chair. I remain by the door as she shifts with unsettled tension. She informs me with a scowl, 'I thought all you young girls were into this Me One thing. Standing up for your rights and burning your Victoria Secrets thongs.'

I don't correct her on Me Too, mainly because she looks so hurt and frustrated. Helpless behind the enforced barrier of her desk. I don't picture her in her heyday as one of the women willing to burn their bra, but I do see, in a way I hadn't before, that she must have been a force to be reckoned with. Joanie The Destroyer.

'I'll speak to Michael about this video—'

The shake of my head stops her. 'Please don't. I just needed to tell someone. Another woman.'

I don't give Joanie a chance to respond and exit her office. I feel better. A problem shared...

But the situation boomerangs back on me less than twenty minutes later when the steel door to the basement bangs open against the wall. Michael comes in, legs braced in the doorway, the spitting image of a man on the warpath. The room shudders still in a way I've never witnessed before. I swear even the beating heart of the walls stop. He looks at me, eyes glazed with blistering temper. Then gestures with a finger at the two zombies who were watching the film. I have to nod in agreement but don't want to. Obviously, it was too much to ask Joanie not to inform him about what I'd told her. Or maybe he found her still brimming with outraged distress. Whatever happened, the cat is well and truly out of the bag.

Michael's hiss is a whiplash across the room. 'You two. In my office.'

They look at each other in alarm. Good. That'll teach them to think moving images of women being brutalised is entertainment. The two hurriedly follow Michael out of the basement. There's murmuring from the other zombies who clearly realise something is up.

Minutes later, the faint echo of shouting rings dully down here as if the basement has become a tin can. It's Michael. He's bawling out the two zombies about the film. This violent dressing-down is going on two floors above but we can all hear it. The volume rises.

It ends with Michael yelling, lungs fit to burst, 'And if I ever, ever find out you've been watching that kind of filth on my premises again, I'll give you a beating worse than anything in any film. Do you understand?' There's a pause. Then, 'This is your one and only warning. Now get out of my office.'

My head drops. I suppose I should be grateful to Michael for taking such prompt and effective action. Still, I was hoping he'd dismiss them on the spot.

The door to the basement opens and the two zombies, heads bowed, I hope in everlasting shame, shuffle in and go back to their desks.

But as they do so, one of them looks at me with something approaching hatred.

Seventeen

After finishing an exhausting day, I end up a twenty-minute brisk walk away at Liverpool Street train station, sitting on a bench. Tiredness tempts me to lie on it to catch some much-needed shut-eye. I resist, instead watch the tumbling mob of commuters thin out as the sun and daylight drift away, replaced by the chilly darkening late evening.

A member of the station staff gives me the eye. I know what she thinks – I'm homeless, looking to bed down on the bench for the night. But she's wrong. I have a new home. It's all mine come the fall of dark. No landlord, no housemates, no neighbours. Nobody, but me.

I wait another hour at the station and then walk with a purposeful stride until I'm standing back outside the building I work in.

It looms over me in the dark, like the wicked uncle in a fairy story. A Dickensian tenement that's survived bombing and developers as if daring anyone to take it on. The streetlamps don't shine enough light to tell, but it's clear there's no-one in there now. Michael has gone home. The place is firmly closed for the night. Hushed and shaded in night-time ink. I nod a respectful goodnight to The 22.

I head down the street, turn left and left again, into a lane until I'm at the rear of the building, stealing furtive glances as I go. The last thing I need is to be caught breaking and entering. I stop at the rusty iron grill that guards pedestrians from falling into the narrow courtyard below that leads to the room I discovered during my frantic effort to escape during the lunchtime I was locked in the basement.

After I left Jed's houseshare, I briefly considered going to my home, but the reality is there are no facilities there, it's inhospitable, a shell that widens the bleeding hole already in my heart when I think of how that house and I started with such promise.

I do one more snap glance behind me before removing the grill, from which my rope dangles. I swing with one hand down, use the other to shift the grill back into place. It's a bit of a balancing act, like a monkey trying to get the grill back into its correct position and shuffling to the centre of one of the bars when it is. Then I drop, easy-peasy, onto the smooth Victorian cobbles below. Tonight, the courtyard puts me in mind of a prison cell. Newgate come back to life.

The back door to the storeroom is unlocked. Originally that was so I could get out in a hurry. Now, it's so I can get in. In the blackness, I feel my way along the wall until I find the light switch and put it on. My new home lights up with the sepia brown of a fading old photograph. I'm free in here. No-one will ever find me in this storeroom. In fact, I'm probably the only person who knows it exists.

All the things I brought with me last night from Jed's place are neatly laid out. There's a mat with a tatty duvet on it. An Aran jumper, a sixteenth birthday prezzie from Mum, that serves as a pillow. A bag full of clothes. A battered clock with illuminated hands that are out of alignment. Sachets of wipes to keep me clean, toothbrush and a two-litre bottle of water. And, of course, my faithful bucket of filled water.

I lie down on my mat. Wrap the duvet's softness and promised warmth around me, keeping, as best I can, the frigid air from the storeroom floor seeping into my limbs. I try to figure out how to get the password to get inside Keats's computer but sleep keeps washing my thoughts away.

I wake up a few times because I think I can hear noises but of course I can't. My imagination is so scrambled.

I jump awake. Sit up, skin trembling, teeth on the verge of chattering. What was that? I extend my neck slightly to hear. Wait. Relax. It's the sound of a drunk outside. His feet clang on the metal grill above. He sings, in a broad mournful Irish accent, *I'll Take You Home Again, Kathleen*. It's stirring, comforting, haunting. I want to join in but don't know the words. I ease back down, allowing the lullaby lament of a man high on spirits, the most beautiful thing I've heard in a long time, to lull me back to sleep.

Something wakes me up again and it's not a man singing for his ladylove this time. My clock tells me it's either five past two or five past three.

There's the noise again. Of course this is a building in a city so no surprise that there's an accompaniment of sounds through the night. I'm on extreme alert when I hear it again. It's long, thready, high pitched. A cry? Whining? It passes over my body like ice-tipped fingers. For the first time I don't feel so free, so secure in my new night-time home.

A few minutes later I understand what it is.

A dog.

It's keening softly as if it's standing over the body of a well-loved owner. Then it's gone. Nothing. Comes back again, distinct but distant, not a gentle lullaby but a bitter wailing of death. The words from the website blaze through my mind.

For years after the fire, Scrap sat outside the tenement, keening and howling for his lost friends. Residents and neighbours claim that on stormy nights, he can still be heard keeping a lonely vigil in the darkness.

Is that what this is? A dog raised up from the dead? I climb out of my duvet, shaking, and put on the brownish light. I shove off nonsense thoughts of ghostly doggy spirits. This is real. It must be. *What, like the times you kept hearing the whispers of, 'Rachel, Rachel, Rachel,' in the tunnel beyond the basement? They're not real. It's the paranoia brewing in your head.*

Whatever's happening here, I proceed to the back door, press my ear against the woodwork and listen. The wail of death rises again. My eyes go skyward, my heart lurches out of rhythm. It's not a stray on the street. It's coming from above. My flesh creeps and the skin on my arms grow cold beyond the freezing room temperature when I think of Scrap desperate to save his sweatshop girls in the basement next door. There's definitely a dog in this building. Real or unreal, he's here.

Above, I hear movement but it's much too heavy for an animal. I scoot away from the back door, move deep into the storeroom. Wood creaks above my head. That's not the sound of a dog, it definitely isn't. I pull open the door that divides the storeroom from the basement. The room's a strange canvas of black with dots of colour from the watchful flashing lights of routers and servers. My vigilant ears become attuned to the infernal hum that seems to be built into the brickwork.

I hurry over to the steel door, bumping my legs into desks along the way. Press my ear up against it. Not only is there the muffled sound of a distraught dog, but another animal joins in too. This newer sound is higher, hurting. Horrible. I wouldn't be surprised if tears start weeping down the walls. Is it a wounded sick frightened cat? A dog and a cat dying together upstairs? The dog repeats its mournful cry. Another ragged wail joins it. I listen hard. Goodness me. That's not a cat or any other type of animal crying a bereaved lover's lament along with the dog. It's a human being. A woman. Crying. Weeping so eerie it makes me want to hide. These laments run through me like chilly electricity, unearthly, not of this world.

The girls were trapped! Scrap's frantic warnings had come to pass! As the lights went out and they were plunged into darkness, the girls screamed and howled for help!

Are the dead sweatshop girls weeping now? I'm imagining this. Or dreaming. It's a thin line between this side and that side of sanity. I've crossed it. Too many bad things have happened over the years. Too much stress, too much strain, too much guilt and too much pain. Too much everything. More than I can bear. I've crossed that line without realising it. Or perhaps I'm in that place where things are true without being real.

Except I know for certain that I can hear a woman's wails upstairs echoing through the pores of this building. The sobbing cries of a woman – girl? – who's also known too much pain.

Abruptly it all stops. Only the chaotic heavy huff of my breathing disturbs the silence.

I wait, listening by the steel door for a long time before going back to the storeroom on my toes. Shut the door tight. Wrap the duvet over me from head to toe. I came to this place because I knew it would be deserted at night. Checked the windows outside to ensure everything was black and empty. To make sure that I was the only one haunting this building.

Now I discover there's another tortured soul in here with me.

Or the spirit of one.

Eighteen

Oddball

That's password number three I've typed into Keats's computer trying to get into the 'P Funeral Service' file. Another big fail. It's approaching eight in the evening, Monday, the start of a new week. I'm in the basement alone. I'm doing Michael's version of a million and one Hail Marys after confessional to make up for the professional sin of producing work that Keats has whispered in Michael's ear is shite. After the others were gone, I did spend about an hour or so watching some of the online training videos, trying to transform Rachel muck-up into Michael gold.

Then I'd turned my attention to finding Philip. My heart seizes despite doing my hardest not the dwell on his name. Being dragged into our traumatic yesteryear isn't going to help me find him. That's if he's here at all. So it's emotions ruthlessly battered down, active do-do-do in place. It was easy enough to get into Keats's computer because he doesn't seem to have a main password. Instead there are individual passwords for the files he's working on. Clever boy. Hopefully not too clever for me.

I'm surprised I haven't been going stir crazy down here, underground, all on my own. There's an intensity, a thickness to the light as if the darkening evening outside is seeping through the cracks in the walls and ceiling. And floor. But I don't feel that trapped sensation, probably because knowing

Michael is upstairs means I'm not alone in the building. I type in another possible password.

Weirdo

The computer gives me the digital finger yet again. Frustrated to high heaven, my fingers jerk off the keyboard and contract into my palm. So tight my nails leave cutting tracks in my skin. I flatten my lips to hold back the curse words jumping furiously behind them. I want to SCREAM in this room. My head flops back, mouth open, sucking in the stale air to regularise my breathing. This is where most would put their head in their hands and admit defeat. Not me. I'm going to keep going until this bloody file goes open sesame.

But I'm tired, so very tired. Sapped by… by what? Being me? My head crashes forward with the crushing weight of that damning question. Why can't I be like everyone else? Forget the past by kicking it under the carpet? Maybe I'm the honest one and everyone else just pretends they shoo-shoo the past with the throwaway flick of a hand? Philip comes back to me in that instant of weakness, smiling with the glow of the best day of his life, hair rustling in the wind in the garden he tended so well.

My head pulls itself up with renewed determination. I pop a BB, pump one drop of CBD oil. It feels heavier than the earlier dose I took to help me get past the trap door, in taste and slickness, as I give it the minute it needs to move from my watery mouth to the stream of my blood. There's a slight light-headiness about me, but I feel more relaxed – maybe too relaxed – as I take a more logical route to discovering Keats's password. I think about what I know about him.

Bandana.

Sunglasses – DKNY always.

Hoodie

Water bottle

I type three of my choices one after the other until Keats's computer tells me that I've had all the shots it's going to give me. I thump my fist against the workstation in frustration, accidentally hitting the mouse, which in turn clicks and opens Keats's photo file. My body changes into a block of ice. Staring at me, as if it's that summer all over again, is a photograph of Philip.

'Can you help me unlock the treasures inside this? Or know someone who can?'

I shove the memory stick I hold with the funeral file under Jed's nose. Keats might have been clever with a password to protect the file but that didn't stop me being able to download it. The photo I printed off of Philip is in my bag. A photo that's proof that it was his face on the funeral programme that's inside the memory stick. How can Philip have died recently? I don't understand any of this but am determined to unlock the secrets of the past.

Jed's head inches back, startled to see me at his door, which I get; I don't live here anymore and it's late at night. Bleary-eyed, the untidy hair a given, in his boxers and a Prodigy T-shirt, the scent of eau de weed pouring off him, his expression shifts to bewilderment.

His rough voice tells me, 'If I can't eat, snort or drink it, I'm not really that interested.'

It occurs to me that he may have company. I lean in closer. 'Sorry if I've interrupted but I really do need your help.'

Yawning, he pushes the door to. 'Footloose and fancy free, that's me. I'm on a babe hiatus at the moment. My last girlfriend chucked me a couple of weeks ago. Said I kept eyeing up her bestie. Never dawned on her that it was her best mate making a play for me.'

I cough to get the earthy smell of cannabis permeating the room out of my nostrils and throat. The offender is a squat fat bright yellow smiley-faced bong with a nozzle shooting out of its forehead. His sparse room is surprisingly neat and ordered.

When we're next to each other on the sagging sofa, I explain my predicament.

'Do you know what this is, Jed?' I present the memory stick to him again.

Instead of answering, he gives me a quizzical look. 'How did you get into the house?'

'I've still got my key.'

He holds out his hand and, with a resigned tut, I pass it over. He says, 'I don't need more trouble here.' Key forgotten, he switches his gaze back to the memory stick with an intent fierceness that suggests he has psychic powers that will open it. 'Is this a game?'

This time, an impatient sigh escapes me, though I was already expecting this; I've never seen Jed near a computer or any other electronic equipment, bar his mobile phone and gadgets associated with music.

'It's a data stick for a computer. You stick stuff on it. You know heaps of people, so I'm thinking you must know someone or someones who can open it.'

Jed's carefree nature has made him an extremely popular guy about town. There's also something about musicians, some kind of cool that makes people want to hang out with them.

He thinks for a bit. 'You mean someone who knows their way around computers?' I nod. He thinks. Then, 'There's Bonnie, but she isn't talking to me anymore, not since the incident in the supermarket.' Best not to go there and ask what the incident was; I let him carry on. 'Rick's on holiday. John and James – twins – own their own tekkie shop.' Hope takes hold of me. 'But they're on remand because of hacking into some government agency. Allegedly of course.'

The hope's snuffed out. My shoulders slump and only then do I realise how shattered I am. Not tired, weary, or exhausted.

I'm a plate-glass window that's been blasted apart. I must've made a noise of distress because the next thing I know, Jed's on one knee next to me, a lifeline holding my hands.

'What's on this memory stick, babe?' Too many people view Jed as this big cheery dumb bloke, stuffing clogged between his ears instead of brain cells. They don't know what I do – he's a man who senses the hurt in others.

I want to tell him, I really do, but the truth is I don't have the words yet to talk about Philip, the past. Only in my head does the story straighten into a logical sequence of sense. A fleeting thought crosses my mind. I wonder how he knows Michael. It was Jed's good word that got me the job with Michael in the first place. But this isn't the time to raise the question with Jed.

Instead I tell him, with a softness I don't feel, 'I can't say. Not yet anyway.'

The pressure of his much-larger fingers tightens ever so slightly on my own. His gaze falters, flicks away. Comes back with the slo-mo of a door creaking open. 'There is one other person.'

Hope burns feverish again. 'Who?'

He shrugs lightly. 'You're not going to like it.'

We're both standing outside the room on the third floor. I'm not sure which one of us is more jittery, Jed or me.

I whisper, 'Don't forget to pile on the charm. Wiggle that crooked nose of yours.'

He sends me an infuriated dirty glare. 'I don't know why you couldn't have done this on your own.'

I step into his space. 'We both know the answer to that.'

Muttering, Jed rubs his hands down his T-shirt, finger flicks through his hair and knocks. We wait.

Finally, my bête noire, Sonia, opens up. One of the longest smiles I've ever seen pings on her face at finding Jed on her doorstep, only to semi die when she sees me.

Sonia's battle armour is swiftly donned. 'What the heck are you doing back here?'

'Do you mean me?' Jed counters with the tone of the broken-hearted. *Thank you, my great friend.*

Sonia is shaken, her mouth opening and floundering. 'Not you, Jed. You know—'

He leans that body of his closer to her, making her suck back whatever she was about to say with a gulp. Jed's good at this; she can't take her adoring eyes off him. 'Sweets, I was hoping you can help me out. You work in computers, right?'

Sonia stretches her neck with obvious pride. 'Software. Know it like the back of my hand.'

'Can you open a file on this for me?' If he leans any closer to her he's going to fall flat on his face, taking her with him. Mind you, Sonia will probably love that. He waves the memory stick like it's an engagement ring.

Suddenly, Sonia's neck lashes back as her glance slicks to me, back to Jed. 'Is this for her?'

'No, it's for me.' I can tell by his tone that Jed is tiring rapidly of the charm offensive. 'Will you do this for me or not?'

Sonia stares me down. Decision time: does she dislike me enough or fancy Jed more? After a few seconds' hesitation her thing for Jed wins, she lets us in. I don't know what I expect but not this, her room's a chaotic mess. Clothes, shoes on the floor, drawers open, and piles of papers and books taken root everywhere. It's not exactly clear where she sleeps. Sonia finds her laptop, crosses her legs on the floor and stretches her hand out for the memory stick.

We stand either side of her, looking down as she plugs it in. Taps away. Does what I suppose is some tekkie wizardry with her fingertips for five minutes. Ten. Twenty.

Looks up at us. 'Who does this belong to?'

'A mate,' is all I tell her.

'Well, they're a genius. Never seen an encryption like this before.'

I frown. 'What does that mean?'

There's a smug expression coating her twisted lips. 'I can't open it. Only the person who set it up can.'

In the weak brown-yellowed light spilling from the ancient bulb, I stick Philip's photo to the storeroom wall. Take a step back and stare at his features. His eyes, nose, mouth, lips, strong determined jaw.

My voice is faint. 'I vow I'm going to find out what happened to you. What really happened that summer.'

Nineteen

It's morning. I begin the climb up my knotted rope to the top of the grill. Fingers finally curl around the bars. A tingling skates down my arms as freezing metal touches skin. My rucksack bangs against my back as I leverage the bottom of my shoes flat against the wall with the knowhow of an acrobat on the cusp of thrilling the crowds. Teeth gritted, I use the force of my feet to shift the grill to the side. Move one hand to clutch the pavement and then the other. Haul my body out. I shove the grill back into place. Almost skip down the side of the building and turn into the front. Nod to The 22 and go inside when I gain entry.

As I speed-walk through the tunnel beneath the trap door, my thoughts turn to the dog and woman – girl? – I heard at night. Upstairs, keening and wailing. A requiem of weeping for the dead garment workers? That's a frightening thought. I shake it off with an all-over shiver. Reach the steel door and walk inside.

The blue arc lights and their offspring shadows seem even more pronounced today. The static humming beat of the walls a pitch louder too. No-one acknowledges my presence as usual except the zombie who was watching the disgusting video of the woman being attacked. The loathing pours off him. Screw him. Let him look. Let him hate.

When I take my seat, Keats perches his head sideways to look at me through his shades. I stare right back. Does he suspect I was messing with his computer after he went home? Knows that I have a copy of the funeral file? That I printed off the photo of Philip? I imagine the blatant shock sitting uncomfortably, defining the expression on his face. The tension of his compressed lips behind his outlaw bandana. It's blood red today. A warning for me to keep away? He'll be disappointed then because I won't. Not today. I have plans for him.

'*I can't open it. Only the person who set it up can.*'

Sonia's frustrating conclusion reminds me what priority number one is. Persuading Keats to either open the file for me or give me the password. Yeah, a difficult one from a man I think is persecuting me and probably hates women in the bargain, but I have to believe he'll help me. I mean, why should he give a flying damn if I see the file or not? I see Philip's face taped to the storeroom wall, which gives me courage to tackle Keats. *Softly softly does it, Rachel.*

I start with the inoffensive, the bland. Begin messaging.

Me: *How long have you been working here?*

He checks his message box, hesitates.

Go on. Talk to me.

As he taps his keyboard, a mini jubilant smile curves my lips, creeping up to my eyes.

Keats: *Why?*

Me: *I'm just trying to find out more about you. You're obviously a very clever man.*

Yeah, the last sucks but so many men love to have their feathers stroked. Zero comeback. My side-eye sees his fingers hesitate over his keyboard.

Go on. Please.

His fingertips touch base.

Keats: *What is this??? Are you trying to build a relationship with me here??? Your idea of tying a yellow ribbon round the old oak tree??? Here's the thing, I don't want to build a relationship with you. Okay? I don't like hangers on.*

That's the cut-off line of a conversation if I've ever heard one. Philip's face stamps back into my mind. I can't give up.

Me: *Maybe we can go out for a coffee or drink sometime to get to know each other better.*

Keats: *If you're asking me out I don't fancy you.*

Me: *What's your type?*

Keats: *Someone with a lot less mouth on them.*

Me: *I was only referring to us doing something social to cement our professional relationship so we feel easier about working with each other.*

This guy's like a robot, no emotions, no social skills. There's no other way to do this – I'm going to have to go in for the kill.

Me: *I need to apologise.*

Keats: *For what?*

I'm careful and think before I write.

Me: *I'll be honest – I snooped on your computer.*

There's a heavy-duty puff of air behind his bandana.

Keats: *I know you did. Don't sweat it. My fault. I shoulda locked in the main password before I went. Don't bother trying again. Password protect is in place.*

Me: *I couldn't help seeing the funeral programme you're working on. So sad when a loved one passes away. Are you doing the job for someone? Or are you connected to the family?*

Keats sits back. I imagine indecision playing across his features, drawing the blood high into his cheeks. Finally he leans forward.

Keats: *Do you want some advice?*

Me: *Sure.*

It's surprising what you can tell about someone when they think they've hidden their emotions on their face. Other parts of the body speak volumes too. His fingers are hitting the keys hard.

Keats: *Mind your own business.*

His pissed attitude doesn't deter me, although I don't message back. I've got the whole day to wait. Wait for him to leave promptly at five and follow him. Maybe I can persuade him when we're away from this dungeon-like place.

The heartbeat of the walls is in sync with my own as the minutes, the hours, tick away.

Finally. Finally, just after five, Keats heads out. I count to ten before following him. I follow on through the steel door. Stumble with a horrified squeal. A puff of fur and tail, in a flash of brown, shoots up the stairs. Or was it a shadow? No, I saw something moving. I'm rocking in shock, unable to move. When I hear a brief scuffle and soft bark, another squeal shoves past my quivering lips. Vermin. I shudder. I imagine them in the walls, in tiny holes in the bottom of the walls, beady eyes, hairy tails, flea-bitten coats waiting for me to go by. Ready to spring on me. I shouldn't be surprised there are rodents hanging out down here, this being an ideal des res for them. Don't get me wrong, I'm not scared of our ratty friends, it's just they live a very diseased life that I don't want anywhere near me.

Hang on, rats don't bark. I'm frowning as my heart thumps way too forcefully in the hollow of my chest. I think back to what I saw. It was a bit on the large size for a rat too, although there are urban myths of rats as big as cats haunting London's sewers. Something tells me to rule that out. The mournful keening of the dog in the night bounces in the acoustics of my head, a death march at a funeral.

I rush through the tunnel to the stairs. Look up. Nothing there. Punch my hand against the trap door and peer out and around. Nothing. I think for a moment of the reports of Scrap's ghost. *The heroic dog that had led the way, keened in helpless anguish.*

Properly freaked out, I scramble past the trap door, bang it closed behind me and am on the narrow street in three seconds flat. I'm not ashamed to admit I'm petrified.

I feed on natural air, breathing harshly, lacking control. For the first time, I question this quest to find out about Philip. To untangle our crooked past. I step away. Stare, eyes wide, at the Victorian building. It stares blatantly at me almost to attention, shoulders back. This once-upon-a-time sweatshop isn't scared of anybody. My mind conjures up Philip's face taped to the storeroom wall. No, I can't, won't let him down. Won't run this time.

The irate blast of a car horn returns me to the street. Only then do I remember my mission to follow Keats. He's nowhere in sight.

'Bloody, bloody damn.' Followed by a stream of ear-blistering cursing.

I'm not giving up, so I walk with speed to see if I can locate him. Then my phone goes off. I shake my head in consternation.

It's Dad. Should or shouldn't I take it? I take the call.

'Rachel, I'm at your house.'

All thoughts of following Keats fly out of my mind.

Twenty

Pulse rate kicking up a storm, breathing like it's the hardest thing I've ever done. I come to a panting unsteady stop outside my house. It's shrouded in the falling evening light. My arms and legs ache as if I've been running since I bolted from trying to find Keats. It's my mind that's been running and running with how I'm going to stall Dad from going inside my house and holding at bay the inevitable bombardment of questions he'll fling at me.

I spin in an unsteady circle, feet finding it difficult to balance against the ground, my terse gaze searching and searching. Where is he? Where's Dad? I can't find him anywhere. I don't understand. Then it hits me. I remember. I become as stiff as a corpse waiting to be embalmed. He has a spare set of keys.

I swallow hard, knowing there's no way out of this. Correction: no way out. Of course there's a way – it's called The Truth. I drizzle some CBD oil onto my tongue, not under it, and coat it across my gums, top and bottom, before going inside.

I find him in the main room. Cross-legged, he sits on the bare floor, back against the wall in the exact spot where once sat a huge majestic prayer plant he'd bought for me on a spur-of-the-moment fatherly indulgence. He's the image of a boy whose toys have been crushed right in front of him. Neither of us speaks. But it's not silence really. How can it be with the creaking weight of the life I haven't told him about crammed in between us. He's set up an LED lamp on a tripod, which he carries in his van, a relic from his days as a site foreman.

'Dad?' Nerves have a stranglehold on my throat, diminishing my voice to a raspy reedy mess.

He waves a hand indicating not just this room but also the whole house. 'What happened here?' There's no accusation in his tone, no anger. It's flat, seeking the facts; no wonder he's considered a master at negotiating deals in his line of business.

The strident LED light stings my eyes as I shuffle deeper into the room, though I make sure not to invade his space. 'I'm... I...' Can't stop stuttering. I pull in a heavy punch of air. 'I was going to tell you.' *Liar.*

Dad slowly uncoils his body and my breath hisses in the depth of my throat; I got it so wrong, he's angry. Furious. It's there in the movements as he straightens – taunt bunching of his muscles, the jerk of limbs against their joints, the flexes and twitches of his fingers by his side. And a face made of granite ready to be chiselled and hacked apart.

'Who did this to your house? I want to know who did it, because...' his voice is a dizzy escalation of fury, 'I'm going to do the same to them as they did to this property! Rip them apart.'

Then he sees the fear in my eyes, noticing how scared of him I am.

'Do you have any idea what I've been going through?' His voice is as clipped as the walk he uses towards me, the light dragging his sliding shadow behind. 'As soon as I saw your house, I knew something was wrong. When you didn't answer, I spoke to the neighbours. You can imagine my horror when they told me they hadn't seen you for months—'

'But—' My hand reaches beseechingly in the charged space between us, but he cuts grimly over me.

'I thought something terrible had happened to you. And when I got inside and saw the wreck...' The memory of it torments him, forcing him briefly to close his eyes. He looks at me again, steady and unrelenting. 'I thought someone had harmed you. Hurt you.'

I open my mouth but words fail me. I'm horrified that I've put him in a position where he must have been twisted so badly with pain.

'It's only when I heard your voice on the phone that I knew you were okay. What the hell's going on here, Rachel?'

So, I gather the courage to tell him the truth. About my home at least. It's time to halt the turning of the emotional ringer I've already put him through. I shake my shoulders back as I suck in a narrow tunnel of air. I want the telling of this to be calm, the tempo and tone of a dad and daughter together at the Sunday dinner table.

I start, deliberately fixing my gaze to the side of him, to a corner where the artificial light hasn't penetrated the dark. 'I rented the house out to a couple I know – knew – who turned out not to be such mates after all. They used it as a get-rich scheme. Instead of taking up residence themselves, they moved in other people, getting them to pay well above the odds.'

'Okay, I get that. I'm not happy about it but I've heard of these things happening before, common practice in the trade I'm in. What I still don't understand is why this house looks like a disaster zone.'

The final lingering embrace of bravery deserts me as I gaze at the floor. Shame, that's what's eating me up. Shame that I've let him down. The mighty Frank Jordan has given me every advantage in life. A leg-up any young person would use as a dizzying spring to a successful future. And what have I done? Let him down. Again. The same way I did that summer.

Dad confronts me with a question that blindsides me. 'How much money do you owe?'

My head shoots up in shock. I don't know what's holding me up because it certainly doesn't feel like my feet. 'How did you know?'

'Come on, love.' Love; I cling on to it. 'In my business I've seen it all.' He takes a full step closer, hugging the light. 'Why else would you rent out your home? Why else are you living like someone who's one day short of being repossessed?'

My palms rub along my thigh. I'm so desperate to touch him, to feel the weight of his parental security around me. But I know the time isn't right. The words on my tongue miss a beat. This is hard. So hard. 'I got into money trouble—'

'How?' Dad howls. 'How can you be up broke street if you've been working and rubbing shoulders with Lord and Lady posh nuts in the City? Those jobs pay a packet.'

'Because none of it's true,' I cry out. The lightning shock on Dad's face would usually stop me but I'm a street called honesty and have to keep going right to the end. *Breathe, Rachel, breathe.* 'I tried. I really did. But nothing's been right since—'

'Your mother passed away,' he supplies sadly, wiping his hand over his face. He's partially right, but that's not what tipped me over the edge.

I nod, leaving him thinking he has the right of it. 'At first no-one wanted to give me work because I left uni early so didn't have the qualifications. But there was plenty of work in bars, call centres, delivering door-to-door to meet the demands of the online shopping industry. I've been spending more than what comes in.' Completely true. Spending hand over fist to maintain the basics of life. 'Before I knew it, I was in trouble with the mortgage company.'

'So, you tried to pay off your arrears and keep your head above water by renting your place out to a pair of deadbeats who ripped you royally off. And the bastards they moved in stripped this house of everything of value to sell on the midnight market.'

Surprise at his knowledge shines bright in my eyes.

'In the construction industry you see it all the time. One of my first jobs in London was working with a crew who also dabbled in stealing copper piping anywhere they could find it and making a tidy profit, no questions asked.'

'I'm sorry, Dad.' My wretched words ring high round the room.

'Sorry.' Dad paces, rubbing behind his neck. He swivels so swiftly in my direction, I stumble back. 'I don't understand why you didn't tell me? Have I been some kind of tyrant to you?'

'Never—' A whisper of painful dismay clogs up my throat that he could even think such a thing. But if truth be told, I was terrified that he'd go after my so-called friends and do them some serious damage. I know what violence feels like against flesh.

His voice rises, the thunder in it discolouring his expression. 'You're the only person I have left. I would do anything for you, precious, anything.'

He opens his arms and I fly into them. We hug each other tight. Tears of exhaustion and relief mark a watery path along my cheeks. We stay like that for… I don't know how long, until Dad leans back, his fingers smoothing the tears into my skin.

'I should've spent more time with you after your mum left us.'

'But you did. You gave me all the time you could but you also had a job to get on with.' Talking about the past and being in his arms, maybe that's what gives me the strength to ask, 'Do you remember Philip, the guy I knew when I was eighteen?'

Dad's arms fall away as he backs up slightly out of the light. 'Philip?'

Of course he'd never met him and it was such a long time ago. 'My friend who died.' A burning sensation scalds my lips.

Dad looks perplexed, his brows touching in confusion. 'I still don't—'

'You remember, the summer I was eighteen.' Gulp. 'After Mum died.'

'That's a year I'll never forget.' The faint ghost of bitterness masks his features. Of course he remembers laying his beloved wife to rest. Clutching my hand as sobs tore through me. His chin comes up. 'You're talking about the accident in which Danny was involved too.'

At the mention of his friend, Danny, Dad looks upset. I want to acknowledge his private pain, but that would mean talking about Danny. That I can't do.

'Tragic business,' Dad utters with sorrow. 'How upset you were at your friend's death. What's made you think about him, this Philip, now? After all these years?'

I choose my words carefully, obscuring my eyes behind my lashes. 'I met a friend Philip and I had in common and he told me that Philip didn't die then. That he only passed away recently.'

'What?' Dad comes back to me, striding with a pressing purpose. 'That doesn't make any sense. When I contacted his family, because you asked me to, they told me he was dead.' Dad scratches his head in thought. 'I don't recall who I spoke to, but that was definitely what I was told. And that the funeral would be a private matter which was why you couldn't attend.'

I soak up the information. Sift through it. Finally conclude it makes no sense. Why would Philip's family tell Dad he was dead if he wasn't? My head pounds at the back, throbbing in my twin temples.

Dad places his big caring hands on my shoulders. All the heat from our earlier exchange is gone. 'Do you want me to see if I can contact them, his family, again, to find out what went on?'

It's an offer I can't turn down. I hug him again, with his words soothing in my ear. 'We'll sort out this situation with the house. There's no more need to worry.'

I squeeze him with heartfelt gratitude.

But why don't you tell him what really happened when you were eighteen?

I ignore the truth whisperer inside me.

Twenty-One

It's five o'clock. Keats is on the move. He checks his watch, closes his computer and hauls a bulging sports bag out from under his desk. I wonder what's inside the bag. I can't see him pumping iron down at the gym. Nothing's going to stop me today. Not a phone call from Dad, not Michael, not the ghosts of twenty-two sweatshop workers or Scrap the stray dog. Nothing. Dad reaching out to Philip's family is not going to stand in the way of me personally pursuing the truth. I'm going to get that password out of Keats even if I have to beat it out of him. When he leaves the basement, I count to ten, pick up my bag and follow. Along the tunnel. Through the trap door.

Michael's in the foyer as Keats closes the exit door behind him. With an arched flourish, Michael looks at his watch. At me. 'Knocking off early, Rachel? You've got things to do in the basement.'

Interesting how he's stopped calling it the systems room.

I don't let his appearance phase me. In fact I've planned ahead for this possible moment. 'Just popping out to stock up on supplies for the evening's work.'

He doesn't say anything in reply. He's run out of mind-numbing online management theory videos for me to watch but I'm still expected to be down there until an unearthly hour. But, for now, that suits me fine.

For a moment, it looks as if my chance has gone. There's no sign of Keats in either direction. I stop cursing under my breath when I spot him at a bike stand at the end of the street unchaining a sporty-looking red and white model and climbing on board. His sports bag looks bigger than him as he sets off. I'm surprised he rides a bike. Maybe he's worried about the planet, which explains his anarchist style get-up.

I run over, shouting, 'Keats! Stop! Please! We need to talk!'

My voice is loud enough to get Lazarus rising from the dead again, but there's no indication from Keats that he's heard me. Perhaps his hoodie muffles his ears, or he's lost in the world of music via earphones. Or he's keeping up his policy of ignoring me. I chase down the street. Damn! He's already heading out onto the main road, expertly weaving through the traffic. My moment has gone.

I don't give up. I can't.

At the corner, I swing onto the main road clogged with traffic, hoping that perhaps Keats will be trapped in it somewhere. No such luck; he recedes into the distance, lost in a flurry of lorries, vans, buses and cars. But I keep running, bumping into angry passers-by and dog-tired-looking commuters. A hundred yards down, at a crossroads controlled by traffic lights, it's clear he's long gone.

Cyclists from left and right, some jumping the lights – I hate it when they do that, so bloody dangerous – and Keats will have no doubt done the same. Someone who goes around dressed like him won't be a stickler for the rules of the road. He could have gone in any direction. Frustration bites hard when I can't find him. In despair, I hold onto a lamppost and rub my eyes.

All I want is a password for one lousy file that means nothing to him and the world to me.

Something catches my eye. Over the street. Red and white. A bike chained to railings beside a row of restaurants, takeaways and an e-cigarette shop. I'm not kidding myself that it's *the* bike; this city is full of red and white bicycles. Still… I make it to the other side of the street. Check out the bike. It's so spotless it positively gleams. Gleams like the prized possession of a weird computer whizz. It's been customised. Various stickers are stamped all over it, showing it's been ridden in Norway, Russia and Japan. I might be wrong, but my sixth sense screams this is Keats's two-wheeled friend. I realise the fact that he's cycled in other countries is the first human thing I've learned about him.

I switch my attention to the street. He's in one of these buildings. I begin my search.

In a Turkish takeaway, two city-type guys and a woman are waiting. The Italian restaurant next door houses a scattering of early-evening diners. None of them are wearing hoodies, dark glasses or bandanas concealing the bottom half of their faces. But hang on a minute. What if one of them is Keats? After all, he can't eat with his disguise on. I observe the restaurant's clientele more closely. None of them match Keats's statue.

I move on. In the e-ciggy shop, a spotty nerdy underage kid is trying to persuade the owner to sell him some vapour. Is this Keats in his civilian guise? No, Keats is no smoker and this kid is exactly that, a kid, way too young. I'm running out of buildings. A florist is empty and looking to close up. A boutique has a few customers but they won't be Keats. The shops and eating holes give way to an array of anonymous office buildings. I feel dizzy. Shake myself back into focus.

Across the road is a scruffy rundown launderette. I imagine Keats's mum does his washing but I dodge the traffic, cross and peer inside. There, still in his full rig, sitting on a bench, looking at his washing go round and round with the empty sports bag at his feet, is Keats.

With no hesitation, I go in and sit next to him. 'Hi, Keats. It's me, Rachel. I hope I'm not bothering you.'

That's a stupid start. He can see full well it's me and of course I'm bothering him. But he doesn't turn or acknowledge my presence. Just sits and studies his washing doing the rounds as if it's a particularly absorbing TV show.

I try again. 'That's a lovely bike you have. I noticed you've been to lots of interesting places on it. Did you travel alone or with friends?'

No answer.

I'm light-headed, breathing too loudly. I plunge on. 'I don't want to make any trouble but I need you to do something for me. You see, I had this friend. Ten years ago. He offered me friendship at a crucial time in my life. Philip. That's his name. Anyway, he died. Tragically in an accident.'

No answer. Again.

I plough on. 'On your computer, I know you're working on his funeral programme. This suggests that he died recently.' My tone rises. 'But he died ten years ago. He can't have passed away recently and ten years ago. That doesn't make any sense.' My eagerness to get Keats to understand, open that closed mouth of his, makes me shuffle so close the heat of his thigh melts into mine. 'Here's another crazy: what are the chances of the person doing his funeral programme sitting next to me, his friend, at my new job? In that building of all places? Is someone playing a sick game?'

I'm freestyling. Don't even know what I'm saying. Perhaps my words are just for my benefit, not his. But it doesn't matter because he isn't listening anyway.

I'm pleading with him now. 'If you could just send me the open file or give me the password, then perhaps I can unravel it all. I don't know Philip's surname or where he lived or anything about him really. He was just my friend. I couldn't go to the funeral. If there was a funeral.' My mind's a patchwork of confusion, my words hoarse with emotion. 'I won't tell Michael or anyone. And anything you know about it, like the details of who commissioned you to do it and suchlike. Is that too much to ask? Is it really?' I get to my feet, trembling. 'I hate this feeling that I'm abnormal. I just want to be like other people. Get my life in order. Do you understand? Are you going to help me?'

Ten years of pain, of knowing I let Dad and Philip down, well up and flood out. My skin feels like it's been torn away, leaving me bleeding raw. Why won't Keats speak to me? How can he sit there, still, emotion free after what I've just told him? Something bursts inside and I shove him. It's only a gentle touch of my hands. At least, that's what I think it is. But he tumbles off the bench, his legs and arms akimbo. His sunglasses go spinning across the floor. His hood tears away to reveal a mop of short curly hair. The bandana's sagging under his chin. His eyes dart around looking for his shades. They're beautiful doe eyes like a woman's.

My gaze slams into Keats's face. My world skids to a shuddering screeching stop.

The shades are gone. Bandana. Gone. The landscape of a face revealed. I'm stupefied. Can't believe what my eyes reveal to me.

Keats is a young woman.

Instinctively, I rush across the launderette to pick up his – I mean her – shades and pass them back to him – her. She snaps them out of my hand and shoves them back on. Angrily yanks her hood over her hair. Then she plonks herself down on the bench again as if nothing has happened, eyes firmly on her washing going round and round. But there's a rigid set of her shoulders that wasn't there before. A tightness to her body as if she's trying to disappear.

I stand there. My apology a whisper. 'I'm sorry. I didn't mean to do that.' There's nothing else to say. 'I'm sorry, that's all.'

When I get outside, the tears are belting down my cheeks. Only it's not the soft tears that caress your cheeks but the bitter spare ones that sting and slice. I don't know where I'm going or what I'm doing. I don't even know if I'm here anymore. Tangled in there is something else – I hurt. How could Keats have left me thinking I was the only woman in a sea of men? How could a woman of a similar age not have revealed herself to me?

'Rachel!' A woman's voice calls behind me.

I turn around and through a misty glaze find Keats standing outside the launderette, beckoning towards me. I stumble back the way I've come. It strikes me it's the first time I've heard her voice. It's rasping, low, soft. It's the softness that astounds me; I'd expected her voice to be all back-throat growls.

I hear what she has to say. 'You shouldn't think like that. It's not you that's abnormal. It's everyone else that is.'

I pause then say a quiet 'Thanks.'

'Are you going back to the basement?'

When I don't answer, she takes out a notebook and pen from her pocket. 'If you are, this is the password for the file.'

I can't believe it. I could hug her, but she angles her body in such a way that screams, 'Back the bitch off.'

She hands me the scribbled piece of paper. 'Go on my computer. I was working on the file earlier.' The step back she takes builds a wall between us again. 'Don't ask me for any more help. You know how one thing leads to another?'

Keats isn't quite done and draws a deep breath. 'Watch your back in the basement, Rachel.'

Before I can ask what she means, she returns to the steamy warmth of the launderette, leaving me in the cooling air of the evening, holding a piece of paper with the password in my shivering hand.

Twenty-Two

'Watch your back in the basement, Rachel.'

Keats's warning leaves me on edge as I sit in his – her – chair in the basement. What did she mean by it? Is she talking about the zombies and the film? That I need eyes in the back of my head around them? The incident with the two guys seems to have turned the other zombies against me too. The reception I get from all of them has gone from frosty to glacial. I can't figure out what she means and now isn't the time.

The blue lights blink, flicker, hiss and fry. They've been doing that sporadically since I returned. The room transforms around me, enclosing me in a web from another time. The basement colour becomes a dusty depressing monochrome black and white. Workers, heads bent, toil at long benches. The machinery and the tools in workers' hands make no sound, all I hear is the dog in the corridor bravely belting out its warning to all inside. The only colour comes from the girls. The red ribbons in hair. The red moves. Leaks from the ribbons. Shiny, heavy, it slips and drips, scarring their faces below.

I snap out of the tricks my mind's playing on me. The only girl here is me. I pray what I find in the funeral programme gives every question a rounded answer because I don't want to come back to this place. I unfold the paper Keats gave me and stare at the password.

LeTmEiN

Very funny, Keats. Very funny. I suspect that once she knew I'd been dabbling in her computer, she changed the password to one for her own amusement. I find the file. Open it. Oh God. Philip's face stares back at me. A shuddering and discordant warmth fills in my heart. Oh Philip. My head's shaking. Tears brim in the bottom of my eyes but don't fall. I wipe my hand over them. I shake myself up. It's time to start getting practical. I notice that the programme is a leaflet of four pages, but I don't investigate what they contain. Not yet. After I've printed it off, I'll say my goodnights to Michael and then sneak round the back into the storeroom. Only when in the solitude of that forgotten room will I allow myself to delve deeper.

I press print. Move across to the printer, which whizzes as it starts its work. There's a wave of expectation I'm finding hard to control. I shake my shoulders back. Breathe in through my nose, out through my mouth. There's silence as the printer stops. There's a slight tremble in my hand I can't control as I reach for the programme. I pick it up. Raise it to take my first look at it.

The blue lights flare so bright I have to shield my eyes from the glare. They go crazy blaring blue with a high-pitched sizzling that makes my ears ache. They cut off, plunging me into darkness. The basement into a thick sightless abyss.

Trapped. Trapped. Trapped.

Packed coffin-tight, head-to-toe, side to side in thick inky walls. The stone-hearted wall beats its continuous hum-hum-hum louder than it's ever been before. I'm surrounded by a seeping encroaching nothingness. No light. Means no air. Means I can't breathe. I suck on the oxygen as hard as I can. That horrible noise can't be me trying to catch my breath, it must be a terrified creature cowering in the room somewhere.

Tap. Tap, tap over my right eye. Tap, tap, tap over my left. Tap, tap, tap in the crease in my arm. Both arms won't stop shaking. Please help me stop shaking. I dredge up the image of the horse on the beach, but the horse disappears because the seashore is a roaring darkness too. Panting, shallow spurts of air slice my chest. The oxygen is draining away. Please give it back. Give it back.

Can't breathe. Can't breathe.

Sweat loosens all over my body. Hot. Cold. Flaming. Freezing. No light. Means no air. Means I'm going to die. Die.

I'm rocking with the final motion of a person on a bridge ready to end their life. I stumble. What's that noise that joins me in the dark? Whispers.

'*Prayers for divine intervention were feverishly howled by the doomed girls.*'

That's what the haunted website claimed the sweatshop girls did before they were consumed by fire. Is that what burns my ears now? I listen closer. No, that's not the clandestine sound of whispers. It's mechanical. A motorised zip-zipping. Zip-zipping. More again. I know what that is.

The spark of colours of a memory flash through my head. Young me sits in Granny Jordan's sitting room as she makes clothes. Zip-zipping. An old-fashioned sewing machine. Is that what I hear now? The sound of sewing machines from the sweatshop? I have to get out of here. Now.

Find the light, Rachel. Find the light.

Find the light.

I'm confused. Can't figure it out. Light. Where? Where? I know. The cowering creature's back with that frightening ballooning sound as shuddering air fills my lungs. I dare to lunge into the shadows, hands becoming my eyes to guide me. The rustle of the funeral programme in my hand ripples in the darkness. Easy. One step at a time. One at a time. That's the way.

A sharpness digs into my hips, twisting my thigh muscles with pain. But this is good because I know I'm nearly there. My desk where my bag sits. I lean forward, my hand patting against the table. Seeking… Finding. I know exactly where to locate my phone. Trembling fingers switch on the phone's light.

The light. Means air. Means breathing. Not going to die. I don't care how stale the air is here – it's the most precious sensation my tongue has ever feasted on. I throw the light back on me, my face. You see I have to make sure I'm real.

I call Michael. Dead line. Recall there's no reception down here. The last thing I want is to go out into the tunnel on my own but I don't have a choice.

Somehow I make it to the door. Open out into a tunnel swept black. The yellow lighting is gone here too. Then I do something many will think with my affliction of being terrified of being underground is strange. I close my eyes. This way I plunge into the darkness I understand; my own darkness. I have control here because I have created it. I'm shut in not shut out.

I tread carefully, slowly, learning the irregular pattern of the lumps and bumps in the hard stone ground. The coldness is so much heavier than in the daytime, so harsh my teeth chatter together; or maybe that's the fear. My private dark swallows me as I get closer and closer.

Suddenly I stop as the trap door in the distance shrieks open. Heavy footsteps pound against the stairs. Now in the tunnel. My eyes punch open to a blinding strong white light that makes them instinctively want to curl back into the dark again.

'Rachel.' Michael. The shadow he casts against the floor and walls makes him appear so big. 'Are you okay?'

I nod with relief. 'The lights went out, which means I couldn't finish the work—'

'Don't worry about that. The electricity is shot. The wiring in this place is so old. The electrics were probably put in by Thomas Edison himself.'

'But surely that's against health and safety. It's dangerous. It could lead to a fire down here.'

He practically shoves the torch in my face, demonstrating his anger. 'If you want to pay for an electrician to rewire the place, be my guest. Now, if you've finished with the safety lecture, shall we go to your office to collect your stuff.'

He's already moving off, stomping really. I turn as I remember what I hold in my hand.

With Philip's face looking down at me from the storeroom wall, I sit crossed-legged on my duvet. His funeral service programme sits idly in my lap. I'm afraid to touch it, open it. It's as if I'll be going through his death all over again. I mourned hard for him ten long years. I went around like my co-workers in the basement, a zombie programmed to do the basics – eat, sleep, perform daily tasks – but inside I was a weeping hollow shell. I took great pains to hide it all away from Dad with glittering gilt-covered smiles and chatter that went on for too long; the last thing he needed was more grief piling up against his door.

But I have to do it. Take the funeral programme in my hand and examine it. Find the clues to why I was told he was taken from me a decade ago. I fold my head down. Give the programme a long shaky stare. Pick it up. It doesn't burn me, cut into me. Infect me with the awful grief-stricken emotions that come with the death of someone you love. His gorgeous open face stares back at me on the cover, a replica of the photo I have already on the wall. It's not his familiar features that hold me enthralled, but that slight smile of his. It's lopsided, mischievous, above all gentle and kind. It sounds syrupy, I know, but hand on heart that was Philip.

Now to the real task, finding out if it holds the clues I need. Names, family members, undertakers. Where the service is to be held and the date of the funeral. These will all make it possible to get in touch with people to find out what's gone on in the past ten years with my friend. Answer the question why I was told he was dead. Out there somewhere is somebody who can tell me what's going on. There has to be. Dad might be reaching out to Philip's family but I'm not taking for granted that they will speak to him.

The hope drops away because I find none of these things. Not a single piece of information that might lead me to a friend, relative or a man or woman of the cloth. There are readings, poems, songs and testimonies but nothing to identify who will be performing them. No hints as to the cause of death. Date of death.

There are spaces left which Keats has marked as '*Family photo 1*' and '*Family photo 2*' and '*Family photo 3*', pictures that would definitely help me in my quest. In fact, a lot of white space has been squared up on this document. It looks half finished. No indication who has asked for this order of service to be compiled or where the information came from. The details box only shows Keats has done the designing and worked on it today. The file was created a week ago.

At the bottom of the last page, there's a request that donations be made to a musicians' benevolent fund and a charity for stray dogs. I laugh softly. That's so Philip. He loved his guitar and had a puppy he doted on. Ray, that's what he'd christened the puppy. Ray for Rachel. Then one of the songs draws me as if hypnotised. Alice Cooper's *Eighteen*. Philip's song. Any lingering doubts that this funeral is planned for Philip disappear.

The noise of my phone ringing pulls me away from the programme. I grab my mobile.

It's Dad. 'Rachel, I need you to come to your house. Right now.'

Twenty-Three

Something's wrong. I know straight away as soon as I enter my house. The house I wish I could put a spell on to make go away. The first red flag is a blanket of warmth that covers me. I don't understand. The gas hasn't been paid for months, so was cut off. Hence no central heating. So where the fecking heck is this heat coming from now?

My disbelieving gaze finally catches up with my brain. The walls of the hallway are... Goodness me, they're the same gleaming gloss white they were when I moved in. The broken bannister has been repaired. A spanking new runner with diagonal lines covers the stairs. That's when I look down and notice the hardwood floor has been coated to a liquid-sheen of polished perfection it has never been before.

Reeling, I rush through each room, down and up. I'm in a state of shock. Everything is new or repaired – bathtub, taps, wardrobes, window frames, locks, kitchen units, sink... My beloved front room is restored, not exactly to my tastes, but you know what they say about beggars and choosing. I spin around near the gigantic rug relaxing in the middle of my favourite room. I stop when I catch my dad's satisfied broad grin peering at me from the doorway.

'How? When?' I can barely get the jubilant words out. 'Did you do this?'

He laughs. 'Well, it weren't the building fairies in the night now, was it?' He chuckles this time, as pleased as punch with himself. 'I got some of my lads to put everything back to rights. They've been working round the clock.'

We embrace partway across the room, a chorus of thank you, thank you muffled against his immense secure chest. And it's just as well he's holding me because there's a weight dragging me, a weight of pure and utter relief – no, disbelief – that's so intense the only way to respond is to collapse on the floor.

Dad must sense what I'm going through because he soothingly whispers, as if guiding my first steps into the world, 'I've got you, love. I'll always have you, my darling baby girl.'

A while later we're side by cosy side on my new sofa – neutral white with large red buttons marking the cushion of each seat – nursing mugs of steaming coffee made from water run from my state-of-the-art mixer tap and brand new kettle with the temperature gauge up the side, a bit like the one in Michael's kitchen in the bright light office above the trap door. The sizzling thrill that's been running through me fades slightly. The last thing I need tarnishing the polish of my restored home is the brooding bleakness of the basement.

'I thought you were angry with me the last time you were here,' I say softly.

'I was.' Dad stops and places his cup on the sparkling glass side table. He visibly collects his thoughts before he starts again. 'Years back, when I first arrived in London with me knapsack like Dick Whittington,' we share a smile, 'I found work on a big construction job. Massive building site. I got matey with a younger guy. We sorta looked out for each other.' Dad's features become cloudy. 'But I couldn't look after him the day he had a terrible accident—'

The harshness of my indrawn breath unsettles the ease in the room. 'What happened? Did he die?'

Dad picks up his cup and sips slowly, then rests it against his thigh. 'He was in a bad way. I only saw him once in the hospital. Then his family took him away. Never saw him again.'

Dad places his cup to rest on the table. 'See that's the thing with life, it can cut up rough, go sideways sometimes. One minute you're on cloud nine, the next – bang! – you're broken on the ground with no idea of how it happened.' His whole body twists to face me. 'I learned that early on as a kid. I needed you to be tough enough to survive. But I was wrong.'

His naked anguish hijacking his face makes my eyes widen. 'This isn't your fault, Dad. I should've come to you sooner—'

He bats my words away. 'How could I have allowed a child of mine to end up in such a terrible situation? I shouldn't have tried to mould you into something you're not.'

'What do you mean?'

He looks so helpless. 'I should've realised your mum's death hit you hard. All I could think about was her wanting you to be a woman of the world, so I had high expectations.' The shake of his head is somehow more damning than what he's telling me. 'I couldn't even see that they weren't expectations but rocks and boulders I put on your grieving shoulders. I wasn't there for you when I should've been.'

'You were,' I tell him with quiet conviction, although the truth is he was away a lot, as much as when Mum was alive. 'Just as you are now. Thank you, Daddy.' And I mean it from the bottom of my mending heart. Clichés are right and proper for moments like this.

Dad rubs his hands like the businessman he is. 'Right, first thing I do when I leave here is put ten grand in your bank account. I'll contact the mortgage company and put that right too. Then we'll sort out the rest over another cuppa.'

#BrokeNoMore #CanAffordSex No more money worries. No more waking, covered in freezing sweat, in the dead of the night. No more. No more. No bloody damn more. Now it's all done and dusted, it's easy to sit here in the sparkling bliss of hindsight and beat myself up about not having the guts to come to Dad before. *You know why you didn't, Rachel,* inner me niggles away. *You know this was never only about your mum dying.*

I suddenly notice a tension about Dad, like he's gazing down the sheer drop of a cliff.

'What is it, Dad?'

'I managed to track down Philip's family. I spoke with his mother.'

My heart drops onto the newly varnished floor. 'What did you find out?'

Dad's tongue peeps out to wet his lips or to gather the taste of coffee on them, I don't know which, but I know this much – Dad is as nervous as heck.

Finally: 'She told me that he didn't die ten years ago. He passed away less than three weeks ago.'

Correction: ~~Philip died ten years ago.~~ Oh dear God. I'm shaking so bad even the wrap of my arms can't help me. All the sobbing that tore me apart that summer comes back, choking and bulging in the very soul of me, threatening to rip every seam of healing I'd stitched into place. But I never healed, did I, not really. How can I when what I allowed to happen has haunted me ever since?

Seeing my distress, Dad is on his feet, already moving to the door. 'I'm going to get you something stronger. There's a bottle of brandy—'

My chaotic voice stops him. 'No. I need to know what Philip's mum told you because, Dad, I don't understand how this can be. After…' The words are there about what happened, but they refuse to be brought up to the light. 'After it all happened and I asked you to contact his family, you told me that they said he was dead.'

I'm not accusing my dad of anything – let's be clear about that – But…

'What aren't you telling me?' I know he's holding something back because he wears that same expression he wore when Mum passed – guilt. Like he blamed himself for what happened to her.

Dad retakes his seat, his hand reaches out for mine. Deliberately I lock my fingers in my lap; I don't want comfort, only the truth.

He begins. 'All those years ago his family, for whatever reason, refused to talk with me—'

'But you told me you spoke with his mother ten years ago.' The shocked words rush out of me with a burn that scorches my skin from toe to head.

'I couldn't make his family talk to me. What I could do was try to find out for myself. So I tracked down which hospital Philip was in.' Dad shakes his head with a heavy-hearted sigh. 'I wasn't permitted to see him but one of the doctors told me that he was burnt so badly he wasn't expected to last the night.'

My hands cover my quivering mouth with the horror of it. Images of Philip with tubes going in and out of him, motionless. God, so still, in a hospital room only fit for the dead, the flame in his dancing eyes snuffed out forever.

Dad keeps his distance. I respect him for that. This awful grieving is one I have to do on my own.

'I really did think what I told you was the truth, love. I wasn't keeping anything back. It's just I had to deal with Danny...'

I reach out and take Dad's hand. Squeeze. Wrapped in my own selfish grief, I've forgotten that Dad carries the burden of his friend's tragedy too. The moisture in my mouth dries because I wish I could tell him... I don't. Can't. He'd hate me. I hate me. We sit there for... I don't know how long, but it's enough time for us to give a shoulder to each other's grief.

'Did his mother tell you how he died?' I don't recall my voice ever being so small.

Dad's response is quiet too. 'Philip was badly injured. After what the doctor told me, I can only conclude that Philip made it through all those years because he was strong—'

'He was that.' A strange smile flutters against my lips. Then is gone. 'One of the strongest people I know... Knew.'

Dad's expression tightens. 'I never realised you were so close to him. I assumed he was a workmate you were merely concerned about.'

My face shutters. I've given too much away. Then again, this is Dad, the man who held my hand when I took my first steps as a toddler, so I give him a partial truth. 'Philip was what I needed after Mum passed away.'

Dad scowls hard; there's something beneath it I can't identify. 'Rachel, you and Philip never...' He leaves it hanging, a father's modesty with his daughter.

I shake my head. 'No. It was never like that between us. What happened to him?'

Dad reaches for his drink and knocks it back in one. Keeps his palms round his mug. 'His situation must've got too much for him. He booked himself into a euthanasia clinic in Switzerland.'

I try to control the quiver of my mouth, the involuntary clenching of my tummy. I can feel the walls of my tears crumbling inside. Then they come, a dam of pent-up emotions finally erupting. A horrible noise cracks at the base of my throat. My shoulders shake. And I'm crying and crying. Can't stop. Finally understand I don't have to stop. Dad takes me in his solid arms, which I'm eternally grateful for because I need someone to lean on during this time of intense self-revelation.

When there are no more tears left, I pull back and ask, 'I'd like to go to his funeral. Can you fix that for me, Dad?'

The flash of irritation on Dad's face startles me. 'Rachel, that isn't a good idea. His parents want a private family service. And you need to respect that. Just as they wanted their privacy ten years ago.'

He's right, I know. Nevertheless it's a crushing blow. Dad gently lays his large callused palms on my shoulder and turns me towards him. 'Your life's back on track, princess. It's time to leave the past in the past. To look forward. This is our chance to steamroller ahead – together – no more secrets. To be open with each other.' He leans over, kisses with the lightest touch on my cheek. 'Let's put the Rachel and Frank Jordan show back on the road.'

I hold the lighter in one hand and the funeral programme in the other over the sink. I'm alone now, ready to do one of the hardest things I will ever do. I press the lighter on and the flame holds me in its yellow-tipped blue-based flare. My hand trembles as the memories come and go like the swaying motion of the flame that warms my thumb. I shove the memories back with all the strength I have. Take the plunge while I'm still strong and touch the flame to the programme.

The growing flame hypnotises, chewing into the paper. Curls. Blisters and blackens over Philip's beloved face. Nothing left but lifeless ash that drops and smoulders in the metallic matt of my new sink. Debts sorted, Philip laid to rest, it's time to move on. Hand in my bye-bye letter to Michael. Time to shut the trap door on my job.

Still, a disquiet descends. You know, like the latest hit song that everyone's raving to death about and you're the only one that can hear the beat is lazy manufactured pop. I can't quite figure it out at first. Then it hits. What are the chances I get a job and it turns out that the programme for Philip's funeral service is being put together by the person sitting next to me? Coincidence? Six degrees of separation? It's downright weird. Isn't it?

Twenty-Four

'Bye, Philip, my mister eighteen.' My voice is soft and full of sisterly love. 'I'm sorry. Forever sorry.'

I'm back in the storeroom later that night. Back staring up at Philip's face pinned to the wall. It's as if I'm staring at him laid out in his coffin, one last moment before the lid slides over, consigning him to earth and dust. There are no more answers to search for here. Thanks to Dad, I know what happened to Philip, why he didn't die ten years ago, why he did pass only recently.

It still chokes me up to think of Philip being in such a bad way that he chose to end it all. The guilt is still part of me, but the elastic tightness of it is loosening. One day, if I'm lucky in life, it may go away. One day.

I lean up and carefully take down the photo. I could stand here in the dead-yellow gloom of this room and weep until my heart hurt but what would be the point? Regretful tears aren't going to bring him back. I run a finger over his face and then carefully pocket it away.

I'm here to pack up my gear, never to return. I've already written a letter of resignation to Michael, which I'll post to him tomorrow. As for the strangeness of Keats doing the funeral programme... a sad coincidence, that's all.

I pick up my things and haphazardly stuff them into my bag. Only the Aran jumper Mum gave me gets the folded treatment. I do a three-sixty stare around. I can't wait to get out of this room that scares me at night. The whole bloody building gives me the creeps. There are no footsteps above. No mysterious woman weeping or dog keening. I didn't imagine those noises when they echoed through the building. But now it's easy to think that possibly I did. Tricks and tics of a very tired and grief-stricken mind.

I make my way to the basement office, pop on the blue lights and clear my personals from my desk. I stare at the walls of this silent space because even the humming of its heart and the blinking bulbs on the digital devices seem to have faded away. In fact, it's rather like those Westerns where our hero cowboy says it's too quiet just before the gunfire blasts into town. It's not only this former sweatshop; the whole city surrounding it seems to be silent as if waiting for something to happen. As if…

A crash above like a tray of drinks being tipped down the main stairs makes my muscles harden and jump. A voice floats down, muffled, full of ripe curses, and although I can't be sure, I think it's that of a woman. The weeping lady? Wailing girl? I look upwards in alarm. And something else my mind tries to crush. Curiosity. It grabs me, refusing to do the decent thing and let me go.

I'm beyond the steel door before I can talk myself out of it. Feel my way down the jet-drenched tunnel. Take the steep stairs carefully until my head's perched at an angle beneath the trap door. I prise up the door an inch, maybe less, and peer out into the reception area, half lit from the front dormer window that gives out onto the street. There's nothing to see, of course. I'm not sure why I'm doing this. It's not as if I'm going upstairs to find out who this woman is, now is it? Is it?

I'm distracted by a noise the other side of the arched entrance doors. I tune my ears to it. A car blaring heavy rock music and from the sound of the engine, it's a high-performance vehicle. Keys rattle in the lock. Heart racing, I drop the trap. Flatten my back to the damp wall. Wait. Listen. Footsteps inside. A clear distinct voice shouts – not too far away — must be up the stairs.

'Mum? Mum? Are you up there?'

It's Michael. Calling for his... mum? Yes, that's what he said. Is that who haunts the building at night – his mother? Why would his mother be living here? I'm assaulted by a roll call of questions that have no answers. Michael's footsteps fade upstairs the same time I hear another vehicle stop outside. The pulse of its engine thrums against the wooden step beneath me.

A violent slam of a door disturbs the quiet of the night in the street. The sudden hammering on the main door goes right through me. Pushes me to sink closer to the wall. I imagine the security buzzer being repeatedly pressed as well because whoever's out there, I sense their volatile impatience.

Michael's back on the stairs. His voice is strained and something else I haven't heard in his tone before – fear. 'Who is it?'

I creep closer to the trap door. My palm lifts it ever so slightly. I see Michael's spit-polished black designer shoes and jeans-clad legs. The answer to his question is a fusillade of thumping knocks that shake the Victorian door in its frame. Michael's feet shuffle hesitantly forward. I think he's looking through the peephole. His feet skip back in alarm.

'What do you want?'

The letterbox opens. 'Open the door, Michael, or so help me, I'll kick it in. And then I'll kick you in.'

My chest constricts, leaving it hard to find air as I go absolutely still. It can't be. Not *that* voice.

Michael opens the door. Another pair of feet and legs covered in grey trousers come in.

It can't be.

Michael's legs abruptly jerk up like a puppet on a string, almost on tiptoes, his body swaying. Whoever has arrived has grabbed Michael.

The visitor growls, 'I want to know what you've been saying to my girl. She's asking questions about Philip's death. Now why would Rachel be doing that after all this time? Unless you or your mother have been whispering in her ear.'

But it is.

Dad.

What's Dad doing here? What if...? No, I shake my head in denial. Maybe... Maybe he's here to give Michael a good telling off, or worse a sound thumping about putting me in the basement. But how would Dad know I'm working here? I've never told him the name of my employer or the address of my job. I gaze sharply down the sheer drop of stairs, which seem to be beckoning me to go back. *Get your gear and get out.* But a magnetic need to find out what's going on holds me.

I pull apart Dad's words to Michael. Why does Dad seem so angry that I asked him about Philip's death? And why would he think this has got anything to do with Michael and his mother upstairs?

Michael says, 'Rachel? Why would I be talking to Rachel? I've never met her, now have I?'

Of course he has; I work for him.

Michael squeals, the noise an animal makes when a predator pounces and takes it by the neck. I don't hear the blow but the gurgling groan from Michael's guts means there's certainly been one.

'Don't try to make a fool out of me, lad. You of all people should know how angry that makes me. You of all people should know what I'm capable of. No-one makes a fool out of me, not in public or private. And never, ever, does someone make a fool of me in front of my girl. You'll find that out the hard way if I discover you or your meddling mother talk trash to my daughter. You'll find that out for sure.'

Michael staggers across the floor, legs wobbling. Dad's let him go.

Dad's voice detonates and explodes. 'Is your mother here? Does she hang out in this rat hole too?'

My legs are wobbling. In a state of confused disbelief. That can't be my dad out there. That man who grabbed Michael with a vicious violence that bordered on hate. I don't want to believe this.

Michael's spluttering. 'Mum? No, no. She's at our place in Spain. Did you know we had a villa there? Just down the road from Malaga, lovely place.'

No she's not. He's lying. She's upstairs. I heard her drop something and swear a blue streak. Why is Michael hiding the fact his mother's in the building from my dad? And why would Dad know Michael's mum? And why is Michael denying knowing me? What would happen if I Jack-in-the-box surprised them now by pushing the trap door back and leaping out? I wouldn't dare.

'I don't care about your housing arrangements, you little tramp.' Dad's volume refuses to dial down.

'Why don't we go up to the office? Have a coffee? Talk?' Michael's back in the guise of in-control professional CEO.

Dad's not interested as he warns, 'Don't make me come and find you again, Michael. And tell your mother the same. I don't care what she thinks about me. I don't care what anyone thinks about me. But if I find out she's been twisting my tail over this matter, she'll feel my claws across her face and they're razor sharp, as you know. As for you, don't make me break you, Michael. I'd hate to see you end up in the gutter. Do you understand?'

Michael's voice is solemn and chastened. 'I understand. I won't let you down.'

Dad's gone with a slam shut of the front door. His car bursts into life and he skids off at speed, taking out his anger on the road. When he's gone, Michael walks partway up the stairs, disappearing from my view.

'Did you hear any of that?' he calls out tightly.

'Enough. You'd better come up.'

The lady from upstairs. His mother. She keeps her response flat, monotone. I don't know this woman but I'm sure it's to hide her emotions from her son. But I hear them. It's funny what you can really see when your vision is taken away. Buried beneath her answer is a cold bitter harshness. Michael disappears up the stairs. There are no more voices. No more words. Mother and son have blended in the hidden secrets of this building.

The basement I re-enter is back to its usual trickster self. The walls' heartbeat pounds, blue lights blatantly gawking, the digi lights morbidly brighter, the ceiling a visual illusion of being lower. I leave it behind and go into the storeroom. Stare up at the wall. I take out Philip's photo from my pocket. Smooth it as best I can. Tack it back on the wall.

I'm staying. It's as if Philip's ghost has grabbed me by the collar and dragged me back. I won't leave until I find out what Michael, his mum and… I swallow hard… my dad have got to do with Philip. His death. The death that never was a decade ago. Can I believe anything Dad told me about Philip's recent self-inflicted death?

Michael has promised my father that he won't let him down.

I stand back, looking at Philip, and silently promise him that whatever has happened, I won't let him down either. I could give Michael my notice, leave the job and sneak in here at night to find answers. No. The best way will be to continue working here. In plain sight. Carry on as normal so Michael doesn't catch a whiff of what I'm really about.

I grab my bag. Climb up the rope. Head out into the night to talk to the one person who might be able to tell me more about Michael.

Twenty-Five

The doorbell hangs limply by its wires off the door frame like an eyeball dangling out of its socket, so no surprise it doesn't work when I press. So I knock with a smart urgency on the front door of the house, the one until very recently I had a key to. The night air is mild, temperature perfect for spring to bring forth new life, not me though; I'm head-to-toe a case of ice with an icicle piercing my heart. Michael and Dad. Dad and Michael. And Philip. WT Holy F is going on?

I knock on the door again. Correction: ~~knock~~. No, this is no knock that connects with the door but a fist that bangs and barges to the beat of the frustration that boils inside me. The air shooting off my lungs reaches my ears – clipped, ragged, like I'm at the end of a race. This is no end, I suspect. It's the start – I just know it is – of finally knowing what happened to Philip. And it terrifies me.

The patter of approaching feet pulls my mind fully back to the door. It opens, revealing Pauline, the teacher who lives in the attic. Her usually perfecto 'fro is slightly lopsided. Thank God it's not Sonia.

'Is Jed in?' I'd called and called him and got voicemail each time, which left me with no alternative but to come to a place I never wanted to be seen in again.

Pauline doesn't immediately respond, instead gives me one of those arched gotcha looks that teachers reserve for their naughtiest pupils, reminding me pointedly what I did to the kitchen. She finally speaks. 'I don't know. Maybe you should give him a call. It's rather late.'

Oh, it's like that, is it? I'm barred for life from re-entering this dump she and the others call home. Well, tough shit; I'm going to see if Jed's in whether she likes it or not. I'm prepared to hammer on this door, Lionel Ritchie style, all night long.

My 'I'm in it for the long haul' determination must stand out like a pair of knuckledusters on my clenched fists because she pulls the door back, stepping out of my way. My stride lengthens as I pass her and take the shifting staircase to Jed's room, and I knock as soon as I get there.

'Who's there?' Jed's voice is relaxed and I can't tell if he's been on the bong or sleeping.

'It's me.'

'Rachel?' His voice hits a high note of squeaky surprise, followed by a flurry of noise including something tipping hard onto the floor.

When he opens up, it's his broken nose I notice first. I'm not surprised after the violence I'd just witnessed Dad mete out to Michael. And now I also see Dad's explosive fist coming straight at Jed's face five years ago. A guy I'd been going out with at the time had had the nerve to slap me during what I'd thought was a low-key disagreement. I'd been shaken up, and when Dad found out about it, he went gunning for him. But when he came to my home to exact revenge, he'd mistaken Jed for the idiot. Without any questions asked, Dad had let loose with a volley of punches that had knocked Jed flat on his arse and smashed his nose. I'd screamed at Dad, couldn't believe what he'd done. Dad had apologised but ever since Jed has, understandably, been very very wary of Frank Jordan.

I shrug off that horrible memory and realise that Jed's in his boxers, his hyperactive gaze shifting from one side to the other like I've caught him with his hand in someone else's weed stash.

'We need to talk…' I don't wait for him to respond. I push my palm against the door and walk in and… Get an eyeful of the person in his bed. 'Woah!' I quickly avert my eyes. Bloody hell, it's the last person I expect to see sexy-satisfied, sharing his pillow – Sonia.

Jed and I are both out on the landing in record time, facing each other. The warming blood of embarrassment makes his fingers rush through his already topsy-turvy hair.

He clearly feels a need to explain. 'Look, it just happened.' Each word is designed for my ears only. 'You know—'

My hand's a full stop in the air, cutting him short. 'Jed, you could sleep with Mother Christmas, for all I care.' I suck in a deep punch of air to steady myself. 'I need you to tell me what you know about Michael.'

He squints, expression so blank it doesn't even look like a face anymore. 'Michael?'

I sigh inwardly. 'Michael Barrington who you contacted to help me.'

Jed's eyes do the rounds of their sockets. 'Remind me how I asked him to help you.' Jed is a self-confessed booze-hound and pothead, which means half the time he can't remember his own name, never mind anyone else's. So, perhaps I shouldn't be surprised that he doesn't recall ringing Michael on my behalf.

'I asked if you could speak to anyone who might be able to offer me work with a decent salary. You rang your friend, Michael. Remember?'

A smile pings on his face. 'No problem, babe. I always like to help people out.' The merriment drops away as quickly as he studies me very closely. 'Right – remind me, which job did I help you out with Michael?'

I have to restrain myself from grabbing Jed by his chest hair and shaking him silly. 'The management consulting company who I now work for. Don't you remember when I thanked you for getting me the job? How I was going to take you out to celebrate with my first wages?' Although if I recollect, he was only half-listening, his attention on telling me I'd outstayed my welcome at the house.

His finger jumps in the air. 'Oh, right. That Michael. I rang him?'

Why is he putting it to me as a question? 'Yeah, you rang him.'

Jed wears a lost-in-space expression as he stares above my head. Finally he drops his searching gaze to mine. 'Don't know what you're talking about, sweets. Don't know any Michael who owns a consulting outfit. How would I know someone like that?'

Unease jolts my spine straight. 'Come on, Jed, you know half the folk in London.'

'True enough. I know a Mike from South London who's a plumber and DJ, a Mickey from Newcastle who stole my second-to-last girlfriend, the bastard.'

His expression deepens with a seriousness he rarely wears. 'Rachel, I never gave anyone the thumbs up to give you a job. I've never met a Michael Barrington in all my born days.'

'Why would Michael lure me here?' I question Philip's photo pinned to the wall of the storeroom.

Tell me, Rachel, how's Jed? That's what Michael had asked me during the interview, I persist speaking to the picture I know doesn't have answers for me.

In fact, the more I think of it, the more strange that interview was. I'd swallowed his cock and bull about having to do the interview in a coffee shop because his office was having work done to it. Believed him when he said that me not having experience as a management consultant didn't matter. He tells me I no longer have an office upstairs and have to work in a cave-style room beneath the ground. Lie after lie after lie. A part of me, the how-dare-you part, insists I storm into his office come morning light and have it out with him. But the quiet logical me knows if that happens I may never find out what happened to Philip. How Daddy is connected to all of this.

'Has this got something to do with you, Philip?' My words reek of unshed tears.

The answers are out there. Somewhere. Including in this building.

For the first time, I sleep with Philip's photo, a replica of the one on his funeral programme that I stupidly burned, clutched to me through the night.

Twenty-Six

The trap door clangs shut like the hatch of a submarine. I'm a mass of confusion this morning after the revelations of last night. I don't feel steady on the steps made for smaller feet and it has zero to do with the CBD oil bitter under my dry tongue. My footsteps click-quick against the solid-hard ground, the walls of this tunnel, as usual, openly mock me like a dog that senses fear. Now they feel like they're creeping towards me too, a brick cage that's bound to entomb before I reach the steel door. I know it's my mind doing overtime, but that's what I heard last night has done to me – trapped me in a snare I can't cut my way out of.

I haven't slept. How could I with my bedfellows being Michael, Dad and a funeral programme? Or did any of it really happen? Am I barking like a mad woman up the wrong tree? I reach out. Let the pads of my fingers tiptoe against the wall. Ice cold. Yes, I'm real. Last night was real. As real as Jed telling me point-blank he doesn't know a Michael Barrington. The trouble is, I don't know what to do.

However, I do know I owe it to Philip – to eighteen-year-old me – to find out what the hell fire's going on. And that's why I've come back to this place of buried secrets and suffocating lies. I shrug off the lingering embers of sheer shock and feel an inch or two taller because my backbone's now straight. I know exactly how to try to find out about Michael. How he's connected to Dad... and me.

Rachel. Rachel. Rachel. My name's calling me again either through these stone walls or the walls of my head. I wouldn't be surprised at the second with the night I had yesterday.

Two more spits of cannabis oil into my bloodstream help me relax, maybe a tad too much. My name spirits and floats away.

For the remainder of the morning, I observe the black digital clock on my computer.

9:30

9:55

10:25

Ready.

I leave the underneath world and head out of the trap door.

My nerves make a meal out of me, chewing and tearing at my self-control. I've never done this before. Sneaking about to search someone's private office. The pursuit of the truth takes you to many shady places. For the first time, the reception area lacks its bright cleansing poise. It puts me in mind of a hospital room where a family prays their loved one won't die. Now, all I have to do is hope and pray Joanie's office is either closed or she's so preoccupied with work I'll be able to whizz by unnoticed. I've already figured out that Michael will be coming in later to work. Actually the more I think about it, the more it seems he's never in the building in the mornings but arrives later on in the day.

I'm a skulking shadow on the stairs, sure of foot, single-minded in purpose.

When I reach the landing, I look over to the purple rope with the private sign that bars the way upstairs. For the first time, I notice the door behind it has a keypad and obviously I don't have the code so there's no way for me to gain access to what lies beyond. I give my full attention to the corridor up ahead. Creep until I reach the edge of Joanie's office. Am I really doing this? I wonder in disbelief as I quiet my breathing. Going to rifle through anything that gives me a glimpse into Michael's life? But how else will I discover the connection between him and Dad and Philip?

Philip.

That's what grows the power in me to carry on. I do a three count and zip past her office like a spirit walking over her grave. Hold back against the wall. Wait. Wait. She doesn't come, so I pivot towards Michael's office. It's open, just a slice between door and frame, an open invitation for me to proceed. London stares back at me through the large windows, its backdrop a sky with not a cloud in sight, the foreground a jagged, up, down, up line of historic and modern buildings.

I start with the drawers to his desk. They're not locked. I nearly stumble back at what I find – they're empty. Not even a pen, a notebook. I don't understand; how can this be his office if he has nothing in his desk? Maybe he's one of these paperless office obsessives.

A rush of disappointment hits; there's no clue to his relationship with my dad. My search of his in tray is feverish with my desperation to unearth something – anything – that will start fitting this puzzle together. I flick through the papers I find. Frown. That's strange. The contents of the trays have nothing to do with a management consultancy business or indeed any other business at all. They're mostly about gardening and look like they were run off from the Net at random.

What's going on here? Nothing in the drawers. No business documents in the trays.

Before my thoughts can dive any deeper, I still for a moment as the sound of Joanie's lullaby-like humming floats inside. It's so pitch perfect, so beautiful, it casts a chill within me because somehow it makes the emptiness I'm finding in this office seem so much worse.

I up my pace, moving quickly. This shell of an office leaves chill bumps pulling tight against the skin of my arms. The files I take down from the shelves almost slip through my fingers because they're so light. I open one. Nothing in it. Another one. The same. And another. And...

'What the hell are you doing in my office?'

The empty file slips from my hand to the floor as I twist to find Michael Barrington staring furiously at me in the doorway.

We're both suspended in stillness. Michael and me. He appears ready to burst a blood vessel. And me... I can't see what I look like but I imagine what he sees. A woman who looks as guilty as transparent sin. Red-handed Rachel, that's me. What do I say? What do I do?

Think. Think. Bloody rake that brain of yours from one corner to the other and think. My mind's as vacant and wooden as Michael's empty desk drawers.

'Rachel, I asked you a question.'

He marches my way, his gaze doing a cat-tail swish sweep of his office. Thank God I took time to line up the papers I found in his in tray. Shut each drawer back tight. His eyes are on me, talons clawing ready to split me apart.

A voice slices into the room from the doorway. 'I told her to come here to find something for me.'

Joanie. Thank you! Thank you! But when I look towards the door, I'm in for a shock. It's not Joanie.

It's Keats.

Keats stands there, rock solid with an 'I dare you tell me different' expression basking on her pointy-chin face. Bandana under her chin, hands flexing by her six-shooter water bottle and mobile phone, I swear she's going to demand Michael stand and deliver.

However, it's not she who has the questions but him. 'And what could you have told Rachel to get from my office?' Each word is coated with lashings of sarcasm.

Keats doesn't miss a beat. 'The Foxbury summary she's working on was missing a crucial section, the part concerning staff intersectionality and work structure, in other words redundancy, and as that's the main thrust of her summary, I thought she needed to have it. I instructed her to see if she could find the full report in your files.'

Our boss considers her for a moment. Then stalks over to her, stopping a toes width from her space. 'You know I run a paper-free environment in here.'

She nods. 'I thought there might be a copy in your files. Because you do have files for a reason despite your wish to go paperless.'

Ouch! I catch my breath at her pointed response. Expect Michael to do an on-the-spot boss bawling about the reminder of who's the CEO in town here. He doesn't and I recall that he called her eccentric before he introduced her to me, so he must be accustomed to her straight-arrows way. It also occurs to me that Michael must have known all along she was a woman because he shows no surprise at her blatant feminine face. What's left of my functioning brain scrolls back; ah, he never did use the pronouns he or she when he introduced us.

Michael folds his arms. 'Next time, if I'm not around, do not enter my office. If it's urgent, speak to Joanie, that's why I have a PA.' He strides towards his chair. 'Now, I'd like to get on with my private work in my *private* office.'

I don't need telling twice and rush out of there like the room's on fire. I shiver; why did I have to use that description?

Joanie's head is peeping out of her office, her face a portrait of confusion. 'Is everything okay, ladies?'

Was I the only one not to suss that Keats was a she?

'Fine,' Keats almost snaps back, not missing a step, face straight ahead. 'You can go back to your bottles of fizzy water and the cigarettes you sneak a puff on around the side of the building.'

Joanie's mouth flaps south at her rudeness as Keats pulls the bandana back over her mouth. I send the older woman an apologetic shrug as I hurry past, trying to keep up with the woman who has just saved my bacon.

We reach the reception. I tell her, voice low, 'Thank you—'

Keats rounds on me. Yanks the bandana down. 'I don't want your thanks. I don't need anyone's thanks. Got it? What I want to know is what you were doing. After work. Me and you. In a café of my choosing.'

My head's spinning from her quick-fire delivery. I'm still reeling as she bends down and pulls the trap door that folds easily back as if it's been waiting for our return.

Twenty-Seven

The café we sit in is trendy, in a Georgian square not too far from the office, filled with Keats types, not in mode of dress but hardcore tekkies with eyes only for their laptops and tablets. Erasure's eighties classic *Sometimes* plays wistfully in the background. Keats insolently tips back a bottle of strawberry-flavoured water to her mouth, the muscles in her slim neck ripple as the drink makes its journey down. She wipes the wetness glistening on her lips with the back of a hand.

'I don't want to be your friend,' is how she kick-starts our one-on-one. That pointed part of her chin is going to saw through her skin if she keeps up the grinding of her teeth. 'I don't like people much. Don't have a lot of time for them. Most will try to royally screw you over.'

'You're the one who asked for a sit down, not me,' I chuck back.

'Because I need to know why you were snooping in Michael's office—'

My palm comes up to stop her. 'Who said anything about snooping?'

'I did. And do. I might've been slung into a special school at the age of seven but that don't mean I'm a thicko.' Keats's mouth snaps shut, the blink-blink of her lowered lashes telling me she didn't mean to give out that personal info. My heart goes out to her; how can anyone have put a mind like hers in a special school? Whatever the story, Keats isn't telling. We've all got our personal safes where we lock up our secrets.

She asks her question again, less heat this time, and I counter with one of my own. 'What's with the whole bandana look?'

'You saying women can't dress like I do at work?'

'I'm saying I've never seen anyone kitted out like Clint Eastwood's sidekick.'

There's a twitch at the corner of her mouth, which, I hope, is her suppressing a grin.

Keats's shoulders dip back, a tiny movement that pops the outline of her collarbone through her T-shirt. 'Ode to the unenlightened: the world's full of variety.'

'What's an ode?'

'John Keats.'

'The poet? He's an ode?' I'm frowning, bemused.

Then another first happens. Keats laughs. A strained burst, like her lungs aren't working properly. She carries on like we've slipped back into our messaging relationship. I don't deter her. Why not? It suddenly dawns on me I might have an ally here.

'Most of his poems were odes. It's a type of poem. *Ode to the Nightingale*. It's a good way of looking at life. Someone called him a 'vulgar Cockney poetaster'. I say bring it on, Keats.'

She's obviously really into this subject because her eyes lift from the squinted guarded position she's worn since we came here.

'What's your real name?'

I wonder if *her* name really begins with a K as well. Kate. Katherine. Kerry. Kali.

Her face shutters. Eyelids hooded again. I should've left this question until later, hopefully when we were on safer ground. There's a dismissive sound deep in her throat. She picks up the bottle, a deeper slug this time.

Her voice drops to a rough whisper. 'Depends on what you mean by real.'

'What name did your parents give you?'

Something briefly washes over her face. Rolls off the edge before I can catch it, but I suspect it would have clipped into place another piece of the Keats puzzle. Considering it probably was her parents who forced her into special school, it wasn't a smart move, on my part, to seat them at the table as well.

'That I won't tell you. I'm either Keats or Sue.'

She doesn't look like a Sue. Sues are sweet, the girl next door, churning out apple pies with perfect shortcrust pastry with Mum.

'A Boy Named Sue.' Keats answers the query she must detect from my expression.

'You've lost me.' She hasn't. I know the song; Jed's band did a respectable rendition of it one time. What I want to do is keep open every avenue so she remains talking.

She rolls her eyes, clearly exasperated. 'It's a Johnny Cash tune. *A Boy Named Sue*. On YouTube – you should check him out singing it at San Quentin. All-time performance.'

San Quentin? I've never heard of it. It must be a concert venue in the States. Keats or Sue? What should I call her, although I suspect that Sue isn't her real name either.

It's my turn to lean over the table, to lower the pitch of my words. Each one I choose very carefully. 'How did you come to be working for Michael?'

A vein visibly throbs in her neck. 'I'm a freelancer. Software and stuff. He contacted me, so I came to work here a week before you did.' Her gaze pierces right through me. 'And he asked me to keep an eye on you. Hence, let's go back to the starting blocks – what were you doing in his office?'

Heat jumps unexpectedly into my tone. 'And you kept an eye on me all right, going behind my back and telling him my work wasn't up to shit. And that's why he started making me work late—'

'Now hold on one bollocks minute.' The shape that anger twists her mouth into is a sight to see. 'I never told Michael

161

anything of the sort. Although let's be practical here, you're no management consultant.'

I discard her need for honesty and focus on the real issue. 'You never spoke to him?'

Another eye roll. 'Of course I spoke to him—'

'No. About me and my work?'

Her chin goes down as she shakes her head. 'He never asked.' Her eyes flick across the room away from my face. 'Michael did want me to report on you to him,' Keats admits, 'but I'm no-one's snitch. And that's what I told him. So, we agreed I'd look after you… from a distance. Getting chummy-chummy ain't my scene.'

My mind whirls. So, if Michael never asked, he made it up. Why is he playing with my mind? Doing this to me? My temples punch and pull, stirring up a dull ache in my head.

'It's a weird set-up in that office, that much I know.' Her words get my attention. 'That's why I told you to watch your back in the basement.'

'I think he's been playing you against me. Probably using the way you look to knock me off balance. Add to the spooky atmosphere in the basement.'

As soon as the words are out, I wish I could drag them back. No-one wants to be told that they look like a weirdo.

I've obviously hurt her because Keats's chest puffs with an expanse of emotion. 'There's nothing weird about me. Nothing wrong with the way I look.' Her tone is hard, verging on fury. 'I'm normal, it's the world that's all bent out of shape. That's why I let you into my computer. Because of what you said.' I don't prompt her. Let her speak. She lowers her eyes. '"I just want to be normal again." That's what you said to me at the launderette. I know how that feels.'

And that's when I do it. Tell her everything. Well, some of the truth. Half-truths have been the story of my life for so long it comes naturally to me.

When I finish, pulse blasting like I've been running for my life, I watch her. Expect Keats's features to be a mix of horror and the curious. That's not what I see. Her face is smooth with considered calm.

After a drawn-out silence, she tells me, 'I'm doing the funeral service programme for Michael.'

So, Michael is connected to Philip. But how? Then Keats spikes my bubble. 'But he says he's doing it as a favour for a client, with more details to come.' Which explains the white spaces in the programme and the gaps marked for photos. 'And there are things about the info that suggests it was cut and pasted from another e-mail. So maybe he's telling the truth.'

Truth? No, that's the one thing that isn't going on here. Michael is linked to Philip. Michael is linked to my dad. A triangle of three I don't understand yet. But I will.

'What's Philip's last name?' Funny, that summer we were just Rachel and Philip, no need for surnames to be included.

Keats pulls her bottle to her lips and refreshes herself before telling me, 'All I was given was his first name, Philip.'

'Michael lured me to this job, I know he did,' I decide to tell Keats.

Her chin does its pointy thing again. 'What do you mean "lured"?'

I give her the lowdown:

– Pretending to know Jed.

– Interviewing me away from the office.

– Making my lack of experience sound like 'hey, that's no problem'.

– Insisting I work late based on a lie.

The last brings a terrible devastating thought to me – has Michael been playing with my head like switching the lights off in the office and blaming it on ancient electrics? Locking the door in the basement when they all went for lunch? But how did he lock me in if he'd left the building? And why would he do this to me? My mind's a mess.

But I ask Keats, 'Did you lock me in the basement?'

'When?' I tell her. She shakes her head. 'Nope. Not me. And it's a newish lock so hardly likely to lock itself.'

I believe her. Why would she lie to me? I reach a no-turning-point decision. 'Will you help me?'

Keats's gaze drills into me. 'Why are you putting yourself through this? It's obviously causing you a lot of pain. Hand in your notice, pack your gear and never look back.'

She isn't asking me anything I haven't soul-searched myself. I ran that summer. I won't run again. 'Will you help me?' I repeat.

Keats pops her shades on. Flips her hood on. 'I'll do it. As long as you don't get the idea that we're two peas in a pod, you know, mates.'

I can live with that.

'Use your digi skills to find out how Michael's connected to my dad, Frank Jordan.'

Keats cocks her head, evaluating me. It leaves me uncomfortable. Uneasy. Her words, stark advice really, haunt me. 'The search for the truth is admirable, but it can also dig up the most unimaginable soul-destroying pain.'

Twenty-Eight

It's a story about the devil in the funeral service programme that makes the breath catch in my throat. The programme's spread across my desk. I'd confessed to Keats that I'd destroyed my copy, so thanks to her I have another. Michael thinks I'm down here going through more – yep, he gave me more – stupid training videos like an obedient little girl. I'm still trying to understand why he played the Pied Piper to my innocent child to get me here, but if he thinks that he's tormenting me by making me work so late, he needs to think again. Dumb idiot! He's given me the time and some of the tools to knit together his connection to Dad and Philip. I'm not there yet.

Soon.

A chair jammed between the steel door and its frame keeps it open. Any sound in the tunnel or on the staircase I'll hear, however faint. The acoustics in this building are a strange thing. Despite the trap door being closed, some of the noises on the upper floors come over loud and clear while others are muffled like voices chattering underwater.

The website about the sweatshop fire claimed that this former tenement is riddled with secret passageways so maybe that's why sound carries the way it does. All good haunted houses have them of course. Except this building is haunted by a real woman: Michael's mother. And that dog, mustn't forget the dog. Funeral service or not, I'm ready as soon as I hear so much as a whisper, a footstep, the drop of a tear up there. I'll find a way to hear what's being said. Michael and his mother will give themselves away eventually. Or perhaps my father will return and they'll all give themselves away together.

The first thing I did when I settled the pages of the funeral programme on my desk was to closely study each page. I'm still no nearer to knowing where or when this funeral is going to be. Or who will be there. Except that it won't include me. My dad was clear that I have to respect the family's wishes. That's if, once again, Dad is telling me the truth.

I'm frustrated by the gaps left for the inclusion of photographs, photos that may well have helped me work everything out. The service doesn't contain the usual *Abide With Me* or *I Did It My Way* but poems, references to plays, readings from books I've never read. Whoever commissioned this half-finished document expects the mourners to be a high-brow congregation who will soak up every reference. Or perhaps this person doesn't care whether grief-stricken mourners or bored fringe members of his family at this funeral get them or not. I'm not sure Philip would.

And that's when the story about the devil grabs my attention. It's a reading. A passage from the story *Faust* by a writer called Goethe, which I assume is pronounced as Goth. Something tells me I haven't got that right, so I wiki the author and discover he was German and his name is pronounced as Gurta. It seems hard to believe that Philip, who I knew as a handyman-cum-gardener, would know who Goethe was or be familiar with the *Faust* legend, which appears to be very famous. He never mentioned he was a fan of German poetry or dog-eared European classics, although he did a good line in salty limericks and knew a few snatches of nonsense verse. It's another puzzle in the death and life and death of Philip.

I don't know about Goethe or *Faust* until Google puts me in the picture. The story's simple: a guy called Faust sells his soul to the devil in return for the secrets of knowledge and pleasure. He gets to enjoy them for a set period before the devil will return to claim Faust's soul and he'll be damned for all eternity. That's it really.

I read the passage that's in the funeral programme, expecting more of the same. But the extract spurs on the icy chill in this underworld room to circle closer and closer to me as I read. I feel an invisible hand on the collar of my jacket, pulling me back, and an unheard voice warning me not to read on. But the story has me in its grip, demanding I continue.

Faust and the devil join a drinking party in a wine cellar. The drunks want to pick a fight with the devil but he does magic to make them stop. There's more conjuring at the end when the devil pours wine into holes in the floor and sets the wine on fire.

I feel sick but not in my belly. It's in my soul. I know full well what this passage alludes to. No, I won't go back there! The forbidden memories fight me, fight dirty, use every trick in their nasty book to erupt from the secret place in my heart. They've rotted in my memory, poisoned my body, corrupted everything. Now, in this basement, they gush out like the contents of a broken sewer.

Twenty-Nine

That summer

Rachel wasn't sure why Philip was unhappy about her working in the wine cellar. But on her first day there, her second day at the house, she realised she wasn't happy about it either. The door to the cellar was off the hallway. It led to a flight of wooden steps that led in turn to a cavernous and rambling space that ran under the house. Row after row of tall wine racks shaded the lights so most of it was sunk in an uneasy and shadowy gloom. The stone walls and floors made the cellar chilly and cold, even while the sun was burning bright outside.

Of course there were no windows down there. But once you passed the first wine racks there was no sign of the steps or the door either. That, together with the silence and the shadows tinged with garish colours thrown by the bottles, disorientated Rachel. It was easy to feel she was trapped in a grisly fairy tale, locked up in a monster's underground lair with no way of escape. One of those stories that parents decide they won't read to their children because it might give them nightmares.

At the end of the cellar was a desk where she set up her notebook and pen.

Rachel wandered from row to row along the racks, counting the wines, dividing them into reds, rosés and whites, Spanish, French and Italian. In boxes littered around were job lots of wine that Danny had bought at auctions and Rachel fished out the bottles and arranged them on the racks. There was something curious about this collection. But she couldn't put her finger on it.

She shivered slightly when she heard the door above open, a piercing shaft of light appear and the sound of footsteps on the wooden stairs. When she realised it was Philip with Ray the dog in tow, she felt relief but couldn't understand why. Philip was uncharacteristically sombre.

He picked up a bottle of red. 'How you doing?'

'Fine. Although I haven't seen much of Danny this morning, so I'm not entirely sure if I'm doing the right thing.'

Philip sighed. 'I think he's on one of his building sites today.'

'My job here is a bit strange.'

In the half-light, Philip's face remained in the shadows. 'Really? Why?'

'I don't think he drinks wine. All these bottles are covered in dust. They look as if they've been dumped here. Funny behaviour for a wine connoisseur.'

Philip put the bottle down. 'I know. I think he's pretending to be a country gentleman and country gentlemen keep wine collections. It's a bit of a joke.' His tone suddenly changed and he burst into a warning. 'Listen, Rach, I don't want to freak you out or anything but you might decide that it's not a good idea to be on your own down here with Danny.'

Rachel gave a light laugh. But it wasn't a convincing one. 'I don't know what you mean. He's a friend of my dad's. He's my employer; I can't tell him where he can and can't go in his own house. What are you suggesting – that he's a bit handy with women or something?'

Philip picked up another wine bottle and studied the label. 'No, I'm not suggesting that at all. It's just I don't think it's a good idea. Tell him you can't work down here. Tell him you're claustrophobic – he'll believe that. He thinks all women have a phobia of some sort or another, except Dannyphobia of course.'

Rachel became angry. 'Stop it, Philip, you're frightening me. There's no way Danny's like that. My dad thinks sex pests should be hung. If he thought Danny had laid a finger on me, he'd kill him, and I mean really kill him. Danny will know that, my dad's views on the subject aren't exactly a secret. So please, stop it.'

'It was just a thought, that's all. I didn't mean anything by it.'

Rachel said nothing further and Philip drifted back up the stairs to the hallway followed by an unusually quiet Ray.

But a few hours later, when Danny returned from his building site and paid her a visit in the cellar, Rachel was worried. Danny said nothing as his footsteps echoed on the stone floor and he weaved in and out of the wine racks, casting peculiar shaped black shadows on the back wall where she sat making notes.

Then he was standing right behind her. It startled her slightly because she hadn't heard him move. The lack of natural light in this underground world suddenly somehow bothered her. Why that was, she couldn't say.

'How are you getting on, Rachel?'

Her answer was uncertain. 'Good thanks.'

Danny was uncomfortably close. 'You're all right down here, are you? I mean, to be honest, this cellar gives me the creeps a bit. You're not scared of enclosed spaces or anything?'

'No. Well, maybe a little.'

He was silent for a moment. 'Okay. Look, do the best you can down here and then we'll find something else for you to do.'

'That would be good.'

There were a few agonising seconds before he walked away, the stairs creaking and moaning beneath him. When he opened the door to the cellar, Rachel heard Danny shout, 'What are you doing loitering in the hallway? And I thought I told you to get rid of that bloody animal.'

The door slammed shut so Rachel didn't hear Philip's reply.

As the days passed, Danny's visits to the cellar were less and less frequent. On one such afternoon visit, he admitted to her that he didn't even like wine and was thinking of selling his collection and converting the cellar into a gym.

'I suppose the whole thing was my attempt to play the country squire. I'm really into my classic cars, Rachel, that's what I love. On your final day here, I'll take you for a spin and we'll go for lunch in a country pub. Would you like that?'

Rachel pretended she would. 'Yes, that would be nice.'

'I'll tell you what, why don't you go home early. You're wasting your time down here anyway.'

Rachel grabbed her bag and seized her chance to leave.

It was the following afternoon, while Rachel was at her desk in the cellar, that Danny paid her a final visit. He stood right behind her while she sat at the desk writing up her notes. The heat coming off him and his shallow breathing were making her tense again.

'I think you're about done down here. Let's reassign you to something more worthwhile.'

Rachel felt an immediate release in her belly at his words. But she also noticed his voice sounded slightly slurred and the peculiar shadow he cast on the wall in front of her swayed slightly. He rested his head on her shoulder from behind and she caught a whiff of his stale cologne and the equally stale alcohol on his breath, his bristled cheek pressed up against hers.

Then his arms coiled themselves around her waist like a slimy python and he whispered, 'I've got a four-poster upstairs that needs airing. How about you come and help me with that.'

She froze. Her legs didn't obey when she tried to jump up and no sound came out of her mouth when she opened it to scream. She was stiff, caught cold in a hellish moment in time.

'Or are you the kind of girl who prefers it a bit rough on the desk in the cellar? Trapped with nowhere to go. You can tell me, Rachel, I'm flexible.'

It was only when he forced his hands up her blouse and squeezed her breasts so hard that she was in agonising pain that she finally let out a piercing scream.

Trapped. Trapped. Trapped.

Thirty

I fling the funeral programme onto the floor as if I'm being burned alive. I scrunch up in the smallest ball I can on my side on the mattress.

'Make it go away. Please make the memories go away.'

The first thing I see in the basement the next day is the devil sitting, showcasing his horns and tail as he swings casually in my chair. I shake my head, knowing it's not real. I'm a bit doped up on BBs and too much CBD oil, off-centre, because it's the only way I'm going to get through the day without the painful images of the past that spewed out last night crawling back. What does catch my eye is there's no Keats. Chair empty, computer a blank, shut screen.

I feel a twist of anxiety that the woman who is prepared to help me isn't there. I don't know where this comes from – she's plainly stated she doesn't want to become buddies – but Keats has that certain something, the very French je ne sais quoi, I believe will do battle for me in a heartbeat against the malevolence ingrained in this tomb. How can I ever forget the way she took on Michael in his office kingdom, a masked assassin who slayed him with mere words.

I take my seat and bury my head in the latest report Michael has tasked me to do. My head may be buried but my mind's somewhere else. The cannabis oil does its work, loosening my brain cells enough for me to run through possible ways to try to unlace the lock of the relationship between Dad and Michael.

~~Speak to Dad~~: No go – the Frank Jordan I heard here frightens me. *'She'll feel my claws across her face and they're razor sharp as you know. As for you, don't make me break you, Michael.'* That level of violence leaves acid bile corroding inside my throat. If someone had told me my dad, my loving gentle dad, would behave like that I'd have called them a bold-faced liar. No, I'm the liar. I'm deluding myself. I know the level of violence Dad is capable of from incidents in my own life. Jed's broken nose is testament to that. Besides, Dad would probably turn the tables, get me on the back foot and somehow make me believe it was all stuff 'n' nonsense. At some stage I know I'll have to confront him, but the time's not right, not yet.

~~Put Michael on the spot~~: He has no allegiance towards me so why would he cough up the truth? I can see the scene now, him dismissing me with an aloof wave of his hand and sour cut of his eyes. Worse still is, he may send me packing and how will I then find out the truth if I'm no longer here?

Joanie.

My mind skids to a stop. Now *that's* a definite possibility. Sure, she's loyal to her boss but she's gathered me under her wing too. Maybe…

Something on the computer in front of me captures my attention. I can't believe this, that bastard zombie is up to his video tricks again. He's re-running the same film… No, this one is different. The air stalls in my chest, hot and burning, at what I see. It's a different woman this time. No way… Can't be… But it is. Oh God, she looks like me.

The spit of me is terrified. Back pressed against the wall, mouth wide, eyes bulging, fingers clawing the air as a masked man advances in deliberate menacing slo-mo towards her. My pulse picks up speed when I see the blue lights strung out across the wall above her head. My gaze bolts away from the screen to the blue lights in the basement. Back to the screen. Are they the same lights? Has a woman been brutalised in this basement? A woman who's the double of me?

Shivers plunge down my spine, my breathing ragged, erratic. The zombie's chair creaks and squeals as he slowly turns to me. Seizes my horrified gaze with his smugly smiling own. *Move, Rachel, move. Get out of there.* But I can't. I'm frozen in the nastiness of his stare.

He wheels his chair towards me. Tilts his head to the side as he sizes me up. Pungent garlic on his breath, no doubt from what he ate the day before, skins over my face as he whispers, 'Have you got a problem?'

I might be scared but no way am I going to let this moron see me shaking in my charity shop shoes. So I tell him, with the bravest voice I own, 'Are you hurting women down here?'

His smile spreads as greasy as rancid oil. 'And what if I am?'

'Michael has already warned you to stop doing this.'

The zombie's face wiggles into my space so closely that the faint splat of freckles on the bridge of his nose must surely be the mark of the devil. 'Say anything to anyone and you better be ready to have eyes in the back of your head on the way home. No telling what type of accidents may be waiting to befall you in the dark.'

That's it. I'm up and out of my chair. Beyond the steel door.

Clutching the tunnel's damp unfriendly walls, the jump of my lungs and fear leaving me breathless and in a fog of sweating cold. I don't want to be scared but I am. I see it, me leaving work, walking, walking, not checking behind me and, in the moment it takes to click a finger, he's there, a man-monster materialising from the shadows. Dragging me down through the trap door. Along the tunnel. Into the basement. Donning his macabre mask.

Stop. It. That isn't going to happen. *Because you're marching upstairs right now to demand Michael sort this crap out once and for all.* Then the thought of Joanie comes to me. Any problems, she emphasised, I should come to her.

I find Joanie in the kitchen, pouring milk into a steaming cup of tea. Immediately my tongue itches with the remembered sour taste on my first day.

Joanie is alert to my distress immediately and puts the carton down. 'What's wrong, Rach?'

I'll be her 'Rach', her anything, if she can put this right for me. I let rip about the scene I left downstairs.

Her eyes widen. 'But I thought Michael told them to knock it on the head or he was going to show them the door.'

I nearly respond that he should've shown them the door the first time. The furious words die behind my lips. I inhale deep and steady instead so I can make what I utter next really matter. 'It's not right that anyone should be threatened in their own place of work. And I think it was filmed here.'

'Here?' I'm glad she's as horrified as I am. 'How can that be? The building is locked up and secured tight at night. There's no way of getting in.'

I draw back my next words, stiffening with a new alertness. There are times in life when you're on one road but then, out of nowhere, a more promising pathway opens up. And the door that Joanie has pulled back reveals the world of this building at night. Secure and locked up she calls it. What more can she tell me?

Tightly controlling my emotions this time, my tone sure and super friendly. 'We wouldn't want more tragedy happening in this building. It already has a terrible history.'

'What do you mean?' Her question is hesitant, alarm lengthening her neck.

'The plaque outside.' Stage whisper. 'The sweatshop fire.'

Her eyes swim around, then widen with understanding. 'Oh, *that* fire. Awful. Can you imagine it, Rach, being stuck in that basement filling with raging fire with no way out?' A shudder visibly ripples through her.

I'm sure she sees the bob of my throat as I swallow heavily at the image her words dump on me. 'What if the building weren't so secure and there was someone living here—?'

'What? You mean at night?' Her mouth finishes with an O shape of disbelief.

I step closer. 'In this day of homelessness, it's not unheard of.' I shrug. 'Or a member of Michael's family might be living here at night.'

I know, way too close to the bone, but as much as I like this woman, I don't think she's clever enough to pick up on where I'm leading her. Don't get me wrong, I'm not stating that Joanie's stupid, it's more like she's a woman who takes pride in not deep thinking too often, a connoisseur of living on the sunny side of the street.

Her nose twitches slightly as she glances at me quizzically. She clears her throat. 'Why would anyone in Mr Barrington's family be living here?'

I'm in there quickly. 'So, who's in his family? A dad... mother—'

She gets there before me, doing that strange shoulder shift of hers that tells me she's going into professional Joanie mode. 'Mr Barrington's father was the best person I've ever worked with. A caring gentle soul who – God rest his long-departed soul–' ah, so Michael's father has died, 'would do anything for me.'

Keep going. Tell me about his mother.

But Joanie picks up her cup and over her shoulder says, 'I'll tell Michael what you told me. He won't be back until later this afternoon.'

And with that she's gone, leaving the milk carton on the counter. I know no more about Michael's mother than I did before.

Thirty-One

For the remainder of the afternoon, I expect – hope – Michael will do a repeat performance of appearing to demand the zombie who threatened me come to his office, but the performance will be different this time – Michael will give him his marching orders. I know Michael is still my enemy, but in this situation with the zombie, he's my knight in shining armour. No way will he tolerate this type of behaviour towards a woman. At least Keats is back with no explanation of where she's been. Still, I feel safer in this room of men now she's here.

So I wait. And wait. Then I hear a steady click-click-click coming from the tunnel outside. Footsteps that kick up their own echo along the way. A secretive smug smile warms my face; finally, Michael to the rescue.

Then the door moves. The silence of its opening is somehow more unsettling than if it had made a blood-curdling creak. It's not Michael.

Joanie.

She just stands there. Doesn't move. Remains a statue, Madame Tussauds waxwork still. Something's wrong. This is not the same Joanie I spoke to this morning. The Joanie who's so animated, full of life, threatening to hug me. Her eyes are faintly bloodshot, smudged mascara deforming their shape. They're piercing doll-like eyes. Fixed, with laser intensity on one person.

Me.

Instinctively, I look behind me, reasoning she must be staring at something – someone – else. No, she's staring at me. And staring. And staring. My body stiffens in disconcerted confusion. An electric dizzying silence seizes the room as the zombies and Keats also look upon the strange situation. No-one utters a word.

'Joanie?' My voice is hesitant, so quiet I barely hear it myself. 'Is there a problem?' Stupid, stupid question. Of course there's a problem. It's as if she hasn't heard me. Suddenly I become more aware of being in a room beneath ground level with no window to escape through. Trapped.

Joanie finally picks up the click-click-click of her robotic walk, grisly glare never leaving me. WTF is going on here? She keeps moving. Getting closer to me.

Click-click.

Closer and closer.

Click-click.

Joanie's not a large woman but from my seated vantage point, looking up, she seems to inflate, up and across, the nearer she gets to me until it feels like she's blocking out all else in the basement. I'm ready to jump out of my seat when she reaches me. Mercifully she walks right past me.

Before I can start the business of breathing correctly again, she turns, folds her arms and keeps her malevolent gaze locked to me again like a jailer keeping watch over a death row inmate. And she'll be personally carrying out the execution. Her face is a mixed palette of washed-out colour and the unnatural blue light above. The background hum of the wall rises to an irritating drone drilling deep into my head. I'm frigging freaked out.

Hurriedly, I message Keats.

Me: *Why's Joanie standing there like I've just mugged her? She looks like something out of a bargain basement horror movie.*

Keats: *Dunno.*

Keats stops and then types away but not a message to me. Joanie click-clicks to stand right in front of me. Good grief, she looks like she wishes she had a chainsaw buzzing in her hand. The heat coming off her reeks of something I can't identify. I see her chest rise up and fall. Hear her breathing. Short, sharp and as jagged as mine. Her fingers flex and claw at her side as if... as if... Joanie's not going to attack me, is she?

I'm not waiting around to find out and jump sideways out of my chair with a squeal. Yes, squeal. I know I'm an imitation of something that sounds like it needs feeding at the zoo but, you know what, I don't care. Whatever's happening here leaves me on the edge. Creeped out more than full-blown fear.

Seconds later, the overlapping thud of running feet in the corridor beyond the steel door crashes through the silence.

Michael, breathing laboured, bursts into the room. He nods brusquely at Keats and I realise that Keats must've been messaging him after she answered mine. The stretch and pull of Michael's mouth shows he's battling with something... I peer harder. Is that anger? Anguish? A twisted blend of both? Whatever it is soon dissolves behind a neutral expression. Michael moves towards the woman who won't let me go.

He drapes his arm over her shoulder and gently tries to coax her out of the basement. 'Come on, Joanie. What are you doing down here? We've got work to do, haven't we.' He ends with a light laugh that sounds like shattering glass. His dimples don't come out. 'Invoices don't type themselves.'

A violent flick of her shoulder shakes him off. Then she's still again. Except for those eyes, alive with the power of a blowtorch scorching into the centre of me. I've had enough of this and open my mouth, but Michael's calm palm in the air freezes the words on my tongue.

He tries again, more firmly this time, with a gentleness that takes my breath away. 'Let's get a nice cuppa down you. And those chocolate fingers you love so much.'

Joanie rocks, her shoulders slump as she finally allows herself to be steered away. Then, as she stands there with her distorted shadow on the gloomy tunnel wall for company, she sends me a final look. It seizes my breath. It's a look of blistering hatred. Isn't it?

Or has the horror of this situation polluted my mind?

In the aftermath of The Stare, my hand trembles around the glass of water I gulp unevenly from as I stand in the basement's tiny dingy kitchen. I can't understand what just happened. Why was Joanie staring at me like that, as if I'd personally wronged her?

Before I can delve deeper, Keats appears. Slams the door shut with the sturdy heel of her Dr Martens. Pulls down her bandana and whips off her shades.

'What did you do to Joanie?' is Keats's brusque question.

I slam the glass down. 'Nothing. All I did this morning was tell her about the zombie doing "camera, action" with that disgusting film of his again. And him threatening me.' Keats already knows this, I gave her chapter and verse when she put in an appearance at work just before eleven.

Keats demands, 'And what else?'

I flick my nervy gaze away from her. 'What do you mean?'

Keats steps closer which means her breath's coating my face because this is a very small room. 'I know when you're holding out on me.'

With a resigned heavy sigh, I make eye contact. 'I asked her, very subtly if any of Michael's family live here at night—'

Keats rolls her eyes, her go-to style of showing when she's very irritated. 'Are you crackers? She's the last person you should've asked.'

'Why?'

'She's too close to Michael. And very loyal. What if she tells him you were nosing around? That's going to get you fired—'

'Will it?' I lean into the edge of the sink. 'We know he wants me here. Why that is, I – we – still need to find out. So, he won't send me packing.'

Keats stews in her silence for a time. Then, 'But if she's told him, it means you've showed your hand to him...'

The ping of her mobile cuts her off. She pulls it out. Reads. Turns her face back to me. 'That was Michael. He wants you in his office. Now.'

My heartbeat stalls. What if Keats is right? That Joanie told him. That he realises I'm on a quest to find the truth.

I hesitate outside Michael's office. Is this how Daniel felt going into the lions' den? A sense of pure dread laced with a determined will to survive.

'You can come in now,' Michael's strong voice beyond the door calls.

It startles me. How does he know I'm here? Did I make a noise? Did he hear my footsteps coming up the stairs? My jumpy gaze suddenly searches, low and high, as it occurs to me that there may be camera lenses trained on me, mechanical eyes doing Michael's dirty work. Why didn't I think of this before? If he lured me here, the obvious next step is to spy on me. Does he know I'm living in the building at night along with his mother? Is he tracking every move I make? I find nothing that suggests there are cameras watching me, but still I store it in a corner of my mind to dissect later.

For now, I level my shoulders, straighten every vertebra in my back and go inside. Michael's standing, poised, apparently casually, by the window. The natural light frames him, bringing to the surface every imperfection on his face I've never noticed before. The circles of barely there darkness peeping under both eyes, the tiniest bump in the bone of his nose, a tightness about his skin that... I look with deeper intent... The tightness has nothing to do with a high-quality moisturiser. It's the strain of holding himself together. And that's when I realise something else. He's upset. Holding on to his anger too.

Joanie sits in a chair, her back to me. She's so still, so unmoving, it appears unnatural.

Michael's lips spread in what he thinks is a smile but to my flickering gaze appears more like an enforced grimace.

I continue to act the faithful employee. 'You wanted to see me?'

He points at the empty chair next to Joanie. Offers me an invitation I can't refuse. 'Please. Take a seat.'

As I move, I hear the planks of the floor creak and cry, depress and dip beneath my tread. Strange how I've never noticed that before. Then again there's so much about this building that only reveals itself when it wants to.

I sit down and turn to the woman next to me. Her hands lay flat in her lap, her head slightly down. Finally she looks at me and I can't help the gasp that escapes. She looks terrible, pinched and drawn, drained and so very tired. She reminds me of a portrait of Elizabeth I I saw once. The one where the ravages of age are painted for all to see.

Joanie lets out a long drawn-out line of air and says, 'I'm really sorry, Rachel. I don't know what came over me.' Her remorse is relayed in a rasping croak.

I think about offering the usual phrases of conciliation – it's okay; don't worry about it; no point sweating the small stuff. I don't. There's a compulsion to make her understand how I felt. 'It shook me up. I genuinely thought you were going to do something to me.'

Her hands come to life, all a-flutter in her lap. 'I'm going through The Change. You know, time of life.' She's clearly embarrassed to mention it. There's the ghost of a smile on her lips. 'One minute I'm a happy bunny, the next hunting around to bite someone's head off.'

I recall Joanie jokingly calling it 'menohell' before. There's no merriment now. What I know about the menopause – which isn't much, I admit – is hot flushes, sleepless nights and mood swings. I've never heard of one that drives a person to stare. The feeling of it comes back to me. Hostile, chilling, downright disturbing.

Michael abruptly joins the conversation as he remains in the light of the window. 'She did the same thing to me last week. Didn't you, Joanie?'

'Yes, Mr Barrington.'

'Interrupted me during a very important phone call,' he quirks his brow, 'which I had no alternative but to end because I was so worried about your welfare.'

'Yes, Mr Barrington.'

Joanie's answers are the toneless recital of a robot on autoplay. She looks cowed as if she's waiting for someone to strike her. My hot gaze meets Michael. Has this bastard done something to her? Made her feel even worse about being a woman going through a natural physical change? I have this strong urge to take her by the arm and rescue her from this place.

Before I can display any heroic actions, Michael folds his arms just as the brightness of the light recedes slightly from the room. 'I hope that's an end to the matter. Be assured it won't happen again.'

I've been dismissed, so get up. It's my turn to stare at Joanie. I don't want to leave her here. I suggest we have tea and chocolate fingers.

She smiles and nods with reassurance, a glimpse of Joanie getting her groove back. 'I'm fine. We'll have a cuppa together. Soon.'

As I leave the room, I feel The Stare again. This time it's the hotness of Michael's eyes that bore into me.

Thirty-Two

I'm shivering inside the duvet on the mat. I can't get warm in the storeroom tonight. Everywhere seems to breathe Artic ice. What I wouldn't give for some central heating. Maybe I need to buy one of those freestanding oiled-based radiators. *Don't get as snug as a bug here. This isn't your real home.* I know, I know, but still I'm here for the duration until I get the answers I need. I sit up and pull my rucksack over. Fish out another pair of woolly socks and put them on. Do the same with the thick Aran jumper Mum bought me. I snuggle under the duvet... and so does the cold. It's eating its way into my bones.

Will I hear Michael's mum upstairs tonight? The dog? Will their mournful melody seep through the ceiling and the walls again? I hope not, a restful sleep is what I need to start my journey to the truth tomorrow. My breathing relaxes, smooths out...

What was that? I sit up, breathing a waterfall of noisy air as I urgently look around like a bird sensing danger. The sound was definitely not the building's natural rhythms. It wasn't a dog or a woman weeping either. I softly flick off the duvet and stretch across, a female panther ready to spring into action.

Listen. There it is again. Scraping. Something heavy dragging across concrete. I know that sound. It's so familiar... I do it every day. Someone is moving the grill that guards the courtyard. Guards my makeshift temporary home.

It hits me how vulnerable I am. No-one to hear the echo of my cries and screams.

'No telling what type of accidents may be waiting to befall you in the dark.' The remembered threat from the zombie concerning his sickening film slugs me full in the stomach.

I fumble as quietly as I can through my possessions until I find my penknife. Whoever's there will soon discover I'm going to go down fighting. I can sense whoever's on the other side of the wall hanging down, a bat in the night, judging when they should drop onto the cobbles below.

Again, I fine-tune my hearing to catch the sounds of the night. Listen. A soft thud. The intruder has landed. I push out the small blade of my knife. This is what crossing a line and refusing to go back feels like. Stronger. Determined. Bloody double terrified. I stand tall, centre where the room is at its fiercest. And wait. The invader doesn't seem to care about me hearing them because their tread moves with a confidence, a steady fall. Getting closer to the door that separates us. Is that the in-out of their breathing I hear? Yeah, there it is, super faint like a collection of whispers travelling through the night.

Is this what shaking like a leaf feels like? Every part of me rocking to a beat I can't control? The handle moves, a circular motion that has the power to hypnotise. It stops and I can't help but take a step back. The door opens in its silence. A figure appears, drenched in black. The face no features at all. A demon. I've seen this demon in a doorway before.

Keats.

Keats, AKA A Boy Named Sue, pulls down her bandana like an outlaw who's lucked in nabbing the loot and outridden the posse.

I gawk at her. 'What are you doing here?' More importantly, 'How did you know I was here?'

She inches out of her own surrounding shade of black, closer to me. Pulls her sunglasses off and hooks one of its arms onto the upper pocket of her fatigue jacket.

'You probably don't realise that you do it, but you keep looking at the door in the basement which appears like a panel in the wall that leads here when you're sitting at your desk.' She delivers her explanation in a levelled-out tone, matter of fact, devoid of emotion. And maybe this is what I need, her logical upfront style of talking. None of that tedious dodging the issue, talking in circles. 'So, I did a bit of snooping myself and it wasn't hard to figure out who the gear in this room belongs to.'

I reset my calmness. 'So, you're here to tell me about a connection between my dad and Michael?'

Keats rolls her eyes with much drama. 'I'm not here to admire the pipework, am I.'

The pipework. A huge grin travels up my face. Who but Keats would liken anything to pipework? A thrill fizzes through me. I'm not alone anymore. Keats flicks her hood back as she settles next to me on the duvet.

She crosses her legs like she's ready to meditate. And begins. 'Michael runs another series of businesses, so he's a genuine businessman. Quite successful really. But I couldn't find any connection between your father and Michael. There was nothing there.'

The disappointment is crushing. 'There must be something—'

'If there is, someone's doing a brilliant job of hiding it.' Keats tilts her head in a way I think means she's got more to say. It's hard for me to tell because her face remains new to me, so I'm still learning what the tics and turns of her expressions mean.

I prompt her. 'Like you said before, you didn't come here to discuss the pipework, so tell me.'

I hear Keats sigh beneath her breath. 'The task you gave me meant I was going to inevitably bump into stuff about your family. I did find out lots of other interesting stuff about your father. Your mum's medical records—'

'Stop!' It's a screech wrenched out of me, forgetting where I am. 'Who the hell gave you permission to stick your beak into my family? I never asked you to investigate my family. All I asked you to do was find out how Dad knows Michael.' The fury's the first heat I experience tonight. 'How dare you.'

Keats remains unruffled, levelling me with such a frank glance I flinch. 'I told you. That's what happens when you go digging into the past; there are lots and lots of other skeletons waiting to tell their stories.'

It's like she's blown a hole in my chest. I try to control the involuntary clenching of my muscles below my ribs. 'You've got the nerve of the devil.'

Keats shakes her head. 'So, you don't want to know what I found out? Maybe you're scared to hear?'

I scramble to my feet. 'How would you like it if I poked my nose into your family's private business?'

I begin pacing. Wrap my arms round my Aran jumper as if it's Mum, and I'm hugging her don't-ever-leave-me tight. There are things in my past I find hard to talk about – obviously – and Mum is one of them. Alongside Dad and Philip, she was the other bright star guiding my life. My mum was… I evict the joy of her from my fragile mind. It's too painful.

'You're hurting,' Keats says as if she's impersonally tapped my profile into a computer and it's spit out the correct answer.

'No kidding,' I grit back with maximum sarcasm. 'Award her the Nobel Prize for being the world's leading expert on observing emotions.'

There's a lapse back into silence and I wonder if I've hurt her feelings. Over my shoulder, I peak at her face. A glimpse so she won't catch me in the act. She's worrying her lip with concentration.

Then she says, 'You want to know about my family? I'll tell you. My parents thought I was a screwball. The kid who would sit quietly and stare. And stare. They were so ashamed of me, so embarrassed, they didn't let me go out to parties, play sports, all the stuff other kids did.' I expect her to be raging, on her feet like me, shaking her fist at the rottenness of the world. But she's not. I know because of the texture of her voice. It's as soft and gentle as a feather floating between us.

'My family is one of those who can't stop yakking, talking from dawn to dust. So, you can imagine how the silent middle child who liked her own company, told people the truth, freaked them out. Everyone thought there was something wrong with me.' Her throat bobs. 'So when I was little, they dumped me in a state-run boarding school buried in the country for kooky kids with special needs—'

'I'm so sorry—'

Her sudden smile cuts over my words. 'It was the making of me.' A dark cloud smothers the smile. 'But when I got there, I thought I was defective. Washed up. A failure. One day I threw my computer to the floor where it smashed. This feeling – I can't explain it – came over me like a spell to fix the computer. So I found out how to and it took me a long time, but I put it back together. That's how I got into computers. Every time I put a part of that computer in the right place, pieces of broken me slotted back into their rightful place too. It's okay to be hurt. Okay to be broken. It's normal. Anyone who says different is peddling a lie.'

'Are you on the spectrum?' I ask as I resume sitting next to her.

'And what spectrum is that? Being a human being? We're all meant to be different. People have tried to stick labels on me, but I won't have it. My parents wouldn't allow me to be who I am. I'm normal. *My* normal.'

I'm blown away by her speech, her revelation of who she is. And suspect she doesn't tell it very often, if at all. I don't know whether to feel honoured or thank her. In the end I say nothing; her words speak for themselves.

Keats gets back down to business. 'I get it, you just want the stuff about Michael and your dad.' Her fingers fiddle with the arm of her sunglasses. 'So, let's be logical about this. Michael's in the business world and so is your father. Maybe the link is one about business.'

I rewind back to that night when Dad came here. Was talking to Michael.

'*Open the door, Michael, or so help me, I'll kick it in. And then I'll kick you in.*'

I shudder as the wash of Dad's remembered violence drenches me. No, what was between Michael and Dad was much more personal than business dealings gone bad. And if it was about business, why did Dad mention my name? And that's what I tell Keats. 'Whatever was between them had something to do with me and Philip.'

Keats gets up, surprising me. My back teeth grind together in an act of possession as she approaches my altar to Philip. Yes, an altar. There are no flowers, no statues, no sticks wafting sweet incense or flickering candles, but that space on the floor beneath the photo is sacred ground. The special place where Philip is back in my life. I avoid using the word 'worship' because that's not what I'm doing. I'm not, am I?

So I get up and join her. Keats regards Philip's face for a long while. 'Was he your boyfriend?'

I tell her the truth. 'It was deeper than that. He was like the brother I never had. He was there at a time I needed him.'

Keats glances away and regards me instead. 'I know you haven't told me the whole story, but the best place to find the truth is to start at the beginning. So, Rachel, where does your "once upon a time" start?'

Should I tell her? I look up to Philip for guidance. Eyes still on his adorning face, I whisper, 'We were both working summer holiday jobs. At the home of…' Deep breaths. Deep. 'A man called Danny Hall. He's dead. He died that summer.'

Keats joins her gaze to mine on the photo. 'Tomorrow, let's take a trip to the scene of the crime. Danny Hall's house.'

Then Keats is gone like a bat beating its veined wings out into the night.

Thirty-Three

My emotions are on lockdown as I prepare to meet Keats to go to Danny's former house. I woke up in the storeroom with such a feeling of wretched panic, I wasn't able to leave the haven of the duvet for a long while. I made myself get up and gazed at Philip on the wall. His face unburdened me, gave me the courage I need to walk the next steps along the journey to find the truth.

I pick up speed through the tunnel because the shadows lurking in corners seem to bulge with tongues today that mock and jeer at me. The ground doesn't feel safe under the grip of my shoes.

Rachel. Rachel. Rachel comes out at me from nowhere. I know it must be in my head. The eerie call of my name floats after me all the way to the bottom of the stairs. Then it's gone.

I take the steps as never before. Thrust the trap door open. I'm out.

At the touch of natural light, I suck in gushes of air. It's like menthol clearing a path to my lungs, my head too. My mobile pings. Text message. My brows lift at who my messenger is. Polly, my debt counsellor. *Former* debt counsellor. Thanks to Dad, I don't owe the world anymore. I wonder what she could want. I'd already let her know that I was debt free and thanked her for her services. I take out my phone.

I still have your paperwork.

Of course. Paperwork, a nice neutral name for the red letters that had tormented me. She wants me to arrange a time to pick them up. Truth be told, as far as I'm concerned, she can burn the lot. I don't answer and shove my phone away. Right now the only thing on my mind is getting this visit to Danny's former home out of the way as quickly as possible.

I find Keats sitting at the wheel of a very racy sporty car, soft top on despite the great weather. It only occurs to me then that as a freelance computer tekkie, a highly lucrative business, she must've made a packet over the years.

'Nice wheels,' is my greeting as soon as I sit beside her on the soft leather beige seat.

She doesn't look at me, getting the engine going instead. 'It isn't mine.'

'Oh, that's nice of one of your friends to let you use it.'

There's an abrupt noise from the back of her throat. 'They're not my mates. I'm borrowing it for the day.'

Borrowing? That's a strange way of putting it. Hang on a bloody second, does she mean…? A harsh frown digs into my forehead. 'Did you steal this car?'

Keats doesn't miss a beat, keeping her focused expression on the road. 'Like I said, I borrowed it. Mr and Mrs Fenchurch won't miss it. They're on holiday, but they do keep an electronic tag on their car. I used some software so that when they check in it will appear to still be in its parking bay.'

My jaw drops. She recounts her tale of stealing someone else's property as if she's telling me how she purchased a loaf of bread. 'Why didn't we catch the train, call a cab?'

'A cab will cost too much and during a train ride, your nerves may get the better of you.'

I resent the hell out of her for pointing out the obvious. I'm holding onto my wits by a thread. So, I divert the conversation by turning the spotlight away from me. 'Why would a woman want to shut herself off from the world by wearing a handkerchief over her mouth, shades and a hoodie?'

I don't expect Keats to answer. Surprise, surprise, there's a loaded silence. But I'm proved wrong when she says, 'I'm not hiding. It's my way of blending in, being forgotten.'

I gape at her. 'Blend in? You stick out like a tattoo on someone's forehead.'

'Initially, then everyone forgets. This is London after all.'

I consider her words. She's right to some degree. London can be such an impersonal city filled with people minding their own business. If Coco The Clown rode a bike wearing a kilt, no-one would take a blind bit of notice. Suddenly, one-handed, Keats pulls out her mobile, taps away at its screen, her gaze alternating quickly between it and the road. My upper body jolts slightly back when she throws it at me. It tumbles into my lap.

'Scroll through the photos.'

Which I do. The first is an old sepia photo of a young woman decked out in cowboy gear – hat, shirt, trousers and boots, looking incredibly confident as she holds a shotgun across her thigh and her leg hitched up on what appears to be an old tin bucket. The second is of the same woman in braces and sporting men's clothing, again sitting, one leg thrown over the other, on a bed.

Keats notes my confused expression. 'Her name was Pearl Hart. She was an outlaw back in the Old West. That second picture is of her in prison where she became a bit of a celeb.' There's an excitement fizzling off Keats that holds me in awe. 'Okay, Pearl was a proper bad girl, but look at her. The tilt of her hat. The absolute ooze of badass boldness coming off her like the rarest perfume. Bet she gave the finger to anyone who tried to tell she couldn't wear clothes that the world said only guys could.'

Keats angles her head, eyes steady on the traffic. 'I like going about in my hoodie, shades and scarf because I like it. Why shouldn't I be what I want to be?' She becomes sombre.

Flicks me a dead-serious glance. 'I don't know what this story is with you and this Philip character. But, Rachel, wherever your story ends, don't let it snuff out your light.'

I know she's right, but it's not easy to break the shackles that hold me to that life-changing summer. How can I walk in my light when it's overshadowed by the dark clouds of the past?

Keats draws me from my confused memories with an insistent hushed tone. 'Are you really being honest with yourself? Is this all about finding out what went on with Philip? Why else are you putting yourself through the wringer over this?'

Because I let my dad down, I yell inside. *Let Philip down. Let me down?* But my lips remain sealed. I don't tell her, and for the rest of the journey, we sit in our own silence.

'Leave the talking to me.' Keats bristles with confidence, convinced that we can talk our way into Danny Hall's old country house. Coming from a person who didn't exercise her right to talk to me for many days, that's quite a claim. She's parked the stolen sports car right near the front door as if she owns the place. Scattered around on the drive, nestling near rhododendron bushes, are the current owner's vehicles. A metallic Merc, a high-end Land Rover and an old saloon that looks like it's used as a runaround. I can't look at the house itself. Or the patch of waste land about a hundred yards away where the outline of where walls once stood is still etched into the ground. No scorch marks of what happened remain.

I've spent the last ten years trying to erase it from my memory and now it's looming over me. I'm seized with panic.

'Keats, let's go. This is stupid. They'll think we're criminals come to do an inventory of their valuables. They'll call the cops who'll quickly figure out that this car doesn't have your name on its driving documents.'

Keats ignores me, keeping her thoughts to herself. She's out of the driving seat before I can call her back and walks slowly round to the passenger side, which she opens and gently pulls me out.

Keats flicks her fingers through her hair, which I assume is her attempt at looking respectable. 'Relax. No-one's calling the feds. We're two posh gals come to look at the place where I used to live. What could be more natural than that? Just leave the chat attack to me.'

She strides up to the door so I have no alternative but to follow a little behind.

Keats rings the bell and while we wait for an answer, I plead. 'Please, let's go.'

'Shut up.' The tempo of her voice changes when the door opens. 'Oh hi.'

For one terrible moment, I expect it to be Danny at the door. Thankfully it's a middle-aged man who's obviously a city type of some sort. His casual clothes look like luxury items. He glances at our sports car and then at us. 'Yes? Can I help?'

Keats sounds like one of those upper-class women who think the royal family is a little vulgar. 'Darling. I wonder if you can. You see, I resided in this house for a while with my Uncle Danny when I was a little girl – such fond memories…' She pulls me closer. 'As my wife and I were in the area, I just wanted to give her a little sneak peak of where I once lived.'

Our guy is confused. 'Your wife?'

'Yes, we're lesbians. I do hope that's not a problem.'

The poor man is obviously becoming worried we think he's homophobic, so he answers, 'No, no, of course not.'

'Can we come inside?' Keats pulls what she clearly thinks is a sweet face.

He hesitates. 'It's a little inconvenient at the moment. Perhaps another time?'

Keats pouts with disappointment. 'Oh please. We'll be no trouble, just a quick whisk round so I can show Harriet where I enjoyed so many happy days and then we'll be on our way.'

He looks over our shoulders and down the drive, probably worried there's an armed gang lying in wait while we bluff our way in. 'Well...'

Keats doesn't give up. 'We're newly married and at that stage where you have to know every little thing about your spouse – sickening really.' She takes my hand and squeezes.

'I suppose it's all right.'

Keats gives a little trill of delight. 'Oh thanks so much! That's so super of you! I'm sorry I didn't catch your name.'

'Oliver.'

'Oh, love that name! I'm Lauren and this is Harriet.'

The guy stands aside and Keats leads me in, letting my lame hand drop while she follows our host through a door that leads off the hallway. Keats calls out. 'Oh! This is the drawing room. I adore what you've done with this.'

Oliver is confused again. 'We haven't done anything with it actually; we liked it as it was. In fact I've lived in the village for a long time and when this house came on the market, I grabbed it.'

'That's what I meant. You've kept it as it was. Harriet! Darling! Come and see the drawing room where Uncle Danny taught me how to play bridge.'

I haven't followed them into the drawing room because I'm still in the hallway, inert. My eyes fixed on one place only.

'Darling? Are you all right?' Keats's head is poking around the drawing room door. She comes out and follows my eyeline down the hall to a wooden door. 'Oh yes. You want to see the... the old servants' quarters, isn't it?'

Oliver reappears. 'No, that's the cellar. The previous owner used it as a wine cellar but wine's not really my thing. I say, is your wife all right? She looks a little unwell. Would she like a glass of water?'

Keats is solicitous. 'Are you all right, darling? You do look a little peaky. Yes, a glass of water would be divine. Could you put a little lemon in it?'

When he leaves the hallway, Keats whispers, 'Do you want to go into the wine cellar?'

I don't. I want to get out. Coming here was a terrible mistake. My voice is barely audible. 'Oliver's probably calling the police.'

'Don't be silly. We're supposed to be lesbians. Lesbians don't burgle houses.'

What the hell does that mean? I scowl at her, but Keats isn't looking at me.

She's staring down the hallway. 'Is it important – the wine cellar?'

What will going down there prove or solve except to rub salt into my still-bleeding wounds? But I've come this far. Keats puts her arm around my waist and guides me down the hallway to the cellar door. She fiddles with the handle and the door wings open, creaking on its hinges. Inside is complete darkness. My body temperature plummets.

Keats runs her hands along the wall, looking for a light switch. In a hush I inform her, 'Other side. It's on the other side.'

When the light comes on, a wooden staircase greets us, leading down to a cavernous cellar. I don't remember the cellar being so big, but in those days it had row after row of wine racks. Now they're all gone. There are some bikes leaning against each other and a few items of garden furniture. Nothing else, except the flagstone floor and ancient stone walls. Keats seems uncertain but she guides me down the steps as if I am an old lady, and we stand together in the cool air in the middle of the wine cellar.

As soon as my feet touch the cold hard ground, my hand feels the outline of the funeral programme in my back pocket. That touch has me spinning back in time.

Thirty-Four

That summer

Neither Danny nor Rachel could see the door to the cellar opening behind the wine racks but they both heard it together with the anxious bark of a dog. Philip called out. 'Rachel? Rachel? Where are you? What's going on?'

For a moment, Danny looked up in alarm, then back down at Rachel who he was still gripping with his stubby icy fingers. He leant into her face. His voice was quiet but savage. 'You dumb bitch. What did you have to make a noise for?'

Philip's feet clattered down the stairs. As if to punish him, Danny raised his hand and struck Rachel across the face so she tumbled off her chair. Clasping her cheek, she hurriedly jumped to her feet but she was in too much shock to run or shout.

Danny grabbed her hair and forced her back into the chair. 'Shut up. Say nothing, leave the talking to me. I'll sort this out.'

Only when Philip appeared from behind a wine rack, followed by Ray, did Danny loosen his grip on Rachel and stand up straight. 'What do you want? Rachel and I are just sharing a private moment here – Isn't that right, Rachel? Now, why don't you clear off and prune some roses, like a good little boy?'

Philip said nothing, but his chest rose high in harsh breaths. He took Rachel by the hand and tried to help her out of her chair. 'Come on, let's go.'

For a moment, Danny watched him do it before he sneered, 'Is this your Sir Galahad, Rachel? I'd be hoping for something with a little more in the way of polished armour than this puss.' Danny's voice went up a notch with significantly more bite. 'I suppose you've been hanging around in the hall again, have you, Philip? Is that how you get your jollies? Listening to other people get theirs? Or are you more of a guy-on-guy kind of shining knight? Yes, I reckon that's it.'

Danny grabbed Rachel's arm, shoving her back into the chair. Before she could say or do anything, he cuffed her head, making her cry out this time in pain and shock.

'Sit down, you little whore, you're not going anywhere. I'm thinking there's a little confusion around here about who's employing who.'

Danny loomed over Philip. 'Come on then, Sir Galahad, why don't you get your lance out and joust with me? Let's see who's the real man with balls here.'

Rachel found her voice. 'Leave him alone. Philip – go upstairs and call the police—'

Danny burst out laughing. 'Call the coppers? Sir Galahad won't be calling the police.' He drew closer to Philip. 'Why don't you tell Rachel why you won't be calling the police.' When there was no answer, he laughed, a sound that echoed around the dank cellar. 'Go on, boy, tell her.'

When he got no answer, Danny shoved Philip back against a wine rack. It shook, wobbled, unseating bottles of wine that crashed to the floor. Dark red liquid ran wild over the stone flags. Ray yapped and charged at Danny, grabbing him on the ankle with his little jaws.

Enraged, Danny growled through gritted teeth. 'I've had enough of you as well.' Danny yanked the puppy away by the scruff of the neck, drew his booted foot back and kicked the puppy as hard as he could. Ray went flying across the floor. Rachel flew at Danny from his rear. Philip lunged at him from the front.

A dazed Ray ran circles around the three of them, barking. They all struggled and fought on until suddenly there was silence.

Rachel lay on her back from where Danny had elbowed her in the belly. Philip stood unsteadily with a broken bottle in his hand while Ray sat shaking and mute. Danny lowered himself onto the empty chair, holding the side of his head with red wine running through his fingers. Rachel hadn't seen a blow struck but one obviously had. Danny was clearly hurt but at first sight it didn't look too serious. Only when the shock wore off and her eyes focused properly, did she realise the red wine on his fingers was actually blood. All Danny's violence, anger and lust seemed to seep out of his body, along with the blood leaking from the wound over his ear.

His voice was bewildered and almost childlike as he tried to stand. 'What did you do that for, Philip? Eh? There was no need for that. No need at all. I wasn't going to hurt anyone.' He took his bloodied hand away from his temple, raised it at Philip in accusation and choked. 'Look at that!' Then he swayed and whimpered. 'No need, no need for that at all.' He gradually slumped over Rachel's desk in confusion before finally, and slowly, sliding to the floor.

Then he was still.

'We've got to call the police!'

Philip was kneeling down, feeling Danny's pulse. 'We're not calling the cops.'

'He sexually assaulted me. Attacked you. He kicked Ray. It was self-defence, they'll understand. What's the matter with you? We've got to call them.'

Philip rose up from his knees and screamed, 'We're not calling anyone! Do you understand?' His voice broke. 'We're not calling the cops.'

Frightened by Philip's voice, Rachel insisted, 'All right, but we've got to call an ambulance, he's unconscious.'

Philip's voice fell to a whisper. 'He's dead, Rachel. He's dead.'

Her hands flew to her mouth as she staggered back. 'But he can't be dead, we hardly touched him.'

Philip threw the broken bottle that he was still clutching to one side. 'Well, he is. And there's nothing we can do about it. Now we need to decide what to do next.'

He crouched down again, taking a shaken Ray by his collar. 'Right, first you need to take Ray.' Philip's mind seemed to be ticking over on its own as if he were talking to himself. 'There are no other staff on the grounds today, so no-one knows you're here. Here's what you do. You go back home. You tell no-one you were here today. Ever. You never ever tell anyone. Say to your father that you were ill on the way to work. No, better, that you had a puncture and you couldn't get to work in the first place. Say you stopped off somewhere on the way back and had a long breakfast but don't say where so no-one can check. Then you say you went up the woods and did some sunbathing or something. And don't forget – when you hear that Danny's dead, don't forget to be shocked – okay?'

Rachel listened in disbelief. Perhaps it was that or the whole series of shocks compressed into the previous hour but she suddenly burst out laughing. 'You're not serious? I'm not doing any of that. I'm calling the police and I'm doing it now.'

She was swept forward as Philip grabbed her lightly and tugged her towards him. 'Do you care about me, Rachel? Do you care at all? If you do, you'll go home and keep your mouth shut about this. Please, I'm begging you. That's all I'm asking. That's all I'll ever ask of you.'

Rachel sat astride her bike on the drive in front of Danny's house. Ray was tucked inside her jacket for the journey home. But he was already looking at Philip and pawing the lining of the jacket with a view to escaping.

Their voices were quiet and businesslike. Rachel said her goodbyes. 'What are you going to do with Danny's body?'

'I don't know. I'll figure it out.'

Rachel pushed an escaping Ray back into her jacket and whispered, 'Why aren't we calling the police? I don't understand. I'll make Danny sound like the most evil man that ever lived. It was us or him.'

Philip looked over her shoulder into the distance with a wistful gaze. 'You need to get out of here.'

Thirty-Five

'Rachel? Rachel?'

I come back to the cellar as it is now. This place is dead for me, but I can't breathe down here. No natural light. No air. Can't find my balance. The echo of my breathing wheezes inside my hurting head.

In a rush, I tell Keats, 'I need to get out of here. Now.'

Oliver's voice carries down the stairs from the hall. 'Hello? Where are you?'

Keats calls back. 'We're in the cellar, Oliver – we're just coming.'

Keats has to lead me up the stairs; without her support I'm going to tip over. She takes the glass of water Oliver offers and drinks it herself before announcing, 'Harriet's feeling a little queasy, so perhaps we ought to go. Thanks so much for your time.'

Oliver seems surprised our visit is so short but he escorts us back down the hall to the front door. 'Did you know your uncle, the previous owner, well?'

Keats laughs. 'Oh yes, such a lovely man. Everyone loved Uncle Danny!'

Oliver's nod by way of an answer is unconvincing. Keats immediately picks up on it. 'But kids are innocent of course. They don't know any better. But there were all sorts of rumours about Danny, some of them a touch unsavoury; I expect you heard about them?'

We're at the front door. 'I did indeed after we moved in.'

Keats drops her posh girl act. 'Okay. So what were they?'

Oliver is alarmed. 'It was just gossip of course, in the village and among the neighbours. Probably exaggerated, no doubt.'

Keats's squinting gaze won't let him go. She looks menacing, as if she's going to squeeze the truth out of him if necessary. 'Please, there's no need to be embarrassed. What I said about him being lovable isn't true. I was forced to live here for a time because my parents had a very messy divorce. My mum was his sister. What were the rumours?'

His gaze zeros in on Keats and this time it's him who won't let go. 'Let's drop the act. I know you aren't related to Danny Hall.' Keats's mouth surges open, no doubt with plan B, but Oliver hasn't finished. 'I let you come in because I thought you might be lawyers for one of his victims looking for historic evidence against him and I'm all for that.'

It's me who speaks. 'What do you know?'

He switches his attention to me. 'That he molested and assaulted women, especially his female staff. He was notorious for it. Women locally wouldn't work for him. Of course, it may just have been gossip. It was whispered nothing came to trial because he paid his victims off. But I have to say, there were some people around who weren't sorry Danny Hall was killed in that fire. They thought he got what was coming to him.'

'Why did you send me to work for Danny when everyone knew he assaulted and attacked young women?'

Dad's pleasure at my unexpected visit doesn't last long. I'm barely through the door before the question pours out like acid. We're standing in his immense hallway facing each other, behind Dad a mounted framed photo of him and Mum taken the first week we moved here. Dad lives exactly five miles from Danny's former house. That summer it would take me thirty minutes cycling carefree from our place to there. Correction: ~~carefree~~. A word that's all about not having a trouble in the world has no business being in this tense scene.

I step closer, air tipping in and out with such quickness my straining body must be leaking. 'Everyone knew.' I spit it at this man I have loved so very much. 'His staff, the local villagers, the neighbours. Even Philip knew. He warned me not to be alone with your old friend Danny.'

There's no reaction from Dad. Not a change to the colour of his face. Not a widening of the eyes. Not a tensing of his muscles through his blue T-shirt or his loose washed-out jeans. I suspect he's been in the garden tending his tomatoes, runner beans and, his pride and joy, his berry bushes and trees. I was once his pride and joy too, wasn't I?

When his response comes, it's calm. The gentlest of breezes threading through the raging storm I've brought inside. 'I can see you're upset. Why don't we take a drink together in the kitchen and you can tell me who's been filling your head with a lot of silly nonsense. Then I can put you straight.' His tone shifts gear, not exactly stern but there's a stiff belt to it that suggests he's nearing the tipping point of losing his patience. 'And if you've got any manners, you'll be apologising to me.'

With that, he walks with steady long strides to the kitchen.

I stay in the hall for a while, haunted by the images of Mum around me. I sense her disapproval in what I'm doing, but I have to do this.

I find Dad already at the table with a bottle of brandy and identical snifters filled half way. Back in the day, when I was young, I remember how he'd take swift drinks of spirits from mugs not fancy glasses. So much has changed about him over the years. Maybe that's the real problem here; he's moved on while I've remained stuck in time. If he's guilty, Dad's doing a great job of hiding it. He keeps his eyes fixed on mine. My defiant body language tells him clearly I'm refusing the drink and I remain standing. Maybe I'm staying out of reach of his *razor-sharp claws.*

'Now then, where did you hear all these fairy stories about Daniel Hall?' His clenched irritation resounds in every word. 'For the record, he wasn't actually my friend. He was my business associate. Business associates aren't your friends, Rachel; on the contrary, they're more likely to be your enemies. Remember that.'

Unconsciously, I coat a layer of wet over my dry lips. 'But I thought Danny Hall was your friend. Wasn't that the reason you sent me to work for him that summer after—?'

'Your mother left us for good?' The strain heightens the colour of Dad's face. 'We met in passing at the golf club one day. He asked me if I knew of anyone young looking for summer work experience. I thought of you because I knew how much of a toll Carole's death had taken on you. I thought…' Dad sips once from his liquor. The brandy glistens on his bottom lips as he continues. 'I hoped that it would do you good to get away from the house. To have space to breathe.'

A few days ago we were laughing, hugging as he put my life back to rights when all the time it may have been him snapping me, piece by piece, apart.

My voice is clear, but I hear the fragility in it too. 'I went to Danny's old house and spoke to the owner. According to him, everyone knew about Danny and his behaviour, *everyone*. Are you saying that you were the only one who didn't?'

Dad stands, the force of his large body scraping back the legs of the chair against the floor, leaving a noise like nails on a chalkboard. He braces his arms against the table, the length of his veins leaping under the surface of his skin a reminder of the rope that's helped guard my life and my sanity. He leans forward, not with menace but with a power that overshadows my presence in this room.

'Do you really think for even one moment I would have sent my eighteen-year-old daughter to work for a man with that type of reputation? There's no way on this earth you would have been allowed anywhere near a man like that, much less go to work for him. Give me strength. I'd have taken a bat over there and beaten the bastard bloody until his bones cracked.' Dad's arms don't look so steady anymore. I realise he's shaking. 'Did he attack you?'

My lips stitch together; I want to deny it. Only Philip and I ever knew. Our secret and the rest. There's no running away from it this time because I can see from Dad's horror-struck expression he already knows the answer.

So I reveal, 'Yes. Yes he did. Philip was upstairs, heard my screams and stepped in. Otherwise I might have been raped.'

With one mighty sweep of his arm, Dad knocks the bottle of brandy flying from the table. It smashes and spills, some of the liquid splashing across the photo of Mum pregnant with me that lives on the fridge. It's the action of that other dad. That dad who struck Michael and warned him, 'you know what I'm capable of.' The dad who smashed Jed's nose. That other violent father I've been denying I knew I had.

'You should have told me. You're my daughter, for pity's sake. Why didn't you tell me?' He staggers back from the table, his palms roaming wildly over the crown of his head. 'If he were here now I'd kill him.'

I want to go to Dad. I want him to come to me. His distress is so real. But... but I still can't understand how a man like my dad, with his ear to the ground, could have missed the rumours and rumblings about Danny's predatory nature.

My voice is only a hush. 'How can I believe you when seemingly the whole world knew?'

Whether it's the light or the way he's holding them, his eyes seem to have changed colour to flint. His voice has hardened too. 'Sit down, Rachel.' When that doesn't happen, he shouts, 'I said – sit down!'

I do as he says, perching on the edge. He knocks back the rest of his drink as soon as he's facing me. 'I suppose you've been talking to Michael, have you? He's tracked you down?'

How I manage to hold back the show of stunned amazement at the mention of Michael, I have no idea. That Dad's admitting to knowing him. Does he know that Michael lured me to the basement? I test my theory. 'I don't know who Michael is. I certainly haven't been contacted by anyone of that name.'

A scoff is the response I get. 'I know all about Danny and Michael – all about them.'

This unexpected twist shatters the breath inside me. 'Danny Hall knew Michael?'

Dad settles back in his chair, the hardness of his gaze becoming more solid. 'I did a lot of business with Danny over the years. I saw him in action, a man a bit too jagged and jaded around the edges sometimes but it comes with the territory. I'm accustomed to it. We did a few deals together, that's why I was shocked to hear about his death. After that, his son took against me.'

I'm gasping, I can hear it. I know what's coming.

Dad tells me. 'Michael is his son. Danny had an affair with one of his secretaries and Michael was the result. So when Danny got himself killed in that fire, Michael turned against me because I bought one of his father's companies.' Dad lets out a bitter laugh. 'Do you know why I did it? Because when Danny died, it came to light that his finances were in bad shape, so I bought that particular company to help his family out. A few years later it rebounds back on me when Michael accuses me of buying it on the cheap. Since then, him and his mad mother have been a thorn in my side making all types of threats.'

Dad looks lost before stiffening again. 'And you know what really sticks in my craw? After Michael was born, Danny dumped the pair of them for another woman. And you know who it was that helped them out then after Danny died? It was me. I helped them because I thought I owed it to Danny. I didn't expect any gratitude for it. But I didn't expect this either.'

Dad gets out of his chair, large and brooding. He stands tall and erect and seems to have gained a couple of inches in height. He looms over me like Michael's tenement and jabs his finger in my face. 'And I didn't expect any gratitude for all I've done for you. But I didn't expect this either.' He turns his finger towards the photo of my mum, me nestled within the protection of her body. He looks on the verge of tears. 'I'm just glad your mother isn't alive to see you betray me like this.' He loses the extra inches that he gained; weary. 'Now if you'll excuse me, I've had enough.'

The house is suddenly silent when I'm alone in the kitchen. As silent as it was the night my mum died. Everything Dad's just told me makes sense and fits in with what I know. It explains his visit to Michael. Why he asked to see Michael's mum. Except for one thing.

I still don't understand how someone as savvy as Dad could've been unaware of Danny's brutal reputation with young women.

My Uber arrives outside Dad's, so I hurry down the hall towards the front door. I don't know where my father has gone. It's a relief to climb in the cab and get away. As the car sets off down the drive towards the main road, when I look back towards the house, the light is on in Dad's office at the front side of the house. Dad's stalking like a caged animal. I tell the cabbie to pull over out of sight and scamper back up the drive, ducking low. When I reach Dad's office window, I peer inside to see my dad's on the phone. He's shouting at someone but I can't hear what he's saying through the double glazing that keeps out the winds that blow off the North Downs. Then I hear him. A bellow so loud no glass can be a barrier.

'You know I don't make idle threats. If you don't get back on my side, I will kill you.'

I'm in the back seat of the cab. I'm half concealed in the shadows as I pull out my mobile. It's time for me to admit that Dad maybe isn't the man I once knew, if I ever knew him at all.

The phone line connects. 'It's me. I'm ready for you to tell me the information you found out about my mum.'

Thirty-Six

Polly, my ex-debt counsellor's brows shoot up when I walk into her office the following afternoon during my lunch hour. I've caught her topping up her lipstick. Attractive colour. A mix of light and dark reds. A touch racy for her but I like it.

'Did we have an appointment?' She sounds rattled, obviously doesn't like being caught on the hop. As she tucks her lippy away, her upbeat counsellor routine slips back into gear. She's the picture of manufactured summer happiness. I don't mind; I'll take a touch of any type of happiness I can find.

'My letters,' I remind her.

'Yes. Of course. I wasn't sure if you got my message about your paperwork.'

I'm also here counting the hours before meeting Keats later to find out what she knows about my mother. Staying in the basement office, thinking about the possibilities of what she might tell me, was sending me crazy. So here I am in a safe place to occupy my mind.

I close the door. Don't take a seat as I start, 'I wanted to personally thank you for all that you've done for me.'

Polly's jolly cheeks pop with an uplifting smile. 'I'm glad that family came through for you in the end.'

'Yeah, my dad bailed me out.' It's an awkward sentence to say aloud. My dad, the conquering hero, feels as if it can only be the truth in an alternate universe.

I rummage inside my rucksack. What I take out I tentatively and shyly set on the table between us. 'I didn't know if you were a drinker or not...' My explanation slides away.

I'm surprised that her smile appears to congeal as she looks at the high-end bottle of champagne with the shiny pink bow tied neatly at its neck. 'This is very thoughtful of you and I thank you for thinking of me, but we don't usually encourage gifts.'

That hadn't even occurred to me. 'I'm sorry—'

Polly gently waves away my apology. 'Gifts are such lovely things but they also belong to what I term "the unnecessary". Things you don't have to spend your money on. You don't want to start your road to financial health with one of those. It's so easy to find yourself being sucked back under again. You're going to hate my next two pieces of advice.' The fingertips of my hand rub anxiously together by my side. 'Firstly, I want you to watch every penny you spend. Every. And I want you to come back to see me in a month's time. You took a leap of faith, in yourself, coming to see me, acknowledging you had a problem. Let's keep that leap of faith going by ensuring your financial recovery continues.'

I don't want to read between the lines of what I suspect she's really saying – your debt was a symptom of something else and until you pinpoint what that is, you're in danger of ending up in the cash-strapped crapper again.

Her voice, back to carefree, intrudes. 'Let me get you that paperwork.'

I expect to be presented with it in a carrier bag, but Polly has it neatly packed in a black box file, which I take. The burden of my one-time debt feels heavy in my hands.

'There was something…' Polly says as she opens her desk drawer. No doubt the required 'How do you rate our services?' feedback form. But it isn't. It's a postcard. 'I found this stuck to one of the envelopes at the bottom of the pile of your letters. I put it aside because I assumed you wouldn't want something personal associated with the more challenging aspects of your life.'

I pick up the postcard, frowning. It's from New York, a photo of the Chrysler Building lit up in all its art deco glory at night. I don't know anyone in the Big Apple or remember any of my mates saying they were going on holiday there. It doesn't surprise me that I missed it in the pile of mail that waited for me inside my front door because I'd gotten into the habit of stuffing unopened letters in the dreaded carrier bag without checking what each one was.

I wait until I'm outside to find out who sent it. When I turn over the card and read, I become numb to the high wind swirling and slapping around me.

Michael

I'm coming to Old Blighty for my sister's wedding.
It's been years, matie. Let's hook up. Cruise some old
haunts. Touch base when I'm in town.

Benny

Michael. The word grows hideously large and dances off the postcard. Why would this 'Benny' be sending Michael a postcard to my house? But I'm making an assumption, aren't I, that it's Michael Barrington. What if…? My brain scuttles around for another explanation… What if one of the bastard tenants who ripped my home apart was called Michael? Could be… But what if it's not? My head pounds as I rewind the years to when I got the house. I see Dad throwing the keys at me, laughing. And he had the key because he said the house had belonged to a friend who wanted to offload it. I factor in the new info I know about Michael – he was Danny's son. Next logical step is that maybe Danny owned the house? And Michael… And Michael… The next part won't let me capture it, like a fly playing 'Dare' in my face but buzzes off when I reach out to swot it.

Now not only am I freaked out about what Keats might tell me about my mother, I have another worry too.

Is Michael connected to my house?

Thirty-Seven

Something's holding me back. Instead of going into the tekkie café in the Georgian square, I stare at Keats through the window as I stand on the opposite side of the street. I'm finding it hard to take that next step. Fear holds me immobile. A fear of being confronted by things I never knew about my own mother. Stuff that may be too hard to hear. I'd left Dad's upset, brain trying to sift through truth and lies, fired up to mow down more truths including any concerning Mum. But, here I am now, and, God help me, I can't go past the edge of the pavement where the tips of my feet touch.

The tangled arguing voices of a young couple at the end of the street draws my attention. The streetlamp illuminates the shine of tears that wet the guy's face. His distressed features twist into Philip's, silently pleading with me to leave him, run, Rachel, run. The muscles and veins in my neck pull taut and strain as my eyelashes flutter, eyelids rapidly blink. It's for Philip, I brave the unknown demons waiting for me in the café that enable me to cross over and join Keats.

Tears For Fears' *Everybody Wants To Rule The World* plays with a melancholic energy inside. A memory at the back of my mind clicks that an Erasure song was playing the one and only time I was here before. This place must have a thing for retro eighties pop. Why I'm recalling this now I can't figure out. Is it a delaying tactic for what waits for me at the table I'll share with Keats?

The place is empty except for Keats and the woman with the blue and white striped apron behind the counter. Keats looks scrubbed-up clean, her curls damp with water or gel and the only part of her usual get-up she wears is the navy bandana knotted under her chin.

She gives me a quizzical once-over as I take the chair facing her. 'Why were you peering at me from across the street?'

She catches me on the hop; it's not what I expect her to say. Flustered, I respond, 'I was feeling really hot, so needed five to cool down.'

Her blatant expression tells me straight that she's not buying a word of it. But Keats keeps that to herself. She sucks deeply from her water bottle before taking out her mobile and pulling something up on screen.

'Can you use your digi wizardry to find out anything about my house?' I ask her.

Keats fiddles with her mobile. 'In relation to what?'

I hesitate for a second. 'How it might be connected to Michael.' Then my voice runs along as if speeding on imaginary tracks. 'I'm not sure if I've got this right or wrong, but I need it checking out.'

Keats nods, then levels me with an unexpectedly frank stare. 'What do you know about how your mother died?'

There it is, that gut-blasting uncontrollable internal feeling I was afraid of. It's akin to the blow I'm dealt when trapped underground. I glance hurriedly up at the over-bright florescent tube lighting. Light means air. That's what I need. Air. My eyelids hood halfway as a funnel of blessed air, cool and refreshing as peppermint on my tongue, rushes through me. I stay like that for a time, filling my body with oxygen and courage.

Back in control, ready for whatever's to come, I tell Keats, 'She was sick, on and off, for years. Dad took her to a number of doctors who couldn't diagnose the problem.' I shake my head with sadness. 'No-one could fix her. I had to watch her die before my eyes.'

A dead silence lies between us. Keats, for reasons known only to her, whips out her shades and puts them on. Maybe it's her way of covering up that she's as emotionally shot as me.

She looks down at the screen of her mobile. 'I'm looking at copies of your mother's medical records.'

'How did you find them?'

Keats's mouth quirks to the side. 'Trade secrets, but the clinic she visited in the final years of her life,' God, it hurts to hear that, 'really should use a decent firewall in their data system—'

'What did you find out?' I prompt. I suspect we'd be here all night listening to her tales of firewall woes.

Keats settles her chin. 'Right. I've summed up what I found out. She was ill because her immune system was failing.' This I know. 'She was also seeing a therapist at the clinic—'

'What?' The word wobbles along with the astonishment running through me. 'Why would Mum be seeing a therapist? Apart from the illness, she was happy.' Mum visiting a shrink somehow feels like an attack on me, my childhood. Our happy home.

'No she wasn't,' Keats tells me without ceremony. 'That's what her therapist and doctors concluded. They think she was sick because of some type of stress in her life. The stress, in turn, was causing her to become depressed. Her immune system took the brunt of this. It's as if her own body was attacking itself.'

I open my mouth to deny this but the veil of a twisted memory falls over me, obscuring the café, propelling me back to my childhood home.

I was twelve. Dad had been away on business for five days, leaving me and Mum alone. I came in from playing outside with my neighbourhood friends to find Mum looking drawn and pasty as she stepped out of Dad's office.

'What's wrong, Mum?'

The strain as she tried to smile in response dropped the sides of her mouth down instead of up. She looked so sad.

'I'm fine, baby. Just fine.'

Her dragging footsteps told their own story. Then she wobbled and collapsed. Frantically I ran over to her screaming, 'Mummy, wake up. Wake up, Mummy.'

I called for an ambulance which came quickly. I sat with her in the back of it, feeling helpless, sobbing my heart out.

When we reached the hospital, I didn't want to let go of her hand, but the nurses and doctors told me they needed to take her away to make her better again. I'd never felt anything as cold as her hand. I called Dad on the payphone but all I got was an eternal dialling tone. When the doctor came to speak to me to assure me Mum was on the mend, I asked him what was wrong with her. He wouldn't tell me.

I stood in the middle of the corridor shrieking at his back, 'Why won't you tell me what's wrong with my mummy? Why won't you tell me?'

I come out of the awful memory with a huge audible gasp, as if I've been underwater. My hand comes up to my chest to steady my breathing, to halt the shockwaves stunning my body.

Someone's calling my name. 'Rachel, are you okay?'

Keats. I look over at her. She's worried, shaken, sunglasses lying discarded on the table. I grab her water bottle and greedily gulp like it's the liquid of life.

With a gentle ease, I place the bottle down. Slide it back into her space. Know it's time to face my own truths. 'I think I always suspected there was more to her illness than Dad told me. Maybe he was trying to put a gloss on it for his child—'

'Her therapist thought her problems stemmed from a troubled marriage.'

Keats's interjection rocks me back in my seat. I frown so hard the skin above my eyes is twisted and raked with pain.

'That can't be right. They were happy. Loved each other. A more devoted couple you couldn't meet.'

One of Keats's hands spread across the table, her way of trying to connect physically with me. 'I'm only telling you what I found out. It took me years to realise that my parents detested the sight of each other. Years later to find out they married because he got her pregnant with my sister.' It's Keats's turn to fight for air to her lungs. 'A child's vision of the world is so innocent it often numbs the reek of rottenness around them.'

We both struggle to regain our composure before she carries on. 'Your father, Frank Jordan, many believe grew his empire through sheer ruthlessness. There are lots of stories about him having the reputation of a man who will do anything to get what he wants. Anything.'

Keats's solid gaze locks with mine. 'People are scared of your father. Are frightened to speak out against Frank Jordan because he uses the law to take them out by threatening libel action. That seems to be an old trick of his, using libel to shut people up. There was another story where it was alleged a family was destroyed after Frank Jordan made a successful hostile takeover of their business which was in trouble.'

I should be shocked. I'm not. Not after hearing Dad threaten Michael and his mother. *My razor-sharp claws.* And didn't he himself admit to my very face, *Business associates aren't your friends, Rachel; on the contrary, they're more likely to be your enemies.* Other memories and unspoken words cloud my mind. How, after Mum's passing, Dad wouldn't mention the words, 'wife', 'mother' or 'mum'. And 'Carole'. How hadn't I seen, heard, that he'd also stopped using her name? I'd put it down to grief, but the plain and honest fact may have been he didn't care about her anymore. My whole world's falling apart and I sit here calmly as if it's happening to someone else. Someone else's dad. Someone else's mother. Someone else's daughter.

'Do you think,' my question is slow, 'that maybe that's why Michael has lured me to the job? He's seeking some type of business revenge against…' Dad. The word's lodged in my throat. The muscles inside my neck won't let it go. Instead I finish with, 'Frank Jordan?'

Keats nods with approval and I realise that's why she's been mainly referring to Dad as 'Frank', trying to create a distance between him and me. I silently thank her for that.

'Dad – Frank – told me that Danny is Michael's father. Maybe Michael is a proxy of revenge for his father. I don't get it. Dad said he and Danny weren't friends.' My brows come together, pulling the skin across my forehead, although I swear he said they were friends when he got me the job at Danny's when I was eighteen. I shake my head in an attempt to clear the fuzzy memories of the past. The haze gets thicker instead of lighter. 'I can't be sure, but there must've have been more of a connection between them if Dad felt an obligation to financially help Danny's family by buying one of his companies.'

Keats leans across the table with urgent intent. 'I wouldn't believe a word that came out of Frank Jordan's mouth.' She wets her lips and then capsizes my pitching world. 'Your mother's doctors believed there was something she wasn't telling them. Something she was hiding about her life with Frank Jordan.'

Thirty-Eight

Something is tickling my nose. How irritating. I grumble, partially waking up. Swot at my nose. Sighing heavily I flip to my other side. The last thing I want to do is to wake. Opening my eyes means having to face the reality of my mum and dad's relationship. Having to face the question of who my dad really is. After leaving Keats, I didn't come back to the storeroom immediately. Instead I walked the streets of London for a time until I stopped by the river. The Thames at night is a beautiful thing, the rhythm of its nocturnal skin soothing and restful.

My groan turns into a moan. Whatever's fussing with my nose I wish would leave. Me. Alone. Rolling over, a slight tang catches my throat. It's acrid, nasty, followed by a cough that racks my body. I tuck my legs into my chest and curl into a ball. For a moment or two I can't control the coughing. Finally it stops. I feel more exhausted as if I'd never gone to sleep. I open up one eye, then the other. The out-of-sync hands on my clock say it's getting on for midnight. I sniff deeply. Scramble out of the bed in an extreme state of shock. I know that smell.

Smoke.

Smoke means fire.

In that moment of stunned terrible realisation, I'm incapable of moving a muscle. I'm paralysed both in this room but in another room from my past as well. I've been chased from pillar to post by images of fire and smoke. *Move, Rachel. Move.* I hear what my brain is pleading with me to do, nevertheless I don't seem to be able to follow its instruction. Ironically, it's the deadly smell that finally shoves me into action when it gives me the jolt of a bottle of smelling salts under my nose. I head for the light switch. Flick. No light. Do it again. The same thing happens.

Stumbling into the basement, no amount of flicking the switches in there can make those infernal blue strip lights come on either. The blinking red and white lights on the servers and printer won't respond too. Even the hum-heartbeat of the wall is silent.

No light means no air.

No light means no—

I cut off the crippling chant. Refuse to allow it to conquer me. I head back into the dark of the storeroom. Use my outstretched fingertips and hands to feel and search my way to my rucksack. I find it. Drop to my knees. My hands dive inside. There. My mobile. I put on the light. A shattering wave of air escapes from my lungs when I'm back in the light. Air. I hadn't even realised I'd probably been holding my breath since discovering there was no light. My head bows in a moment of defeat because I tried, I really did, to out-psych this connection between light and air. But it didn't work.

I shake off my misery and stand up. My phone light catches Philip's face in the photo, twisting him into an apparition ready to glide off the wall. I snatch it and collect the rest of my belongings and stuff them without a care into my rucksack, which I swing onto my back.

I rush into the basement. The reeking stench of smoke is stronger here. I flash my phone at the bottom of the steel door and gasp so loud it rocks my head back. What I see are wafts of ghostly smoke eerily blowing in the beam of light. It's hypnotic, the way it coils, spirals, twirls, preparing itself for its deadly dance. This is actually happening. There's a fire in the building.

22 garment workers lost their lives due to fire.

Am I going to become number twenty-three? Hell no! I move towards the smoke. My hand hesitates over the handle. What if there's a ball of fire behind it and opening the door unleashes it all over me? I rush back into the storeroom. Grab the bucket of water, which is heavy in my grip. I tuck my phone under my chin so when I'm ready, both my hands are free to use on the bucket.

I wrap my hand round the steel door's handle. 'One. Two. Three.'

Mercifully the door opens. The water dives out of the bucket and into the tunnel. A lashing sound echoes off the walls as it lands on the ground. Through the thick smoke, I see no flames nor does my skin feel the heat of lurking fire. I choke, wretchedly cough as smoke hits me full in the face. This is when one of Keats's bandanas would have come in pretty handy.

I cover my mouth with one hand and make a run for it. The smoke smothers me in its fog. Draws me into its noxious embrace. I keep running and running. My eyes burn, sting and stream water.

Finally I make it to the bottom of the steep staircase. Look up and see my saviour – the trap door. It's hard to see but I make my way up. Nearly fall on a step midway that decides it wants to throw me over. Bent, I balance my free palm against the step until I'm steady. I restart my journey. The trap door gets bigger as I get closer and closer. I'm already smiling. The trap door is the gateway to heaven.

My palm reaches up to push it. It doesn't move. I try again. And again. Use both hands. Push with a desperate strength I never knew I had. I can't believe this; it won't budge, even an inch. My hands roll into fists and I bang, shout... No-one comes for me.

I'm not defeated; I know another way out. My speed is much quicker through the smoke this time. I keep it up through the basement and storeroom until I'm in the cool courtyard in the rear. It's unusually dark in this place tonight, almost black on black. An unease stomps down my spine, spreading throughout my body. I turn my face skywards to the grill. There's not a speck of the outside world peaking through. My escape is blocked. A large car has been parked over the grill, its big wheels resting on the metal bars to prevent it being opened. It belongs to Michael, I know it does.

All kinds of disorientating horror spark through me like an electric shock. That shock you feel when you're in a car spinning at high speed across a carriageway into the path of an oncoming truck. When you wake up in the middle of the night and you realise that one day you will awake no more. That shock that seizes your stomach when you realise that moment when you die doesn't lie in some hazy and distant future but is staring you directly in the face and there's no escape.

I drop my bag and climb up the rope, grabbing the bars of the grill, hauling myself upwards until my lips press against the callous cold metal.

'Help. Murder. Michael's killing me! Call the police. No, the fire brigade.'

My screams degenerate into gasps, the howls of a wounded creature. There's no response on the back street. My helpless fingers slip and slide down the rope until I lose my grip and fall down in a heap to the cobbled floor.

I'm trapped.

I scream one final time. 'Help. Me!'

Thirty-Nine

The smoke coming through the basement and storeroom brushes my face like an evil spirit. That's what drives me back into gear. On my feet again. I head into the basement in a rush, clasping my phone and its light. There's a way out of here. There has to be. I scan around. What to do? What to do? I pile desks onto each other, sending silent computers crashing onto the floor, the glass from their screens scattering everywhere. It's a chaotic scene. I lunge up to the desk at the top. The tower of desks wobbles. Doesn't fall.

Somehow, I have no idea how I manage it, I'm balancing unsteadily on the final desk. I batter and bang the ceiling with a keyboard. Of course it doesn't give – it's made of stone. I chuck the keyboard across the room. Gingerly climb down. I punch and kick the wall.

The smoke gets thicker. I'm choking. Why didn't I wrap something over my face?

Stop, Rachel. Think. Think. Think. My head's throbbing. Threatening to explode. My neck tips back as I remember how I found the door to the storeroom. What if…? Teeth gritted, muscles bulging and hurting, I pull and lug the photocopier away from the wall. No! No! No! There's nothing unusual about this wall. I dip my head with abject soul-destroying defeat. Suddenly my breath stalls inside my aching chest as I see something on the floor.

Drop to my knees. In the light of my phone, I see a large shape with – I count the number of sides – eight outlined on the floor. A hexagon or a type of star. There are lines from the corner of each side leading to a point in the middle. For a moment I forget my terror. I'm curious. What is this? I've never seen anything like it before, certainly not in the ground. In the centre is a small piece of wood. I dare to press. The shape springs open like a star bursting open or a monster's mouth with sharpened triangular teeth. It's another trap door.

I peer inside. It's a rectangular boxed-shaped space that leads away under the floor of the basement. A shiver sinks and expands into every pore in my skin. I don't want to go down there. Down and under. But what choice do I have? I drop into it on my hands and knees. The space is soaked in chills and damp and smells bad. A mental peg over my nose, I crawl along it, followed by wisps of smoke. I reach a dead end.

Trapped. Trapped. Trapped.

The fear digs its sharpened claws in any part of me it can find without mercy. I'm crippled, can't move. I'm going crazy. Losing my mind.

Gonna die. Gonna die. Gonna...

I look up, seeking deliverance. I gasp loud and ragged because there it is. Marked with faded paint is another star trap door. I lunge up at it, forcing it open. The passage continues upwards this time. The ancient rungs of a ladder fastened to the sides take me upwards through this cool musty and chimney-like structure. I'm shaking and terrified. My arms and legs hardly work anymore. My fingers barely grip. My heartbeat shakes my whole body in a continuous tremble. But I go up, banging limbs and legs against the wooden panels.

When I reach the top, there's another trap door. It opens onto a miniature landing and another ladder. This must be on the ground floor of the tenement. I lay my hands on the sides of the landing but feel no heat. No crackling of flames either. But then the way fires burn is a funny thing. I know that from bitter personal experience. This passageway is longer than the others and something shines in the dark distance. I see no way out so I look up.

Another trap door. Another ladder. Another climb. Of course fire goes upwards too. There's no choice but for me to keep going. I climb through another trap door. It slams shut behind me. There's no ladder. When I pull on the trap door it won't open. I kick at it. It refuses to help me. The light from my phone goes out. I'm in the dark. In the skeleton bricks of the building. Trapped.

No light means no air.

No light means no air.

It's the end of the line. I'm in barely enough space to stand. I've spent the last ten years trying to avoid underground spaces and fire. It's ended with my entombment in a casket-shaped box and a fire chasing me. Doomed, I slump against the side and weep. It's over, my struggle is over; my whole ten-year battle is over. I never gave up. Not even in the darkest hours did that happen. Never surrendered; buckled but never broke.

My mum's face suddenly is there with me, the only brightness in this hell dark.

'Mummy?'

She doesn't speak. She doesn't need to. Her being there is enough. Her beautiful face is filled with such happiness, such kindness. I feel curiously light-headed and content. Intensively calm. I'm ready to go, knowing Mum's arms will be waiting to take me. My head jerks. There's scratching on the side of the box. At first I don't believe it. It happens again. It shakes me up so much I bang my head. That's when I hear it, a dog's barks on the other side of the wood. It's Scrap come to save me. Just like he tried to save the sweatshop girls.

That's stupid. This is real. There's more scratching. Clearer, more distinct. I push against the wood. It gives slightly. There's not enough room for me to get any leverage against the wall but I make one final effort with what's left of my strength and barge against the wood with my shoulder. It swings open and I tumble headfirst into a room on the other side of what must have been a wall. The dog scampers and leaps around my prone body, barking like mad. Then it's licking my wrist and tugging at my clothes with its teeth. He or she seems to know me, although that's obviously ridiculous.

When my eyes focus, I understand why the dog's acting as if it knows me. That's because he does. Hanging from his collar is a silver tag. On it is his name.

'Ray,' I say with astonishment as I sit up.

Ray is Philip's dog.

For a moment there's no sense of danger. No fire or smoke. Simply me and Ray hugging, a moment shared between friends who have been separated for too long. He's a Yorkshire terrier who looks like he's sporting a brown beard. Still as bouncy but the age is plain in his coat. So it wasn't Scrap after all, but Ray. What I don't understand is why is Philip's dog here? And where exactly is here?

I look around as Ray licks my bruised hands. I figure out this must be where Michael's mum is staying at night. I come full circle again – why would she have Philip's dog? But that's the least of my worries; I need to get out of this burning building. Dancing in a frenzy as he barks, Ray follows me as I run over to the window. Throw it open and fill my lungs with fresh oxygen. Then I prepare to scream with all my might.

I hesitate as I peer down. There's no-one on the street below to shout out to. What makes my scream die is there's no sign of smoke or flames flicking and blazing from the building. On the other side of this apartment, a quick scan through those windows shows there's no sign of fire there either. Perhaps it went out? Or perhaps there was smoke without fire. Michael playing more of his dirty games with me, except this time I suspect I was meant to be knocked out of the game for good with no way of getting out from the basement. He obviously doesn't know the secrets of this former sweatshop as well as he thinks.

My natural instinct is to hunch low to pick Ray up and get out of here as fast as possible. Michael's mother could be in this flat somewhere. But it's silent apart from Philip's dog and me. A quick tour of the flat shows no-one else is around. I take my chance and search the rooms while borrowing her charger for my phone.

There's very little in the way of personal effects. The flat has an air about it that suggests someone's moved in for a while with no intention of staying permanently, almost like a hotel suite. At first my search is determined and savage. I throw things around and rifle through a sideboard in the hunt for information that would bring me closer to Michael and his mother. And Philip.

But there is none.

In the compact bedroom, the wardrobe holds a selection of clothes that are a mixture of smart-professional, some more classy, but all are expensive. A rummage through her bedside drawers draws a blank. I yank the mattress off her bed to see if anything is tucked away from prying eyes. There isn't.

Ray watches me and looks worried as if he knows that this search isn't the right thing to do but loves me too much to say so. I look at his soft face that's rumpled by age but which I remember so well.

He follows me into the kitchen and becomes excited when I take down tins of doggy food from a cupboard and whimpers with disappointment when I put them back. Michael's mum can't have gone far. Even the wicked witch of the east wouldn't leave Ray in here to starve. I conjure up her weeping in the night, Ray's wailing. Two tortured souls together. Actually, three of us if you count me too.

My hunt loses momentum. So I find out who Michael's mum is? So what? According to my dad, she was Danny's secretary with whom he had an affair and then kicked to the kerb. Of course there's no evidence that's true. I don't believe my dad anymore. Anyway, what's a picture of her going to prove? That Michael has a mother? What's a name going to mean?

My search grinds to a halt. I pick up Ray and carry him to the front door of the flat. Of course it's locked. Behind it is the staircase that leads down to the first floor and Michael and Joan's offices. There's no way out through there. That means going back the way I came. I hesitate. My arms tighten around this gorgeous generous dog. What am I going to do with Ray? I can't take him down through the trap door parallel universe that runs through the walls. Or keep him in a locked basement full of smoke.

I place him on the ground and lie on my belly so that I'm eye-to-eye with my tiny friend. 'Listen, Ray, I'm going to have to leave you here for now. But I'll come back for you – is that all right?'

He doesn't seem sure as his tongue caresses the tip of my finger before I scramble to my feet. I collect my phone and open the door in the living room that leads back to the basement. With the light from the room, it's obvious there's a simple pulley to open the trap door that I thought wouldn't open. When I open it, Ray becomes frantic. He barks at me and scampers off towards the bedroom. He howls. What's the matter with him?

In the bedroom, I find Ray standing over a small photo frame, its glass lying scattered on the floor. I must have knocked it off without noticing during my search. Inside is a photo.

It's an intimate family photograph with a lush English garden as its backdrop. It's springtime. Roses are blooming and fresh green leaves hang lazily from trees. At the front are two small boys smiling as if no-one's told them yet that the world is full of invisible trap doors. One is Michael. The other... My breath sticks way deep in my throat. Philip. The other is Philip. Standing behind them and slightly to the left, with a tenderly and motherly hand on each of the boys' shoulders is their mother.

Joanie.

Forty

Joanie is Philip and Michael's mother.

Michael is Philip's brother.

Joanie's got Philip's dog living with her upstairs, which is where I've left him.

It's a triple whammy! Still no link to my dad other than what he told me.

The unframed photo of Joanie, Michael and Philip is like dynamite in my hand. I pin it next to the adult picture of Philip on the wall. I'm back in the storeroom. Surprise, surprise! There's no more smoke. Michael probably rented a smoke machine like you get in a theatre to scare the crap out of me. Not just Michael, I remind myself, but Joanie too.

A wave of sorrowful despair descends over me. That Joanie was no friend at all. She played an on-point game, I'll give her that. The Stare comes back to me. The way her dead-eyed gaze bore into me with such hatred as if she wanted to lunge forward and squeeze the very light out of me until I was a limp lifeless shell slumped in my chair. Why? I still can't make head nor tail of her motivation. Is this part of her and Michael's revenge against Dad, as he claims, for an imagined slight against Danny? No. The hate she threw at me was very very personal. Why would a woman who I've only just met hate me so much?

I round on Philip's pinned photo on the wall. 'Why didn't you tell me about your relationship to Danny? That he was your father?' My words are heated. For the first time I'm pissed with him, crazy angry. Then my tone drops with agonising heartbreak. 'I didn't drive you to kill your dad, did I?'

But I know it's true. It leaves me wretched and aching. I know what Danny was, but to push a son into killing his own father. I'm not religious but even I know that's one of the most abhorrent sins. *Don't go there, Rachel.* Sensible inner me is back. *You never told him to do anything. Philip did what he did because it was the right thing to do. Sometimes only a wrong can make it all right.*

Still, it's a weight I carry across my slumped shoulders. I pivot from Philip's face. My first instinct is to confront Dad — again — this time about why he deliberately rubbed out Philip in his telling of Danny's story. Didn't mention that Philip was Danny's son. Michael's brother. Lies, lies, and more damned lies.

Something else occurs to me. What if Dad was trying to save me from further hurt about Philip? Hiding the fact that he has the blood of a man who preyed on women running through his veins. I'm so confused about Dad's role in all of this.

My head's pounding, so I dose up with two squirts of weed oil and down a BB. Then I make my way to the courtyard in the back. The grill is still blocked by the vehicle, so I stand in the ink-stained gloom. I move closer until I'm caressing the length of my faithful rope. The air from outside still seeps through, wrapping me in a cocoon of cold that makes me run my palms up and down the frozen skin of my arms.

I'm praying that this hostile air will help me. If air's coming in, it means something else can travel in as well. The waves, or whatever they're called, I need to use my mobile phone. I was in such a twisted state earlier my brain wasn't able to make the connection. The connection. Now that makes me smile although I know I have no business doing that in this terrible situation.

I take out my mobile. Two-bar reception. I pray hard it's enough to connect to Keats. I do a mighty jubilant air punch when the dialling tone buzzes in my ear. Come on, Keats, answer the bloody phone. It keeps ringing and ringing and…

'Keats, I've figured out what's going on.' I don't give her an opportunity to speak. 'I managed to get to the room upstairs.' I don't go into the ins and outs of how I did it. 'I found a photo of Michael with Joanie and Philip. Joanie's their mother. She's been in this with Michael from the beginning—'

Keats manages to finally jump in. 'I know—'

'What?' I freeze in stunned shock.

'I tried to call you, but your phone was only going to voicemail.' Of course it had; I'd been inside the building where my mobile has zero reception. 'Joanie's been playing a very dirty game. Pretending to be your mate while in league with her eldest son all the time.'

My bewildered thoughts turn back to Keats. 'How did you join the dots of Joanie being the mother of Michael and Philip?'

'Your house. They all lived in your house—'

'What? Michael, Philip and Joanie?'

I hear her ragged breathing and the sound of cars. 'I can't talk much now.'

'Where are you?' My racing mind goes through what she's just told me like an archaeologist sifting through the bones of my past. I join more dots. Dad's friend who needed to sell his house must've been Danny who had housed his secret family there. But why make them leave?

'I've borrowed another car.' I wonder whose car she's taken this time. 'I'm on my way to Surrey.'

A frown drags my brows down. 'Surrey? Why are you going there?'

'I'll explain everything tomorrow.'

That gives me an attack of the nerves and leaves me feeling frustrated. 'Why can't you tell me now?'

'Because I want to make sure I've got this totally right.' There's a hitch in her voice, an awkward change of pace. 'I can only tell you if I'm absolutely sure. There's something else I need to tell you.' I wait. 'Michael has put the company into liquidation. I got a text from him where the upshot is I'm sacked. If he's fired me I suspect he's given the zombies their marching orders too.'

'I never got a text from Michael.'

Keats audibly inhales. 'That's what I thought. Don't go anywhere near those two lying bastards. I want you to get out of there now. Do you hear me, Rachel? Get out of there. I'll call you in the morning at eight...'

The line goes dead. I call and call Keats but I can't get her back.

I rush into the basement to use the one and only landline on Keats's desk. I stagger to a stop. The phone on her desk, any of the desks, is gone. I was in such a mad panic earlier I never noticed. Did Michael and Joanie sack their so-called workforce because they knew they were going to trap me down here? Alone. No means of escape. Was their intention to block the back exit and the trap door, to leave me buried alive here to die slowly day after day?

But I know something that those two morons don't – I have found a way out of here. In fact I've discovered another way to get out too. I suspect this building is filled with many secret exits and entrances. I pack up my gear in a rush. Pull down Philip's photo. Hesitate as I place the one of his evil family on top. That doesn't feel right somehow. I didn't want Michael's and his mother's contamination to touch him. So I shove Joanie's photograph to the bottom of my rucksack.

I pick up my empty bucket, hooking its handle over my shoulder. My rope hangs from my neck in the position of a snake waiting to be charmed. I look the picture of *A Wayfaring Stranger*.

I head into the star trap door again. However, when I reach the second level, instead of going up, I deviate sideways along a dark passage. I might be wrong about this but on the journey down from Joanie's hideout upstairs, I caught a glint of something shiny standing out in the heavy darkness. If I'm right...

The claustrophobic foreboding I get from being trapped is still there, but it's not as all consuming. Who would've thought I'd have Joanie and her son to thank for that. Still, I condition my mind and set it to think that the absence of a light doesn't matter.

Light doesn't mean air. Light doesn't mean air.

Carefully I set one foot after another. The atmosphere here is dank, the same frostiness I felt run over the back of my neck the first time I stood in front of this building runs over and in me now. An intense musty smell stings in the inside of my nose and mouth, making me cough lightly. I hope there are no rats. A shudder snakes through me. I know they're God's creatures too, but if one of those critters comes my way I'm prepared to use my feet and penknife. The shine of what's ahead of me comes closer. Closer still. Finally I reach it. Look up. There are two of them, square metal handles sitting side by side. I think it's another trap door.

The position of the handles confuses me for a time. Why would there be two of them alongside each other? Only one way to find out. I grasp them and push up. Nothing happens. My brain goes into solving mode. I think I've got it. I pull both handles sideways in opposite directions. They slide, until hidden, under another floorboard. I look through the rectangular opening; it's the reception area upstairs. How ingenious is this. Why this former sweatshop has an array of different-shaped trap doors I don't question, what I do is carefully lever me and my belongings out.

I remain frozen, listening for noises above stairs. When all I hear is an unsettled hush, I quickly glance around the reception area. How I once found this bright and comforting I will never know. There's a small wooden cupboard over the trap door, its weight holding the door in place, ensuring I couldn't lift it. I don't touch it. Let mother and son think I'm still imprisoned down under.

As I head off to the door, my feet suddenly drag as a daring thought – or stupid, it depends on how you look at it – hits me. If Joanie and Michael have indeed got the most evil of intentions towards me, they'd think I'm still here with no way to get out. But I know different; they don't. What if the safest place for me to be is the most unsafe place of all?

I go back into the newest secret this building has given me. Curve my fingers around the handles. Snap shut the trap door.

Forty-One

I haven't even tried to sleep for the remainder of the night and the awakening of the early morning. I've been resting with my back against the ice-drenched wall, my penknife at the ready in my hand. It's nearing eight. Time for me to go into the courtyard in the back and wait for Keats's call. That's if the reception is being kind to me. If that fails I'll have no alternative but to make my way out, using the sliding trap door where I'm assured the phone will connect.

The damn car is still on top of the grill. It can't be legal the way it's parked. Why hasn't a traffic warden alerted the authorities to tow it away? The wardens are usually red-hot in pursuit of their job in this area because it's the gateway to the City and the trendy shopping areas of Spitalfields, Petticoat Lane Market and Brick Lane.

The phone rings. I breathe a long sigh of blessed relief.

I get straight into it. 'Tell me what you've found out.'

Silence. Then, 'You're still there.' Not a question. I picture Keats's chin shoving down as she grinds her teeth.

I fob her off. 'Look, I don't have time to explain. Just take my word for it.'

Silence again. Then the clap-clap-clap of her stomping feet. 'I've reached Surrey. I know exactly what's going on.' She sounds breathless, like she's running or has been running.

The beat of my pulse joins in her short-winded rhythm. I don't like what I can't see on the other end of this call. 'Keats, what's going on?'

'I can't...' She seems very nervous. 'I think someone's following me.'

I gasp and choke in one fluid motion. I have to lean my back against the wall for support. 'Who? Why?' The volume of my voice twists higher. 'You have to tell me what's going on.'

'I'm hiding in the car park. Or maybe I'm being paranoid.' I sense her shake her head. 'Which wouldn't surprise me because I slept in the car last night here.'

'Where's here?' *Just bloody well tell me*, I want to scream.

It's as if she hasn't heard my question. 'I'm on the move again because I think I shook the guy off?'

'Do you mean Michael?' I can't think of another 'he' it could be. Did he figure out that Keats was helping me? What's he planning to do if he catches up to her?

'Dunno,' is the terse response that flies back. 'Just wait for me to get outside then I'll fill you in.' Her breath catches. 'It's an ugly story, Rachel. Real ugly.'

The sudden rush of the noise of a car in the background obscures what she's saying. 'Speak up, I can't hear you.'

'I can–'

The sound of that bloody car keeps cutting up her words. 'Speak louder—'

'Rachel, you need–'

The car's closer now, I hear its engine breathing heavily in the background. There's the screech of rolling tyres on the road.

The tone of Keats's voice changes becoming high and panicked with dread. 'What the–?'

A roaring engine rips through the air. Tyres scream. Then there's a crashing thud. A mini-second of silence. Another thud, duller this time, as if it's in the distance.

'Keats? Keats?'

My face scrunches up from the impact of the clack-clack-clack noise coming down the line as if Keats's phone is rolling on the ground. Rubber against road squeals and a car's engine fades into the background. That's when I know, dawning horror of what's happened. I don't feel my heartbeat anymore.

'Keats? Keats? Keats?' I'm bellowing by the end.

No response. My back slides down the icy wall.

Whoever was following Keats has just run her down like an animal in the street.

I wipe the back of my hand across my eyes. There's no time for tears. My spine straightens with fortitude. Although I think of the car parked over the grill, I know who hurt Keats – Michael and Joanie. I get practical. My gear's already packed, I'm going to have to leave my bucket behind. The rope's coming with me though, it's my talisman, my good luck charm that has been my lifeline to safety.

I make it out of the sliding trap door in no time at all. Look at the entrance door and face another possible boulder in my way – what if it's locked with a key I don't have. Then, by God, I'm going to kick it in. I undo the bolt at the top and bottom. Press down the handle. The air swarms out of me as it opens. I don't have time to nod to The 22 today, not with Keats lying bleeding, maybe dying, on the ground without a friend to hold her hand. The tears threaten; I won't let them.

Think. Think. Think. My head's a jumble. I need to clear it, to figure out what to do.

First, I pray and hope that someone saw what happened to Keats and called an ambulance, which means I can try to find out if she's in a hospital. I pull out my mobile as I walk away from the building and… I jerk to a halt.

The zombie who watched the distressing film and threatened me stands at the corner looking up at the building. My heart does a funny skipping beat. I keep my skittish gaze away from him as I pass him by and walk down the street. My pulse goes into free fall as I hear footsteps join the beat of my own. Quick peak over my shoulder. Hell, he's following me. The death knoll ringing in my head is his promise of retribution:

'*Say anything to anyone and you better be ready to have eyes in the back of your head on the way home. No telling what type of accidents may be waiting to befall you in the dark.*'

He's obviously not waiting for the dark. I sense his stride lengthening. Other people are about but there's no telling if anyone will help me, even if I scream blue murder. The only person I can rely on is me. I pick up the pace. So does he. Clinging greasy sweat making its presence felt, oozing down my back. The base of my throat becomes cuttingly dry as the noise of his shoes becomes the only sound I hear.

I'm almost running. So is he. I speed around a corner. When he does, I'm waiting for him. He squeals as I grab his jacket, spin him and slam him into a wall. Then I let loose with a one-two series of power punches to the bastard's solar plexus. He doubles over, groaning through clenched teeth. Dad taught me well.

'If you don't stop following me, I'm going to call the cops.'

He raises his head, gasping and gulping oxygen. I notice his hair's different, it's slicked back with gel and he sports a pair of attractive glasses that are askew on his face.

'What…?' His palm rubs his belly as he straightens. 'What did you do that for? I was only waiting until Michael arrived to collect my fee.'

Is this guy for real? 'You said you were going to do serious damage to me if you caught me outside, just like the woman being terrorised in the video. You scum.' I'm so mad I raise my fist to deliver another blow to that despicable mouth of his as a lesson in what happens to men who only have bad words to say to innocent women.

His hand comes up in defence as he shrinks back. 'But it was part of the script.'

I angle my head and give him a very hard stare. 'What script?'

Grimacing, he shifts up the wall slightly in an attempt to pull himself together. 'Come on, you're an actress, I mean an actor. I know you ladies no longer like any gender distinctions.' He winks at me, which riles me up again. Seeing my bewildered expression, he says, 'Maybe Michael forgot to show you that part of the script—'

I cut over him. 'Who exactly are you?'

'I'm an actor. Name's Teddy. At your service.' He performs a little bow that ends with a wince.

The baby hairs tingle on the back of my neck. I'm not sure what this is, so I decide to kill two birds, one stone.

I give him my widest and most dazzling smile. 'Do you have a car?'

Forty-Two

'Here she is,' Teddy announces with pride.

'She' is a knocked about white Renault van. He takes his keys out and shuffles to the back doors, opening them. Inside is a collection of clothes hanging from any space they can find and a mattress with a duvet neatly spread over it.

He looks at me sheepishly. 'I'm in between places to live at the moment and this is as good as any to bed down for the night.'

I sympathise with him. Know exactly what that nomad feeling is like.

As I jump in beside him up front, I ask, 'But I thought you actors got paid mega bucks.' Thinking about it, 'Were you in that frozen pea commercial a while ago?'

'No, not in that one. I was up for it but they chose some other young chap with green eyes, I suppose to match the peas.' He's embarrassed. Then a shine picks up in his eyes. 'I was in the ad for orange juice. Perhaps you're thinking of that? I was the guy in the orange costume singing, "You can't get fruitier than a fruity orange".'

Any other time I'd have been chuckling away at the image he's planted in my head, but this is no humorous moment. First things first, I need to see if I can locate Keats.

So that's what I do as Teddy drives along the M25 towards Surrey. Only when the first hospital I contact asks me Keats's name do I realise that I don't know it. I can imagine if I said, 'A Boy Called Sue,' they'd slam the phone down on me, so the names Sue and Keats are all I have to go on. I become more rattled and fidgety as hospital after hospital informs me that no-one of Keats's description has been admitted.

'What happened to Keats?' Teddy asks with genuine concern. He's been surprisingly good-natured towards a woman who double socked him in the belly.

I can't answer his question of course. So I decide to lay off the hospitals for a time, since we've still got quite a distance until we reach any part of Surrey, and ask him instead. 'Explain to me how you came to be working for Michael Barrington.'

Teddy swiftly changes lanes as he goes into his tale. Being an actor he does it with a certain amount of dramatic flare as if I'm auditioning him for a part in my play.

'To be honest, I was hoping I was going to be playing Hamlet by now but you can't turn work down, can you? There was an advert in The Stage calling for actors to join an academic project on workplace environments. Michael said all he wanted me to do was sit in a basement all day as an extra. His only instruction was not to interact with you in any way. Apart from that, we could surf the Net or do what we liked for a hundred quid a day. Easiest job I've ever had.' His voice lowers, 'Between me and you, I was tempted to complain about the lack of fire exits.'

'But what about the film you were watching?'

He coughs appearing slightly ill at ease. 'I dabble in making films. The first video you saw was a short film I'd just finished—'

I'm outraged and want him to know it. 'You call a woman being scared out of her very skin art?'

His head rapidly shakes. 'The actors were my friends Tess, Leon and Sanjeev. We were recreating a scene from a horror classic.' He flicks his gaze at me, then back on the road. '"The Horror At Number Five". Do you know it?' He can see from the distasteful flare of my nostrils I don't. 'Anyway we were giving it a modern twist. You know with the ambience, the direction, the—'

'No disrespect, Teddy, but I can do without the introduction to the art of film.' I delete the sarcasm. 'You seem like a nice enough guy, so how did what Michael ask you to do involve scaring the sweet life out of me?'

His voice becomes solemn. 'Can you answer a question for me, Rachel?'

I stiffen. 'If I can.'

He glances at me again, longer now. 'I suspect you're not an actor, so did you know about the project in the basement? Know it wasn't a real workplace?'

I dither inside my head about what to tell him. Decide to brazen it out. 'Of course I knew.' I laugh, more of a wild cackle that's grating and ugly. 'I mean there's this Keats knocked up in crazy gear that looks like a reject from *High Noon* and Joanie creeping around and staring like the ghost of Hamlet's father?'

He joins in my fake laughter until I say, 'I don't understand the film though. I suppose Michael wanted to bring some realism to the project and the only way he could do that was by not telling me.'

'Ah, classic method acting,' Teddy responds. 'I have to tell you that the way you reacted to the film was pure brilliance. Storming off to tell Michael. When he took me and the fellow next to me to his office, I thought we were off the project. But he said he was going to pay me an additional fee to create another film.'

I'm seething, filled with such a blazing fury I have no idea how I don't explode. I let Teddy carry on. 'So he pretends to shout at us enough for everyone to hear in the basement. When we returned I was to give you a look of pure loathing.'

That was one acting role he hit on the nail.

'Make sure you saw the next film, which I edited to make the actress look similar to you, which is what he asked for, and appear as if it was shot in the basement. If you challenged me

245

when you saw it I was to threaten you. Michael told me exactly what words to repeat to you.' Teddy looks smug. 'I'd say I did a pretty spectacular job.'

I lapse into brooding silence. Michael and his mother have been picking me off at every turn. Every last detail planned and executed. It confirms my conclusion that whatever they have against me is personal.

I get back on the phone on the hunt for Keats. Two more hospitals to go and if neither one of them plays out, I don't know what to do.

The receptionist on the phone asks, 'A patient called Keats? Is that their first or last name?'

'I don't know.'

There's an audible huff as if I'm a timewaster. 'I'm not sure if I can... Wait a moment.' She goes offline for a while. Then is back. 'We do have a patient carrying ID in the name of Priscilla Green and other documents that had the name Keats.'

Finally.

The receptionist at the desk in the main area of the hospital smiles at me. It's one of those quick smiles that flashes bright and as quickly is blown away. She's obviously stressed and I can't blame her. Tomlington Hospital is busy, packed, a never-ending stream of people. She doesn't ask me how she can help; obviously that's what people come to her desk for.

'Can you direct me to the ward that Priscilla Green is on?'

The other woman mutters Keats's birth name as she checks through the computer screen in front of her. 'Temple ward on the fourth floor.'

The ride in the lift seems to take an age. My rucksack feels like a huge stone weighing down my back. Temple ward has the hushed atmosphere of a mortuary. A place to take people who have already died. It sets me on edge. The impersonal white walls aren't helping much either.

A voice, as disturbingly quiet as the ward, interrupts my observations. 'Can I help you?'

It's a nurse. He looks keen to assist. 'I'm looking for Priscilla Green. She's also known as Keats.'

'Are you a family member?'

That catches me unawares. I should've thought that one through. 'I'm… her sister. Rachel.' I think of her parents who put their genius child in a special school far away from home. How much hurt it still causes Keats.

Now she's hurt again. 'Where is she?'

'She's in the trauma unit…'

His voice fades as a buzzing whelms in my ears. I'm caught up in the implications of the word 'trauma'. That's bad. Really bad. Something dreadful has happened to Keats. I try the best I can to quell my bouncing nerves, the twisted clenching of my stomach whose muscles have transformed into the cutting sharpness of barbed wire.

I make the uneasy journey to her room. Hover outside.

My fingers clutch the handle but don't turn. I'm scared of what waits for me behind this door. *If you're frightened, how do you think Keats is feeling?* I open and… I have an urgent need to clamp my palm over my mouth at what confronts me. And that's when I realise the overwhelming emotion that balls inside. Guilt. This is all my fault. Keats is where she is now because of me.

There are tubes going in and out of her. Logically I know they're supporting her road to recovery but I can't help think they resemble the tentacles of multiple parasites greedily sucking the nourishment from her injured body. The rhythm of the coloured lines on a monitor and the steady beep-beep-beep are the only outward signs she's still alive. Keats is so so still. A disturbing stillness that rings her and the bed in a motionless world that will never wake up. With the softest footsteps, I move towards her in this room filled with isolated silence.

I stand at the side of the bed. She'd hate being here, strangers staring and staring at a face she has the power to reveal and conceal from the world. A large dressing covers the top half of her head and her expressive chin is lost inside a neck brace. I don't see any other evidence of wounds but I know they are there. Her breathing is barely audible. Grief stretches and contorts my face. I did this to her, I did.

Someone enters the room. Another nurse. Her brows knit together, eyes squint slightly in concern. 'I know this must be a terrible time for…'

I say nothing. Let her deliver her kindness in peace. When I feel the time is right, I ask, 'What happened to her?'

'Witnesses report that she was the victim of a hit and run.'

Bastards. How could they do this to Keats? 'How badly is she injured?'

'She sustained trauma to her head. We believe she sustained this when the car hit her not when she hit the road.' The image zooms cruelly across my mind. 'Thankfully one of the members of the public on the scene was a nurse so she was able to make sure your sister's airways were cleared and that no-one moved her. Our team is still investigating possible damage to her internal organs and trauma to major blood vessels.'

This nurse gives me time to absorb all this information before adding, in a tone that suggests there's more bad news coming, 'It's her head injury that is causing us the most concern. Since Priscilla—'

'Keats,' I cut in with force. 'That's what she likes to be called. Keats.'

The nurse nods. 'Since Keats was admitted, she hasn't regained consciousness. This may be due to a brain injury so we're waiting for the neurological team to take a look at her.'

'Is she going to make it?' I wait, breath stuck in my gut for an answer I'm not prepared for.

'We need to let the medical staff here do their work. The neurological team has a reputation on a par with our world-class burns unit. She's in good hands.' And with that, the nurse leaves me alone with my anguish.

I let the tears fall, hot and scalding a path down my cold cheeks. Guilt is such a terrible burden to carry even in the pursuit of what is right. Nevertheless I won't allow myself to escape from the fact that I put Keats in danger. Michael and Joanie have done this to her. Tried to snuff out her life. Anger comes in many shapes and forms. Spitting. Explosive. Raging. Red-hot. The one I feel towards the evil duo is best described as 'doesn't give a damn'. I'm going to get them if it's the last thing I do on this earth.

Before I leave, I place my good luck charm, my rope, under her pillows.

In the corridor, as I pass the reception desk, the same nurse who spoke with me calls out, 'One of the doctors remembers seeing your sister downstairs in the reception earlier which was lucky for Keats because the incident didn't happen far from the hospital.'

That stops me. 'She was here earlier? What was she doing here?'

The nurse's fingers flutter briefly above her paperwork. 'I assume she was visiting someone.'

The wheels of my brain spin into gear. The puzzle starts slipping into place. Of course. Keats said she was going to Surrey to confirm whatever she'd discovered.

Is that discovery in this hospital?

Forty-Three

I'm back in the main foyer downstairs, drilling the receptionist. 'My sister was here earlier. Can you tell me who she came here to see?'

A pleated frown disturbs the woman's expression. 'I've been on duty for the last three hours. Are you sure it's this section of the hospital?'

'I don't understand.'

She fills me in. 'There's the private convalescent hospital in the annexe. Maybe your sister was visiting someone there.'

After she's given me directions, I set off across the car park and soon after that the grounds of the hospital changes from concrete to a pretty well-loved garden with summer flowers basking in their arrays of colour. The garden sits at the back of a small neat building whose glass windows gleam clean and bright in the reflection of the sun.

I should go around to the front to enquire at the reception but I see an open sliding glass door that tempts me inside. So that's what I do, pick up speed and enter a rectangular room with an alcove housing books, polished tables and comfy chairs. The air is so different from the disinfected harsh smell of the main hospital. Here is sweet orange scented that is designed to be inhaled slowly. I suspect that this is the day room.

I check what's beyond the door. A corridor. Long, with a type of muted lighting that warms up the pale lilac walls. I have a problem though. I still can't be sure that Keats came to this private wing of the hospital and if she did, who she came to see.

Maybe, just maybe, one of the rooms off this corridor holds a clue. Right, here goes.

Room number one is locked, as is the next. The third is a patient's room where the bed has been stripped bare. There's a pungent unpleasant tang. I swallow because I suspect that someone recently died in here. The memory of Keats so still slugs me in the gut. I snap the door shut. Then wish I hadn't because the sound may alert a member of staff to what I'm up to. I check room after room. Nothing. In fact no people present at all.

I come to the second-to-last room, the logical me insisting this is a plain waste of time. I don't listen. This room's door is partially opened. My fingertips gently push a touch so I can see inside. It's empty but lived in. I push the door shut after me. It's modern and tastefully thought through. Rich cream walls, a two-seater couch with a curved back that welcomes you into its soft embrace, a hip-high cabinet that contains books and old-style CDs. And a bed that has enough room for two people with fluffed overlapping pillows sitting on top of a stark white cover. Near it sits a table connected to the floor by wheels set at an angle with an opened laptop on top.

Furtively I check the door over my shoulder and then stride to the mobile computer. I twist it to face me.

On the screen is… I deliberately shake my head, hard, because truth is I can't believe the evidence of my eyes. What I see hasn't gone away. It's Philip's face. A replica of the photo once stuck on the wall of the storeroom. On the computer his face sits on the front cover of the funeral programme. The bomb drops. I've found the person creating his funeral programme. My finger flicks urgently across the screen. A strange strangled noise drives from my mouth at the display of the inside of the programme. Two of the missing photos in my copy are included in this version.

The images force me to drop on the edge of the bed. The first shows Philip as a toddler. What a cutie in his loveheartstamped jim-jams. His hair was so black then. He's holding the strong hand of a man whose body and face remain out of shot. I can guess who it is though; Danny, Michael's father. The other photo makes me hurt deep inside. It's Philip sitting, holding his guitar on his knee, one hand draped over it with a tenderness reserved for a life partner I hope he found to love. I have to glance away. It's so so very painful. All that energetic and lively youth snatched away. I remind myself, sombrely, that it may have been Philip doing the snatching recently in Switzerland.

Then I find another family photo that flips my shaky world upside down. No. This can't be. Can't... A shroud of such lethargic despair covers me that I want to fall back. Lie on the bed. Shut my eyes tight and make the rest of the world go away. I don't want to believe what I've just seen. I inhale and stare back at the screen. But it's true, it hasn't gone away.

A quote at the bottom grabs my eye. It's Goethe. Gurta, I remember how it should be said aloud. A quote from *Faust*:

Yet death is never a wholly welcome guest.

It grabs me by the throat and chokes me back into the past.

Forty-Four

That summer

Ray made it impossible for Rachel to make a quick escape from Danny's house on her bike. When he realised that Rachel was leaving Philip behind, Ray made increasingly desperate attempts to get out of her jacket and run back. Every few yards, she had to pull over and gently force him back into the lining.

She grabbed him by his collar, pulling him close and hissed, 'Don't mess things up, Ray. Don't make me go back. Please. This is Philip's crazy idea. I don't want to do this. I wanted to stay and call the police. So please behave.'

For a moment, Ray seemed to understand. When Rachel set off again, pedalling down the drive towards the main road that led back to her dad's, Ray seemed to settle down. When she placed both hands firmly on the handlebar to turn, he took his chance and jumped out onto the road before turning, barking with triumph and heading back up the drive to where they'd left Philip.

Cursing, Rachel turned her bike. 'Come back!'

She set off in pursuit, the effort and focus helping to clear her head after everything that had happened. As she bore down on Ray, he dodged off the drive onto the grass and zigzagged to avoid her. Rachel leaned over and scooped him up with one hand while the bike wobbled, trembled and finally tipped Ray and Rachel over. She held him tight and stared into his disappointed face.

'Help me out, Ray.' But as she unbuckled his lead to tie his body to hers, a blue and orange flash crossed her eye line, followed by the boom-bang of an explosion. Stunned, Rachel urgently looked over to the garage where a thick noxious plume of smoke was rising hundreds of feet into the air.

Philip.

'No! No!'

Ray slipped though her slack fingers and raced off. Rachel climbed on her bike and headed to the garage, consumed in billowing smoke and flames.

'Philip! God, Philip! Speak to me.'

No answer. Rachel roughly discarded her bike and pulled her jacket over her head and went in through the doors that were blasted off. If he was in there, he was dead. So why go in? Acrid thick smoke enveloped her, making her cough and cough. Cinders from above showered down and there was the unmistakable sound of the roof groaning. It was only a matter of time before it caved in.

She called out Philip's name one last time but more as a lament than an attempt to summon a response. She was only a few feet inside but her bearings were gone and overwhelmed in the black smoke and panic. There was hardly any light, leaving her feeling as if there was no air. She was going to die too.

She stumbled forward, falling over a piece of debris. Then she saw the debris had a hand. A few yards away to her left, she could hear a dog barking. She grabbed the arm, followed the barks and pulled with all her might until she emerged from the smoke and flames.

As she did so, the roof collapsed and shortly after that the walls caved inwards.

She'd been seconds from being buried alive in flames and rubble.

Philip's body lay on the grass but it was a body transformed from that of a handsome young man. Scorched, blackened, singed and burnt. But he was still conscious. He raised his arm in an unearthly way and whispered, 'Go away, Rachel. They'll be here in a minute. Say nothing to anyone.'

In the distance, sirens disturbed the air. Ray was howling and keening by the body. When Rachel tried to grab him, he bit her hand in anger. Philip tried to laugh but groaned instead. 'Leave Ray with me. Just go.'

It took Rachel hours to travel the five miles home. She walked her bike, stopping every few hundred yards to shake and cry uncontrollably. *How can I have run away and left Philip?* she asked herself over and over again. When she arrived, her father wasn't there. That spared her having to explain her smoke-damaged clothes and hair. She sat inert in a bath and got out again and went downstairs to find her father coming through the door.

He looked at her curiously. 'Where have you been, Rachel? I've been calling you. Why weren't you at Danny's today?'

She told her first lie on Philip's behalf. 'I skipped work and went and saw some friends.'

'Just as well. I've bad news, I'm afraid. There was a fire at Danny's. He's dead. Not only him but that young lad who worked for him.'

Her voice was a whisper. 'Philip's dead?'

'I don't know.' Frank's gaze narrowed. 'Did you know this Philip well?'

Rachel shook her head, for a second incapable of speaking. 'Not really but I liked him. He worked in the garden so I never saw much of him. But will you try to find out how he is?'

'Of course.' Her father looked puzzled. 'Strange thing though. The paramedics found him on the grass, away from the fire with a dog having a nervous breakdown. They couldn't understand how he got out, given his injuries. If you weren't up there, that only leaves Danny and the kid. There was no-one else there apparently. And it certainly wasn't Danny who got him out.'

She couldn't lie a second time for Philip. 'Perhaps someone who loved him pulled him from the flames.'

Her father was even more puzzled. 'Someone who loved him?'

Rachel realised she'd said too much. 'I'm going to have a lie down.'

Without waiting for his response, she left him, her face crumpling when she was on her own.

A few days later when her dad gave her the devastating news that Philip had died, that evening was the first night Rachel slept with a bucket of water by her bed.

Forty-Five

A noise jerks me back from the life-changing horror of the past, away from the funeral programme on the laptop. Away from that damning photo. It's the hospital room's door opening. I stand up, staunch and ready. Ready to meet the person who has been planning Philip's funeral, playing with my mind. It's the wheels I see first. Then I see the wheelchair. I don't notice the porter who pushes it, only the person sitting in it has my utmost attention.

My head's trembling with such an intensity I don't know how it stays connected to my neck. There's a terrible roaring in my ears. My legs give way and I drop heavily onto the bed.

'Philip?'

This is what happens when you take one too many shots of cannabis oil and pop BBs like they're Smarties, you end up seeing things. That's what my blown mind is telling me.

'Rachel.'

Oh God, he's real.

I'm consumed by such an intense ballooning of elation that it threatens to split me apart. I don't know what to do with my hands. Whether to reach out towards him or hug my fingertips to my lips. My hands don't have the will to do either. They're frozen to the blanket on the bed. I watch as the porter wheels him over and then leaves us. Now he – *Philip* – is less than an arm's length from me. A wave of other emotions crashed down, drenching me. Horror. Disbelief. Complete, total incomprehension. But joy shoves them all out of the way and wins through again.

I'm laughing like I don't have an internal stop button. 'Philip... Philip... Philip.'

His grin is a twisted history of scars, burns and grafts. His poor, poor beautiful face. 'Hello, Rachel.' He speaks as if the last time he saw me was yesterday not ten years ago. 'This is a nice surprise, although perhaps it shouldn't be—'

I interrupt, voice scraping across my vocal cords. 'I don't understand. Why did you let me think that you died all those years ago after the fire?' There's a bitter taste on the tip of my tongue. 'I blamed myself for it all. For running away. Leaving you. I thought I'd let you down.'

His eyes lower to his bony hands and that's when I realise how emaciated he is. His head shoots up. 'Look at me. I'm not a pretty sight, am I. And I don't mean that as a statement of vanity. It's simply a truth. At the beginning I was in hospital for such a long time, and it wasn't only my body trying to heal. Inside my mind was damaged. It took me such a long time to put myself back together and it felt wrong to drag you into it all over again. I wanted you to find peace.'

If only he knew that I'd found anything but. I touch a palm to my heart. 'I'm filled with such happiness seeing you alive.'

His face isn't anywhere near as mobile as it was, but there's a tiny lift of one brow. 'Nearly everyone has paid me a visit today. Your friend Keats dropped by, my dad, my mum and my brother Michael. I suppose you're the last person left who hasn't. It's been a whole series of tender deathbed scenes,' he laughs too but then winces with pain, 'of one sort or another.'

I get off the bed to hug him but he raises a hand covered in a white glove that resembles an oven mitt. 'Best not. There aren't many parts of my body that don't burn again when they're touched. We can virtual hug if you like. Everything is virtual for me these days.'

Then the penny drops with horror. 'Deathbed scenes?'

He's still trying to grin. 'Yes, I'm going, I'm afraid. The doctors will tell you different, my mum can't accept it but it'll be lights out for me shortly.' He taps his chest lightly with his white glove. 'My lungs were severely damaged in the fire. The miracle isn't that I'm alive but that I've lasted this long. I've been given a few months at the most before my lungs shut down. I'm not sorry either. Enough is enough for me really; I've been as good as dead for years anyway.' He points to the laptop. 'That's why I'm making those arrangements for my own funeral—'

'You're the person behind it.'

His expression lights up. 'Imagine having the opportunity to put the things you really want to be remembered for in your funeral service instead of what your family try to guess what you wanted. I want to be remembered my way not somebody else's. Although I had to be careful. If Mummy had worked out what I was writing, she'd have deleted the lot.' His good hand flashes around. 'Plus, it keeps me amused while I'm waiting for the grim reaper and a couple of hospital porters to show up and wheel me off to the morgue.'

I'm gutted. Philip's alive but he's going to die all over again. What a wicked trick for life to play on me. In that moment the sorrow on his face is a burden that needs to be shared but I can't touch him because how can I burden him with my heartbreak as well?

He asks, 'Did Keats tell you what's been going on? She's an interesting lady.'

For the past few minutes, Keats has slipped my mind. Now her accident takes me by the throat. I don't want to tell Philip what's happened, in case he blames himself for that too. 'No, no, not yet...'

His body shifts as he settles more deeply into his chair. 'Best start at the beginning. My mother and brother, Michael, blamed your father and you for what happened to Uncle Danny.'

Woah! I didn't see that one coming and it shows in my face. 'Danny Hall was your uncle?'

He nods slowly. 'He was mummy's younger brother. She was very protective of him, including his memory. When Mummy discovered your father had fallen out with Uncle Danny over some business thing, that you were working there, and then Uncle Danny was killed and I was injured in a suspicious fire – well, they blamed you and your father for it. Obviously, I told Mummy and Michael that was nonsense afterwards but I couldn't tell them the truth, could I? That was impossible. Hey – are you all right, Rachel?'

I'm not. I'm shattered. He obviously doesn't realise that I've seen the picture. I turn the laptop in his direction and, with a shaking finger, point to it. 'Why is my dad in this photo with you, Joanie and Michael?'

I expect him to turn away from me. He doesn't. His hot stare drives into me. 'My mother was his long-time lover and Michael and I are his sons. Because he's our dad too.'

The blow doesn't fall because I was expecting this. I think back to all those years when Dad was away for days, sometimes weeks, 'on business'. He was probably with his second family. Is that what crushed Mum's spirit because she found out? Then it hits me what I confided in Keats about my relationship with Philip:

'*He's like the brother I never knew I had.*' It was all true. Philip is my brother, my half-brother.

He must be reading my mind because Philip chokes, 'Surely you must have known that, Rachel? Someone must have told you? How could you not have known?' He cries, tears soaking down his wounded face in crazy patterns over the scars. 'Oh Rachel…'

I feel the walls of my tears crumbling inside. We cry together, for the mess that has been made of our lives. For two eighteen-year-olds who had just gone through the gateway of adulthood on the journey to find their dreams but instead found a hellish nightmare awaiting them.

Philip has his big-gloved hand around my shoulder and kisses my cheek with his broken lips.

'Don't worry about a thing; everything's going to be okay. Keats told me what's been going on. I've laid it on the line for Mummy, our dad and Michael today. All this nonsense has got to stop. Don't be too harsh on my mum and Michael. They were only trying to get revenge for what they imagined happened to Uncle Danny and me. I told them from the beginning that it wasn't your fault but when they discovered I'm dying that was obviously the trigger that must have started them off with all the bogus company and gas lighting. They just wanted you to suffer the way I did. Don't be too hard on them. Revenge has been going on for ever; it's a natural human instinct to right wrongs.'

My voice has no tone. It's broken, the same way that I'm broken. 'Why didn't you tell Joanie and Michael the truth about what happened at Danny's?'

Philip laughs grimly, though I can see how painful this is for him. 'How could I do that? Tell my mother that her beloved baby brother was a rapist and couldn't keep his filthy hands to himself? That's why I couldn't call the police then, I didn't want her anywhere near that mess or finding out who her brother really was. How do you think she'd have reacted when she found out that I killed him? That I burned his body to cover up the evidence, and was the cause of my own injuries? I couldn't do that, Rachel.'

The grip of the gloved hand on my shoulder gets tighter, although the pain on his face shows what it's costing him. 'The thing is this, I've spoken to my mum and Michael and told them this has to stop. They're going back tomorrow to clear out their fake business. Shut it down.'

He pauses, considering his next words. 'But what you have to remember is that under no circumstances must you let our dad know what you know. He's obsessed with his reputation.' It comes back to me what Keats told me about how my father crushes his business opponents, uses the courts to protect his reputation.

Philip ominously adds, 'And if he finds out you know what he's done…'

My confusion shows on my face. 'I don't understand. Having a secret family isn't exactly the crime of the century.' My expression changes. 'He's done something else, hasn't he? What aren't you telling me?'

Philip's eyes jerk away. 'I've told you everything. But heed this – Frank Jordan's capable of anything. He's a psychopath, Rachel. He's been coming to see me every week since I've been in here. I think he enjoys it. He thinks I deserve to be like this because I was stupid. Seriously, that's what he thinks.' His gaze turns back to me now. 'You're his little Rachel. If he thinks you know everything, you're in serious danger. You're the only one he really cares about. See? He doesn't care about me, my mum, your mum or Michael. Only you.'

Is Philip holding out on me? But I don't feel I can press him because what kind of person would I be to badger and bash someone facing a death sentence?

Suddenly I remember, 'If your mum and Michael are going back tomorrow, I'm worried about Ray. When I left, there was no-one around. Say no-one comes for him?'

Philip's expression becomes grim. 'You're not going there. I mean it. You're in danger. For my sake, please say you're not going. Please!' The marks of his martyrdom are all over his body from that day ten years ago when he stepped in to save me from Danny.

He's probably right. And his mother no doubt has Ray. Still, I need to check for myself.

I gently take Philip's hand from my shoulder and get up off the bed. 'I've got to go.'

Philip's torment is etched on his already-tormented face. 'Rachel? Rachel? Are you listening to me? You're not going to that tenement. I forbid it!'

He wheels his chair backwards to block the door. I grab its handles and pull him out of the way. Climbing unsteadily out of his chair and taking a few steps, Philip lunges for me with his gloved hands but they can't grip and he tumbles down onto the floor. I should help but I'm afraid if I stay, he'll talk me out of going to the old sweatshop.

'Rachel! Rachel! Listen to me!'

Striding down the corridor outside, stealing a backwards glance, I can see Philip as he crawls out of his room. 'Rachel! Rachel!'

Nurses and other patients appear, drawn to the scene by the shouting. Medical staff rush past me to see what's happening. I keep walking, through the unit's reception, not looking back to where Philip's yells echo up and down the corridor as if they come from beyond the grave.

Forty-Six

As I sit in the back of the cab, I think of me. Of the last ten years, of my slow descent into debt, my rope and buckets of water and cold-cold filled baths. My fear of fire and underground spaces because of what happened in that wine cellar and garage. Of my guilt and my mental anguish.

Then I see Philip's scarred and pinched face and what he told me. My dad is his dad. Half-brother and half-sister. Philip and Rachel. Was it that unknowing connection of blood that instantly drew me to him? Did we see mirrors of ourselves reflected in each other? A reflection that has another face in it – Frank Jordan. I have this horrible weird feeling digging from my head right down to the soles of my feet that's telling me that there's more to the story of my dad covering up the fact he's had a second family. A hidden lie that's a truth that will shatter me apart.

Before I can try to unstitch it, my phone buzzes. I hesitate before I take it out because if it's Dad, I'm going to have to spew my own lies; I want to confront him with his duplicity when his face is in front of mine. But it's not Dad, it's Jed on Skype. I inwardly groan. I love my dear friend to bits, but I'm not in the mood to talk to him now. Nevertheless I connect to the video call.

Jed pops up on screen, the camera distorting his face, turning his hair into a gravity-defying mane.

Jed: 'Hey sweets, how you doing? You look like you've had the roughest day of your life.'

Me: 'Something like that.'

His face becomes stark and alert as he shifts his face nearer to his camera.

Jed: 'It's something to do with that place you're working in, isn't it?'

I scowl, pulling the skin on my face taut. What would he know about the conditions in which I've been working?

Me: 'Why would you think that?'

Jed: 'After you asked me about this Michael character, I got to thinking I don't like my Rachel working for this bloke. I mean, if he's lied to you about knowing me I got to thinking what else is he lying to you about?'

Jed is more perceptive than I give him credit for. I get to thinking maybe I should have asked for his help much sooner. Brought him along for the ride too like Keats. Yeah, and look what happened to her. If anything had happened to Jed I'd never have forgiven myself.

Me: 'That's kind of you—'

He butts in, voice overly urgent.

Jed: 'Do you remember telling me about the sweatshop fire that happened there back in the day?'

I don't actually. I blink rapidly, trying to find the memory.

Me: 'What of it?'

Suddenly Sonia appears beside him, her head intimately cushioned next to his. So they're still an item. I'm surprised; I didn't give their hook-up more than a couple of days. Strangely it's not her wearing the soppy 'I'm in love' dreamy expression, it's Jed.

Jed: 'Me and computers aren't really friends so I got Sonia to look into it for me.'

Sonia gives me her full attention. I can tell by the pursed fix of her lips, the narrowing of her eyes, that she still thinks I'm a bad influence on the man she'd fancied the pants from afar for such a long time.

Sonia: 'When I tried to find records or accounts of the fire online, I could only find one website that mentioned it. It's a roll call of haunted buildings in London.'

She isn't telling me anything I don't already know. But I remain patient, allowing her to continue.

Sonia: 'It all sounded strange. A fire where a lot of people had died even back then would be a matter of historical record. So, I checked this haunted website more carefully and found that it had been put up about three weeks ago.'

Me: 'So, it's new. There are websites going up every day.'

Jed and Sonia look so serious I realise that my day from hell is about to shove me deeper into Hell's fire.

Me: 'Tell me.'

It's Jed who does.

Jed: 'The commemorative plaque on the building wasn't put there by the local council.'

I hold my breath. Wait for him to drop his fireball.

Jed: 'No-one died in that building. No young girls. No-one. Someone made all that crap up on the website. The sweatshop fire never happened.'

Forty-Seven

I stare intently at the plaque on the wall of the old sweatshop. Another trick to mess with my mind. I'm tempted to use my bare hands to rip it down. Instead, I look up at the building. It displays every last scar from its long history.

I'm surprised that the door's slightly open. I hesitate a second before I go inside, searching for Ray. His mad continuous barking erupts in the air but I can't see him. I walk further into the foyer, becoming an island in the middle. Remain totally still. Attuning my ear to the location of the distressed dog. It doesn't sound as if it's coming from upstairs. He's barking and whining in bursts. I don't want to... I move towards the trap door. The small cupboard weighing it down is nowhere to be seen. No way in hell do I want to go down and under ever again. But I can't leave poor Ray there.

I hunch down. Pull back the trap door with a flourish. Leave it open because I want additional light to guide me, but I also need a touchstone of the bright world above with me. I hold back at the top of the narrow staircase because it looms dizzyingly below me. I ignore it and the solid pounding of my heart as I carefully take each step one at a time, my palm pressed to the bumpy uneven wall. The tunnel is all contorted shadow clinging to walls and floor and jagged cracks in the ceiling.

I've never felt safe in this long stretch of subterranean London and my insecurities increase with each move towards the basement. Ray is in there. I rush on until I have the handle of the steel door in my palm. I open up. Remain in the doorway.

My brows shoot together in confusion. I can't see Ray. I go further in.

The door behind me slams, startling me. I urgently spin round. A blur. Pain. White light. Then I'm falling into the deepest darkness.

It's the choking stench of petrol that wakes me. I wince and cringe with the thudding searing pain in my skull. I'm confused. Why is my head hurting? And where the hell am I? Slowly I blink-blink-blink my eyes alive. My vision is blurry, watery, made up of shadows mixed with a blue-tinged light.

Rachel. Rachel. Rachel. The eerie voice calling me by name floats above and around me. Then settles on my soaked skin.

Rachel. Rachel. Rachel.

It's the humming I hear that makes my body stiffen. It's the beat of the stone heart in the basement walls. My vision flicks furiously into focus.

I'm lying on the ground, petrol soaked all over my clothes and hair. It's splashed in a circle on the ground around me, turning me into the virgin sacrifice at a satanic ritual. Standing, back against the wall, is Joanie, staring down at me. She looks like a ghoul. Her eyes are sunken deep in a face that doesn't appear of this world. The Stare's back, dead flat doll's eyes blazing and blistering with hatred. At her feet lies a can of petrol. In her hand a lighter she flicks on and off, on and off, the flame, yellow hypnotic-blue, fluttering wildly. Thank God there's no sign of Ray in this macabre scene.

Her mouth opens and she sneers, 'Rachel. Rachel. Rachel.' So it hadn't all been in my head, the BBs and cannabis oil playing tricks on me.

I struggle to rise, but Joanie's strangely even-measure robotic voice stops me. 'Stay down. I wouldn't move if I was you.' She raises the lighter with a threat my prone body can't ignore. 'No need to look for Ray, he's safely tucked up in my home. This is all I need to draw you back here.' She touches the old-fashioned cassette recorder near her, where I assume the taped noises of a dog barking were coming from.

'Joanie, whatever's going through your head is all wrong.'

She calmly punches off the wall. That's what scares me the most, her calm. It's unnatural, as if she's had one too many shots of my weed oil.

She speaks. 'He was born at five minutes to six in the morning.' One of the most gorgeous smiles I have ever seen lights up her features. 'The sun's ray, such a beautiful light, were coming through the windows anointing my perfect baby boy. He fitted so right in my arms. I already had a name picked out for him. Jacob. But when I gazed down at him I knew that wasn't right. I gave him another name. Philip.' The tempo of her voice switches to menacingly hard. 'And you killed him.'

'But he's not dead. I've just seen him—'

'You. Killed. Him.' The demeanour of her body shakes off calm, replacing it with an alertness that tells me Joanie's a hair's breath away from springing on me. 'You think he's been living for the last ten gut-wrenching years? After what you and Frank did to him, he's been a shell. His love of life drained out of him.'

I hear it in her voice. Sorrow. This woman is possessed by a grief so strong it's turned her crazy. God forgive me, but I feel for her. I know what that emotion feels like, how it can tear your insides and heart apart.

Tread carefully, Rachel. Very carefully. 'I know you're my dad's lover and he's your sons' father.'

'Lover?' Joanie scoffs nastily at that. I hear her footsteps until she appears huge, looming over me. 'Me and Frank haven't been *lovers*,' the word is spat down at me, 'since the day he set his own son on fire. You both tried to murder him.'

I touch her eyes with mine, but hers are unsteady, twitching in their bloodshot frame.

'I never tried to kill Philip—'

'Liar—'

'The fire wasn't my fault—'

'Liar—'

'It was an accident. Something that just happened.' This should be my moment of absolute truth but I can't get it out of my head how Philip told me his mother would be crushed if she found out the whole of it. What her brother Danny really was. More importantly, Philip's role in her brother's death.

She screams, 'Liar. Liar. Liar.' And lashes me with petrol from the can over my belly. 'I'll empty this fuel down your lying throat if you don't shut that filthy mouth of yours.' She pauses. Takes a step back. 'You were so easy to manipulate. It wasn't hard to find out that you were down on your luck crippled by debts. Let's do the girl a good turn and offer her a job. And once we had you in our net, time to play with Rachel.'

'Were you trying to kill me?'

'Kill you?' She shakes her head as the can swings in her hand. 'Killing's too good for you. No, you had to suffer just as my Danny and Philip suffered. Put you under the ground like you were back in Danny's cellar. From the start we had to make you think that it was your own mind tormenting you, so we began ever so gently with the sour milk. Let you experience the nasty and bitter taste we've carried in our mouths all these years. I wanted you to feel trapped like Philip had in the fire in Danny's garage.'

'It was you who locked me in the basement when everyone else, including Michael, went to lunch. But it was you both who made up the story about the sweatshop fire. There never was a fire here.'

Joanie bares her teeth. 'And you fell for it hook, line and time to sink Rachel. Every day you came here after being put in the basement, I wanted you to experience the threat of fire, being helpless underground. Blocked in. That's what Philip must've felt in Danny's garage—'

I throw back before she can torment me more, 'But you weren't able to take me down, were you? You took me on and I fought back.'

She considers me with a tilt of her head as if in preparation for the deadly chop of an executioner's axe. 'Tough nut, just like Frank. Did you know that I met him through my brother Danny? He introduced us at a party. I'd just come through a very messy divorce – the said mister Barrington, although I've been using Connor to cover my tracks – and Frank provided a pick-me-up. He was fun. Of course he promised me the earth... Then your mother came along. I should've given him up then but couldn't. We were never his second family, we were Frank's first. Then you came along. My boys overnight became second-class citizens—'

'Think of your sons now—'

'What do you think I'm doing?' she snaps. 'Michael was always going to be okay. He set up his business straight out of university. But Philip...' Her body bows inward, deflated. 'Philip is the artist. More sensitive. Doesn't care about money. All he ever wanted to do was play his guitar. Bring some cheer and love into the world.' She's back large over me. 'Then you had to spoil it all.'

I go on the counter-attack, vicious in my delivery. I don't care anymore. 'It's you who has been trying to murder someone. Me. You blocked the exits and left me down here to die—'

Her upper body elongates with a full-blown breath that she lets out with a roar. 'Why are you lying again? After you tried to kill my boy and put my brother six feet under, you think I could kill anyone?'

'Then how do you explain the smoke? The car over the back grill and the cupboard over the trap door to stop me getting out?'

Joanie staggers back, her face a patchwork of bewildered confusion. 'I don't know what you're talking about.' Her head shakes with horrified denial. 'What smoke?'

'If you didn't do it, then who did?'

Our attention diverts to the door as it opens. Michael walks into the basement.

Forty-Eight

Joanie's the one who rounds on him. 'What have you been doing behind my back?'

Michael's gaze flicks guiltily away from her. 'I don't know what you mean. You're the one who nearly gave the game away by deviating from the plan and staring at her like a mad woman.'

'She,' Joanie's accusing finger stabs in my direction, ignoring his last words, 'says she was locked down here with no way of getting out.'

Michael turns his gaze back at Joanie and becomes horrifyingly still. 'Mother, what are you doing? This wasn't part of the plan.'

She visibly shrinks. 'Don't you get it? I can't figure out how I can remain living on this earth without my son. So, I thought it's time for me and his killer to go. Frank's too clever for me to get so I'm going to have to make do with his accomplice.'

For the first time since entering, her eldest son takes in the scene. The lighter. The fuel can. Me soaked in petrol. Then I notice with horror what I should have before. Joanie is soaked in petrol too.

Michael rears back in panicked shock. 'Mother, what are you doing?'

Instead she throws him a question of her own. 'What did you do, Michael? Tell me about the smoke and blocking the exits because I never agreed to any of that.'

He straightens his neck. 'It was time for her to properly pay for what she'd done. A life for a life.'

The can drops from Joanie's suddenly slack fingers. She's staring at her son as if she's never seen him before. 'He got to you, didn't he?'

'I don't know what you're talking about.'

But I do. It was Michael that my father was talking to in his office when I listened at the window to him threatening someone on the phone if they didn't... how did he put it... '*If you don't get back on my side, I will kill you.*'

'Frank,' Joanie screams. 'Your father. How can you forget how he threw us out of our home and gave it to his precious daughter?'

I would've staggered back if I'd been standing up. The previous owner of my house was never Danny, it had been Dad. How could he have done that to his own children? No wonder Joanie despises me. In that instant I understand her hatred runs much deeper than what happened to Philip in the fire. What she's convinced herself Dad and I did to him.

She continues to lash out at her eldest son. 'Have you forgotten how he barely spent money on us because he wanted to keep it all for his fucking daughter? Remember that winter there were holes in your shoes and I pleaded with him to help me buy you a new pair. I only wanted half of the money and what does almighty Frank Jordan say – "Get a part-time job, Joanie."'

I want to cry then, join my tears to the wetness of the petrol soaking through my clothes. How can any man have the right to call himself a father if he treated his own flesh and blood that way? It's not the stink of the petrol that's threatening to make me want to be sick.

'What did he promise you?' Joanie demands of her son.

A voice in the doorway answers for him. 'His rightful place. As heir of my empire.'

Dad, Frank Jordan, strides in as if he owns the place. He huffs heavily as he looks pointedly down at me. 'This is what happens when you start interfering. You should've told me you were working for them. I would've told you to run for your life.'

Joanie surprises everyone by walking over and levelling a resounding slap across her son's face. 'You idiot! Frank's a born user. That's what he does. Did you tell him that Rachel worked here?' When he doesn't answer, she screams, 'Tell. Me.'

Michael rubs the mark on his cheek. 'Dad called after she confronted him about Uncle Danny. He said I could come work for him. He'd give me the business. I'm his first born.' The desperation for his father's love is blatant.

Joanie says, 'He manipulates everyone, including his children.'

'He manipulates everyone including his children.'

Suddenly my breath bashes against my chest, my brain ticks and ticks over the thread of events from the past. What Philip wouldn't tell me.

My gaze slams into Dad. 'What happened between you and Danny Hall and this business deal I keep hearing about?'

'He stole it away from my brother!' Joanie shouts.

Dad stares at his former lover with disdain. 'At one time you were such a gorgeous lady. Now you're an ugly bitter and twisted shell of a woman. In business there's only one winner and both me and your brother had our eyes on the same prize. And in business you have to use every weapon at hand to get it.'

I get up, defying Joanie's earlier demand. I don't care. She can burn if she wants because I suspect what I'm going to find out next will scorch me forever.

I don't take my flaring gaze from Dad. 'And is that what you did? Use everything you could against Danny Hall?'

Dad tips his head arrogantly. Opens his mouth. Then his lips close tight. He sees it on my face. Sees that I've finally figured it out.

It's left to me to put it in the room. 'When I was eighteen, you deliberately sent me to work for Danny. You knew about his reputation. That he was a man who had raped women, especially young women.' There's a soul-piercing sound — I know it's Joanie – her reaction to hearing, probably for the first time, what her *darling* brother was, but I don't give a damn.

'Was that the plan, Dad? That he attack me, brutalise me, and when I got home and told you about it, you get the police onto him. And there it is.' I click my fingers. 'As quick as that, your competition for one of the biggest contracts in your life has been eliminated.'

What Keats had told me when I embarked on this journey hits me hard: '*The search for the truth is admirable, but it can also dig up the most unimaginable soul-destroying pain.*'

My heartache stands out in my voice. 'All these years I thought I'd let you down when in reality it was you who let me down. Placed me in the most ugly situation possible.'

Dad insists, 'I don't know what you're talking about—'

'But you didn't count on Philip being there, did you?' Then the pieces of something else click together. 'Philip told me you visited him yesterday. It was you who ran your car into Keats.'

Dad doesn't pretend anymore. 'I heard her talking to him, sticking her nose where it had no right to be. So I followed her.'

Before I can process this, the tunnel outside echoes to the beat of drag, drag. Tap. Drag, drag. Tap. It gets closer and closer. There's someone at the door. We wait. The door handle pushes down.

'Philip,' his mother cries with concern as she rushes over to hold him. And it's just as well that she does because he looks terrible. The 'tapping' is the cane he holds to keep him upright. He is so thin, his clothes hanging off him, face drawn, his surgery and scarring prominently displayed.

He pats his mother with comfort. 'How come no-one invited me to the family get-together?'

'*We're like a family at my firm.*' That's what Michael had informed me at the interview. At least that was one truth he'd told me from the start.

Philip might be slower on his feet but his eyes do a quick sweep of the scene. 'Mummy, how many times have I told you that Rachel had nothing to do with this?'

She looks at him pleading. 'Is it true about your Uncle Danny?'

'That he attacked Rachel? That it isn't the first time he'd done something like that? All sickeningly true.' Philip leans his cane on the wall.

Joanie's face crumples and tears stream a retched path down the taunt skin of her face. 'Why didn't you tell me?'

'How could I? Apart from me and Michael, your brother was the only person you had left in the world.' He inhales deeply. On the out breath, says, 'I didn't mean to kill him. It was the only way to stop him. He'd already hit Rachel. She had nothing to do with me burning his body. In fact, if it hadn't been for her dragging me out, I would have died in there too.'

A stunned silence meets the truth. It's finally out there where it should have been years ago.

Philip informs us all, 'I think the best thing to do is to leave this place. Now.'

He tells his mother directly. 'I don't like what I'm seeing here and I worry about you, so if you could give me the key for this door, which I suspect you have, it will rest my mind.'

Trembling, Joanie puts her hand in her pocket to retrieve the key and gives it to him. We leave the basement, a family that is no real family at all.

Part way through the tunnel, Philip announces, 'I left my cane behind. Dad, would you take my arm so I can get it. I'm feeling very weak all of a sudden.'

Dad looks as if he's going to tell him to piss off. Then, grudgingly he does what his son asks him to do. We wait in an awkward silence as they head back.

Then Joanie, in a choked voice tells me, 'I didn't realise, Rachel. I really thought—'

'I'm not going to say I'm not hurt because I am. What you – both of you – put me through was bad. Horrible. However, grief can take us to the most miserable of places.'

Up ahead there's a click-click noise. Then through the basement door, we hear Dad yell, 'Open this door!'

What the hell's going on?

Now it's Philip's voice. 'No, I won't. Your nasty fingerprints are over all of this. Setting Rachel up at Danny's, which I figured out years ago. I suspect turning my brother against the only parent who has loved him. Treating my mother like she's shit instead of the beautiful giving person she is. Turfing us out of our home a week before Christmas. When we were growing up, Mum having to fight you for every penny to clothe and feed us. We're all collateral damage in the service of your greed.'

'I said open this fucking door.'

There's a thumping sound and a shout of pain from Philip.

Joanie steam rollers forward. Tries to open the door. It won't move. She bangs furiously on it. 'What are you doing to my son? Leave him alone. If you touch him I'm going to bloody rip you to shreds.'

Michael and I are soon at the door too. More screams of pain.

Philip: 'Do your worst, it doesn't matter. I'm a dead man walking.'

That's when I figure out with sickening realisation what Philip's doing. He's sacrificing himself for me all over again. No, I won't allow that to happen again. Ever.

I bang on the door. 'Don't do this, Philip. Please, I beg you.'

I suck in my breath at what I'm sure is the brutal sound of a kick. 'Open this door, boy,' Dad roars.

Philip: 'I won't allow you to hurt anyone anymore. Rachel, can you hear me? Grab life with both hands and love it.'

Then there's a monstrous yell from Dad. 'What are you doing? Let me out of here.' The handle of the door jerks and jerks down.

Then I understand why Dad is so frantic – Philip has set the basement on fire. No way out. We all bang our fists against the door. Over and over. Smoke seeps under the door.

Philip's voice comes as a light in that terrible moment, quoting from his funeral programme: *"Yet death is never a wholly welcome guest."'*

The heat inside sears into the steel of the door so we can no longer touch it. Then the screams come. And come.

Joanie's feet go from under her. Michael takes her in his arms, whispering, 'I'm sorry, Mummy, so sorry.'

I tell them both, 'We need to call the emergency services. If we don't…'

The horrific screams inside the basement follow us out of the tunnel and through the trap door.

Joanie's face is wiped clean of emotion as she shivers with a blanket about her shoulders next to me, given to her by the paramedics team. Michael's on the floor at her feet, rocking. We watch as the fire brigade battle with the fire that claims the building. Then the rear of the former sweatshop that never had the history of a fire, collapses inwards and upwards in a fountain of flames, sparks, rubble, dust and billowing, billowing smoke.

Philip is forever gone this time. I know that. I felt his spirit leave this world. A hyper warm sensation, so tender, bloomed within me, holding me tight. So tight. Then it was gone, leaving me drenched in a dreadful cold, a hollow emptiness.

That's how I should've figured out he never died all those years ago. I didn't feel his spirit vanish from this world.

Why is it that the best of us has to die first?

Joanie falls against me, sobbing. I understand now that the weeping I heard from her when I lived in the storeroom was real. Tears for her son. Now she cries for him because she knows she'll never see him alive again. I place my gentle arms around her. I don't cry for my father. It wasn't Joanie who was ever really the ultimate threat to me. It was always my dad, Frank Jordan, the true monster.

Forty-Nine

Three days later

Keats is sitting up in bed with her shades on. After being knocked down by a car, unconscious for hours, the first thing she tells me in a thin croaking voice is, 'I put my bandana on and one of the nurses ran for her life like Frankenstein was on her tail.'

Typical Keats. And I'm glad for it. I do something next that she won't like – take her into a soft embrace and hold on, my eyes squeezed as tight as I'd like my arms to be but I don't want to hurt her. She surprises me by sinking into it without a word of fuss.

After that, I get comfy on the side of the bed. 'How are you bearing up?'

I sense her eye roll behind her sunglasses. 'Apparently I've been lucky, just cuts and some very painful bruises. I'm very hard-headed, so no serious damage to that.'

It's my turn to be embraced but by guilt clutching me tight. 'I'm so sorry—'

'It isn't your fault your dad's a psycho wanker—'

'Was.' I swallow hard. 'He's dead.'

I tell her what happened at the Victorian building. Keats doesn't say she's sorry about my dad, which I'm glad of because I'm still sorting through what I feel for him now he's gone. You don't just switch off the tap on your love for someone because they did terrible things. I wish I could; I'd do it in a heartbeat.

Now it's all over, I understand myself a little better. 'I hated that trap door at our so-called job at first. But do you know what I've realised? What happened ten years ago meant I've been living with my own mental trap door for way too long. Keeping bad things locked inside creates a poison that will only keep growing.'

Keats surprises me by picking up her mobile. She fiddles with it as the stare she gives me becomes grave. 'Philip sent me something—'

'What?' I can't hold back the shock.

'When I visited him I gave him my e-mail because he wanted me to finish his funeral programme. Firstly, he instructed me not to have the word 'funeral' on it. Instead he wanted me to use the word 'celebration'. A celebration of the life of Philip Barrington.' Keats paused, taking a deep breath. 'And he wanted this photo to be on the front cover.'

She passes me her phone and I stare down at the photo. It's a selfie Philip took of us with Ray snuggled between us at the gazebo in Danny's garden during that summer. Our first paid job as adults. Our smiles are jokey and bright, the setting around us appearing to be the most innocent place in the world. I run my finger with love and devotion over his face on the phone screen as the tears sting my eyes.

'Don't do it,' Keats commands with a harsh softness.

'Do what?'

'Cry.' She makes the word sound like a curse. 'No more tears, Rachel. That's not how Philip wants to be remembered. He wants you to hang on to the great times you had.'

Keats is so right. Philip will always be my brother and I will lock him away in the good place in my heart.

'What are your future plans?' she asks as I pass back her phone.

I mull it over. 'I haven't had time to think things through. I've made a kinda peace with Michael. Joanie too. I suspect what'll happen is Michael will become co-owner of Dad's business and I'll leave the everyday running of things to him. As for the rest,' I shrug lightly, 'who knows.'

Keats's chin pushes down. Her lips silently move together as she talks to herself, which leaves me puzzled. Not for long though as she informs me, 'I'm planning on stopping being freelance and setting up my own company. Maybe go into the gaming market too. I've got enough money to set up in a good part of town, although I'm wondering if it might be better to be based in my duplex.'

My brows shoot up. 'You've got a duplex?'

She looks pleased with herself. 'Yeah. By the river in Wapping. A view of Tower Bridge to die for.' Abruptly she stops and mutters again for her ears only. I figure out she's working through what she wants to tell me, which means it must be something she's dreading. 'I'll pay good money—'

'Good money? For what?'

'I know you're loaded now, but would you be my assistant cum PA cum...' She bites her bottom lip. Then coughs that sounds like she's being strangled. 'Friend?'

I smile properly for the first time in a long time, the same real smile I gave Philip years ago the first day I met him. 'You've got a deal.'

Epilogue

Six weeks later

We all stand in a circle around a newly planted olive tree in the garden of Joanie's house. Me, Keats and Michael. And Joanie of course. I've made my peace with my half-brother and his mother. It hasn't been easy but the world doesn't need more ugliness after what we've all been through. I don't think me and Joanie will ever be great friends but I respect her as Philip's mother.

Philip's remains were found in the fire, but Dad's weren't. Still, I had a burial for him at a church near where he lived. With the police involved, news had leaked out about what had gone on, so many of his business associates decided to stay away. I refused to bury him near Mum. She deserves to rest in an eternal peace she didn't find in her marriage.

We've just got back from the church where Joanie laid her son to rest. The celebration service he'd prepared had guided the proceedings. Joanie had invited a few of us back to her home for the last simple request Philip made in his celebration programme. To plant an olive tree so that his mother could still see him grow. There are the stains of long-dead tears on Joanie's face now but there's a ghost of a smile too as she stares lovingly at the small tree. Ray is lying near the tree, his tail wagging but he makes no sound. Maybe he senses what the olive tree represents.

Now for the final part of the ceremony. I wave my hand for Jed and his band who stand at a respectful distance in the corner of the garden. They play *Eighteen* and we all sing with our best voices to Philip's song.

Also by Dreda Say Mitchell

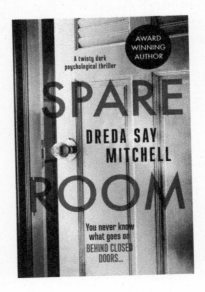

International number one bestseller, Spare Room

'The scariest, creepiest and best psychological suspense you'll read this year.' - Lee Child

Acknowledgments

Thank you!
Thank you for reading *TRAP DOOR*. We hope you enjoyed it.
We LOVED writing it!
Checkout Amazon Author Central for all my books
Amazon UK
Amazon US

Message from Dreda
For news and loads more, head off to my website and sign up.
https://dredamitchell.com

I adore hearing from readers, so please do get in touch with me
if you'd like to.
My website: https://dredamitchell.com
Facebook: Dreda Facebook
Twitter: Dreda Twitter

Reviews: I write for you!
I love to hear what you think about the books.
So please leave a review.

About the author

All About Dreda

I wrote five books before partnering up with Tony Mason to continue my writing career. I scooped the CWA's John Creasey Dagger Award for best first time crime novel in 2004, the first time a black British author has received this honour. Since then I have written twelve crime novels.

I grew up on a working class housing estate in the East End of London and was a chambermaid and waitress before realising my dream of becoming a teacher. I am a passionate campaigner and speaker on social issues and the arts.

I have appeared on television, including Celebrity Pointless, Celebrity Eggheads, BBC 1 Breakfast and Sunday Morning Live and Newsnight, The Review Show and Front Row Late on BBC 2. I have been a guest on BBC Radio 3 and 4 and presented Radio 4's flagship books programme, Open Book and written in a number of leading newspapers including The Guardian. I also review the newspapers every Friday night on BBC Radio 5 Live's Stephen Nolan Show. I was named one of Britain's 50 Remarkable Women by Lady Geek in association with Nokia, and am an Ambassador for The Reading Agency. Some of our books are currently in development as TV and film adaptations.

My name is Irish and pronounced with a long ee sound in the middle!